SAINT HIROSHIMA

SAINT
HIROSHIMA

Leigh Kennedy

HARCOURT BRACE JOVANOVICH, PUBLISHERS

San Diego   New York   London

To Christopher Priest

June 1986

H E stopped the car at the side of the road on a rise that overlooked the town where he was born and bred. His watch said five minutes to twelve; he waited.

So many towns he had known like this across the country—he had eaten in the truck stop cafes, rented boxes in one-story brick post offices, bought underwear at J. C. Penney's, sat in the third row at the movie houses, and picked up magazines at the drugstores. But this town had a real shape and sound and feel to it that could be like no other, as indescribably individual as a familiar face, no matter how long he spent elsewhere or how long he stayed away from here.

The smoky-blue mesas cupped the town like the side of a giant hand, shielding it from the distant, more purplish Rocky Mountains to the west. The highway whose sandy shoulder he had just parked on continued down this hill and through the town, where it was dotted with filling stations and motels and where neon signs shaped like cactus or cowboy boots were dull in the bright sun of midday. The southern end of the highway bent around and away, skirting the eastern edge of the mountains, looking hotter in the distance than it felt where he stood in a high, dry breeze. New to him this time was a mobile home park, shiny rectangles fanning out from half-circle drives, on the southeastern outskirts of town. That had been a field where his father had taken him to learn how to work a clutch on the old Plymouth.

He looked at his watch again and leaned against his car. Any second now. In the tidy squares of intersecting streets, the houses set in generous lawns, he could pick out his old school, the Little League baseball field, and from there, his house. The configuration of his town from this hill was familiar from the days he would walk his bicycle all the way up just to ride down and also, later, from sitting with his girl at night—a place to be alone and look down at the lights or up at the stars if he had his eyes open at all.

There she goes.

Noon straight up. The whistle on the hill blew a long note that always sent a shiver across the back of his neck and across his shoulders. Whenever he came home for a visit, he aimed to get to this spot around noon and hear that siren's voice. It had shipwrecked him once.

The second shipwreck in his life had happened less than two months ago, but it was only the memory of the siren that had led him on to the rocks that time.

He slid back into the seat, warm from the sun, and headed down the highway to see his mother and his father. And to visit old friends.

1950–1961

1

S H E sat in the middle of the front room floor bundled in a scratchy blue blanket. The electrician installed the television in the corner where they used to have the big chair. Now the big chair sat closer to the piano, where it looked a little confused and out of place. Katie had only seen one of these things before, at Aunt Margaret's house, but she had thought it was a radio with a shiny speaker.

"Have a mirror, Mrs. Doheney?" the electrician asked.

Katie's mother brought out the gilt-framed hand mirror from her brush set and handed it to the man. "I heard the Youngs are getting a television, too," she said to him.

"Yeah, I installed it yesterday. They have a lot of snow on it though. They'll have to get some rabbit ears."

Katie wondered where the Youngs got snow at this time of the year. Then she realized that it probably came from Rabbit Ears Pass in the mountains. Her father said there was

7

snow in the shady spots under rocks all year round. Katie
was a quick child; she knew how to figure things out.

The man propped the mirror against Katie's knee. "Here,
sweetheart, would you mind helping me out?"

Katie shook her head. The man went behind the television
and looked over the top of it at the mirror. The glass popped
alive with grey light. He instructed her to hold the mirror
up a little. Katie held it up and he said, "Whoa," and fiddled
with things in the back, glancing back and forth between his
hands and the mirror.

She could see light blurs in the screen. A man's voice,
like a voice from the radio, said, "That July it was tested in
New Mexico." There was a pause and a long hiss.

"Doggone," the electrician said.

Her mother had told her that it would be like having the
picture show at home. Katie couldn't see anything but vague
shapes without face or form. The electrician scowled at the
mirror. Katie's arms were beginning to tremble from holding
the mirror up for so long. Something changed on the television window and dark bars rolled down the screen, making
Katie dizzy.

She squinted, trying to make sense of the fuzz. There was
a booming explosion sound in the television that reminded
Katie of the sound the truck had made yesterday when it hit
the white car. With the squealing, crackling and rumbling
sounds coming out of the television enhancing her memory,
she recalled the scrape and crunch of the accident she had
seen while walking home from kindergarten. Then she understood what she saw on the television.

That dark blob was the truck bearing down on the white
blob, which was the car with the woman in it. The white
blob swerved and tried to escape. A woman screamed, but

it was a weird electronic howl this time. Then she could make out (it happened a lot faster yesterday, she thought) the black blob crushing the white one under its front wheel in a deadly smash.

Katie barely noticed the radio voice talking on again as half a woman was flung towards her, her pretty white and blue flowered dress fluttering like a dancer's as she sailed through the air toward the curb where Katie stood.

Then the truck exploded. Katie didn't remember that from yesterday; she had been staring at the bloody head at her feet in the gutter. On the television, they showed the truck blowing up through the clouds so quickly that the middle shot beyond the edges, which fluted out into a puffy, mushroom shape.

"Hiroshima was destroyed," the television said.

Katie could no longer hold the mirror. She dropped it and stared down at the braided rug that lay on the polished floorboards of her own house. She knew that it wasn't really happening again, that the woman was not lying at her feet right at this moment. Even though the television played it all over again, it had only happened once. Just as her father had explained to her that when they saw the newsreels of the war, they were just moving pictures. The war was all over.

But now that Katie knew the name of the woman it made her shudder and feel sick all over again. Before, the woman had been anonymous, thrown into her mortal pieces by chance at Katie Doheney's feet. Now she had a name, a pretty name, and Katie could imagine her friends calling to her as she got into her car that day, wearing the full-skirted, swirling dress.

"See you later, Hiroshima!" her friends said. She waved to them and drove away.

The eyes that Katie knew only as glazed, shocked and spattered with bits of gravel had once been alive. Then Hiroshima was destroyed.

Katie's father was trying to be quiet, but they were speaking just on the other side of her bedroom door. "How is she now?"

"She's asleep, I think," her mother said.

"I thought she would be crazy about the television."

"She will be. She's still upset by the accident."

"Well, I thought it would help."

They went into their own bedroom where their voices were quiet murmurs. Katie wanted to go to her parents, but she was afraid to get out of bed.

She had a ghost in her room.

2

"So you're Master Benson, eh?"

From the garden below the window in the music room came the smell of roses and sunlight. Phil was too small to see out the window without climbing on to the chair, but he was old enough to know he shouldn't. He stood and stared down at the carpet, which was well-worn around the piano.

Mr. Tackett (old, because he had gray hairs) sat on the mahogany piano bench with his back to the piano and smiled at Phil the way uncles or family friends smile at boys.

"Your mother told me all about you."

Phil rolled into a tube the envelope his mother had sent with him. It contained money. Phil wanted to give it to Mr. Tackett, have him open it, and be surprised at how much there was in it. At the same time, he wanted to keep it. So he stood and rolled it even more tightly, glancing at Mr. Tackett when he thought the old man wasn't looking.

"Your mother tells me that you play your granny's piano very well."

Phil nodded.

Mr. Tackett lit an unfiltered cigarette and blew smoke toward the window where a warm breeze carried it through the screen. "What do you play?" he asked.

"I make it up. Thunder and Lightning, mostly."

"Thunder and Lightning." Mr. Tackett grinned. "Seems to me that I used to play that, too."

"You did?" Phil was amazed. His father always said, "Shut up that noise!" But here was a piano teacher who knew Thunder and Lightning. Phil was exhilarated by the possibility of being understood by someone with this knowledge, but also disappointed. He thought he had invented the song himself.

"Come over here and sit down, Phil." Mr. Tackett patted the bench beside him. As Phil slid between the piano and the bench, the man hoisted him up with huge hands, which were strong around his ribs. It was the kind of lifting that would have made him say "Whee!" when he was younger— last year.

"OK, for a little while we're going to do something simpler than Thunder and Lightning, but it will still be just as much fun. I'm going to show you how to read notes of music that tell you what keys to play. You know how to read, don't you?"

"I know my ABC's," Phil said confidently.

"OK." Mr. Tackett seemed to notice the envelope for the first time. "Is this mine?" When Phil reluctantly nodded Mr. Tackett took it and tossed it lightly into the overstuffed chair across the room as if all the money meant nothing. "Put your hands on these keys all in a row. No, not your thumbs."

Phil looked over his shoulder at the envelope balanced on a corner against the cushion. He thought about how his mother had given it to him so nervously, reminding him never to tell his father about it or the piano lessons. "My pin money," she said. "He would wring our necks, P. J."

"Yes, that's right," the piano teacher said. "Now the keys all have letter names and this one is C. Middle C."

Mr. Tackett lifted his hairy, bony-knuckled hands away from Phil's like a magician releasing ten white doves. All that remained were a boy's grubby fingers on the cracked keys of an old and well-used piano. Phil pressed all the slippery keys down at once.

Thunder.

3
___

P H I L learned to play baseball out of self-defense. He had
learned somehow that other boys didn't dream about the
things of which he dreamed—of Chopin dying of consumption and writing about raindrops while his lover, a writer
who used a man's name, was away. Of Darius Milhaud sitting
in smoky jazz clubs in America and taking back the sounds
to France long before jazz was fashionable in the United
States. Of Robert and Clara Schumann and their devoted
friend, Brahms. He never quite understood the nature of this
devotion. It always seemed odd and gave a glimpse into a
world that he would learn about "someday" when he, too,
was a famous pianist and composer.

Other boys talked about Joe DiMaggio and going to see
the stock car races in Englewood and building model airplanes. Phil learned their language and dabbled in it because
he liked some of the boys and wanted to be friends. But he
had another side that he couldn't really explain to them.

He also learned to play baseball to please his father. He, like his father, saw that there was something subversive in classical music. It was not American. Even the American composers, like Copland, had ethnic backgrounds and weren't what his father called "one hundred percent American"—or they were like Gershwin and wrote music about black people or Cubans. Dipping into subversion frightened him. He had overheard some men talking about Senator McCarthy, and one said, "Next, children will be turning in their parents as Communists." Phil knew that he would never turn in his father, but he doubted that his father would hold back from punishing him. So he left this feeling of not being one hundred percent as a secret.

Neither was he natural with Mr. Tackett. He became a temperamental, romantic musician who had never been a boy on a hike with the Scouts on Pike's Peak nor had a bicycle nor knew how to heft a Louisville Slugger and bat over the shortstop's head. The inquisitive, conciliatory kid whom the teachers praised to his parents became dark and brooding and had a certainty that at some time during his life he would go deaf or blind, or die of consumption after many unhappy love affairs. He could imagine the blindness much more easily than the lovers, but he was aware that these things took time.

His most immediate struggle was with Mr. Tackett's constant criticism. As soon as he thought he had mastered something, Mr. Tackett would throw another wrench into the works, telling him to play it differently or giving him something else too hard to learn. He wanted to hear Mr. Tackett say that what he had accomplished was near perfection, or perfection itself. His teacher was an impossible taskmaster with a ready, gentle smile.

Phil loved him but knew better than to show it.

Mr. Tackett put up with the temper to a degree, but the day Phil threw his score over his shoulder onto one of his teacher's ever-burning Camels, it was enough.

"Philip," he said in a level voice, "boys your age do not say 'damn' nor do they throw tantrums when they can't master something the first time through." He brushed the ashes and cinders from his overstuffed brown chair. "In fact, we're not supposed to do that sort of thing at *my* age."

Phil ground his teeth.

"Pick it up."

He sat, staring at the black and white keyboard.

"All right. Apparently I can't teach you any more. Maybe you would rather spend your Wednesday afternoons playing ball or riding your bicycle. It would certainly make my life easier."

Phil fought to hold on to all the dignity that an eleven-year-old boy could muster. Stiffly he stood and picked up the music. The creamy vellum paper had a few singed marks on the coda. Phil was sorry and embarrassed. He shuffled it together and opened it solemnly on the piano.

"Try again."

Phil sat with his back to Mr. Tackett and picked at a wart on his knuckle.

"Hey," Mr. Tackett said gently. "Listen to me. This is going to be hard for you because your hands aren't fully grown yet. Look at the difference between your hands and mine, eh?" He held up his long, driftwoody fingers as if Phil had never seen them before. In fact, Phil had been watching them intently for five years and now gave them a grudging sideways look.

"But I know you can do it with practice."

Phil was suddenly horribly conscious of his own boyish hands.

Mr. Tackett rose, brushing still more tobacco crumbs from his trousers. He closed the door as he left the room.

Phil stared out the window at the sparrow on the cold metal post of the Cyclone fence. Beyond the Tacketts' garden, the mesa that was a prelude to the Rockies was shrouded in a low autumnal cloud. Between the cloud and where Phil sat at the edge of the Great Prairie, the air was clear but cool and turbulent. The coming change in the weather affected Phil to the marrow; he felt expectant and impatient. As he stretched his fingers over the keys he measured how far they would reach. To grow a little more, to get that extra note without banging his thumb against the corner of a wrong note . . .

He turned the score to the beginning.

As he practiced he ticked out the time with his tongue against the roof of his mouth just as he had done when he was a beginner. Several times he stumbled and started over. It was considerably better than the first time through.

He finished and stared down at his hands, aware that his hour was probably over. He didn't want to leave. He wished that he could live with the Tacketts and always have access to this room, for it was where he played his best. The little brown piano with keys like old teeth was all he could think of some days. In school, his fingertips played desktops in silent striving for mastery. Always there were stretches of music in him waiting for release into sound.

Mr. Tackett returned.

Phil's heart pounded against his ribs. "Well, you know I won't be able to practice it anyway," he said, his throat tight.

"Sure you can. That was better, wasn't it?"

"No, I mean my father's on strike and I can't practice at home and I won't have an allowance and he'll take my odd-job money anyway. So I guess I'll see you around." Phil dashed for the front door.

"Wait a minute, young man."

Phil would have taken his jacket and charged through the front door, but he was startled by the girl sitting on the sofa. He recognized her as one of the kids in the grade behind him. She looked at him with an equally startled expression, her eyes too big in a thin face, and slender neck burdened by thick braids.

"Phil, come back here." Mr. Tackett guided him to the music room and closed the door.

Phil stood, head hanging, and prepared for a lecture full of impossible adult reasoning.

"I've told you before that when your father won't let you practice you can come here. Don't worry about paying me. You can help out around here—take out the garbage, shovel the walks when the snow comes, whatever. I'll ask Mrs. T if she has any jobs for you."

Phil nodded uncertainly, thinking of the lies he would have to tell at home. He hated it when his father was off work. He and his mother both had to bear the result of his father's easily found boredom, but they found themselves in counterpoint rather than in harmony and so it was better to avoid his mother, too.

"Phil, look at me."

Phil raised his head. He observed for the first time how much younger Mr. Tackett's eyes were than the rest of his face. They were spry, happy eyes as they looked down upon him.

"I'm as proud of you as three fathers, but I get pretty

discouraged when you give up so easily. It's a lot of work, music, and you have to stay at it. Never, never let other people get in your way."

Phil nodded obediently.

"OK. Go. See you in a few days, eh?"

Mr. Tackett followed him to the front door. As Phil put his jacket on, Mr. Tackett said, "Do you know Katie Doheney?"

"Hi." He didn't want to make conversation with some fifth grader. Contemptuously he glanced at her hands and derived satisfaction from the fact that they were even smaller than his own.

Snow scrunched under her red rubber boots as she walked along Kit Carson Boulevard. There was a strange lull in town—she wasn't often downtown at half past four in winter when the light was beginning to fade. Most of the kids went straight home from school or to play at other houses. The cars with men coming home from work wouldn't start sloshing up and down until five. It was late November, too early for the eager Christmas shoppers to be compelled to come out in the snow like this.

Katie liked the snow but feared it. She loved to look at the flakes and count their six sides before they melted into droplets on her coat sleeve. With her sisters, she used to make snow cream with snow, vanilla, powdered sugar and condensed milk. But now they said that it was dangerous to eat the snow; it had fallout from the bomb tests. The fallout came right over the Rockies in the clouds. Covered with boots, mittens, muffler and knitted cap, Katie was protected from the snowflakes except on her face and hair. Each one stung her where it touched her bare skin.

She hurried along to get out of it and to fetch the medicine for her mother, who was ill with influenza. When she reached the glass front of the music shop, she slowed down. Inside the shop was Phil Benson, walking around the three pianos in the shop with his hands behind his back, leaning over and peering but not touching them.

Then his hands released and fell to the polished wood. His fingertips stroked it very lightly. His face was intent, his hair scattered forward boyishly in what was otherwise to Katie a grown-up look.

She felt a thrill at watching him secretly, feeling that she knew him better than anyone else on earth. She spied him caressing the instrument, loving it more than people ever loved each other. Katie felt a pang of envy. She loved nothing so much—except at that moment she loved his passion for the piano.

Knowing that if he saw her, it would be spoiled—he would be a boy, she would be just a girl, his musical conspiracy with the universe would be locked away as it was at school—she turned from the window and headed for home.

For several steps, she forgot to put her head down and guard against the irradiated snowflakes that were burning holes of slow death into her skin.

4

MRS. T let him in with a smile. "Hello, Phil."

"Hi." He listened to the lesson being given. That Doheney girl was still laboring over the same Mozart piece he
had heard her start on last week while he was painting the
back door.

When Mrs. T took a basket of laundry out the back door,
Phil edged down the hallway toward the music room. Sometimes he listened to Mr. Tackett with his other students like
a jealous lover listening in on telephone conversations. At
one time he had suspected that he might be Mr. Tackett's
favorite pupil. Then he heard him praising others even
though they made mistakes in timing or accent or couldn't
quite get the feel of a piece. For example, Katie. She always
got a big pat on the head for the simplest things. She even
confessed that she wanted to switch to violin next school
year, which was like treason to Phil. He couldn't understand
how anyone would abandon the wooden gods and goddesses

with their taut strings across curved diagonal frames decorated with shiny bits of metal and pads of felt.

Violins weren't bad, though. At least she wasn't going to take up the flute or something like that. Phil knew a lot about instruments from hanging around the music store and talking to Tony, the salesman. Tony didn't treat him like just a kid—they had even had a Coke together once at the drugstore. But Tony had to be careful about Mr. Sawyer, the owner of Rocky Mountain Music, because he didn't like to see Tony talking to kids instead of wiping the fingerprints off trumpets or flirting with the ladies who brought their kids in for rental instruments.

Katie fumbled and Mr. Tackett said nothing. Phil stood outside the door, flooding with resentment. He picks on me, he thought. I could never get away with that.

As he tiptoed back to the front room she stretched another sixteenth to a quarter. "Count!" Mr. Tackett barked. Phil felt better.

When they emerged Phil was reading *Life* magazine. He didn't look up or speak. Mr. Tackett made an "oh" of surprise and said, "Did I forget to tell you that I have another appointment this afternoon?"

"Oh. Yeah. You told me." Phil put the magazine back on the coffee table and picked up his music folder.

"Have to go, boy. How about tomorrow?"

"I can practice at home tomorrow."

"You can practice at my house now if you want to," Katie said.

Phil ignored her. He didn't like this girl talking to him all the time. She said hello to him at school, which embarrassed him. The other kids told stories about her. One day, during civil defense drill, the teacher had to send her home because she got hysterical and wouldn't get under her desk. She just stood in the middle of the room and screamed for her mother. That was a few years ago. When she was a first grader she ran home every day when the noon whistle blew because she thought it was an air raid siren.

One of his friends had a sister who was in Katie's grade. His sister brought home a copy of Katie's essay on the Bomb. Phil and Cal laughed themselves sick over her phrase, "I know what the Bomb is like. It explodes and there are legs and heads and torn dresses and blood everywhere."

What a baby. She was wrong, too. The Bomb *melts* people.

"Come on, Phil," she said.

Phil shrugged. "I gotta go home, I guess. Bye, Mr. Tackett." As he went down the sidewalk he heard Katie clomping after him in her saddle shoes. He looked at her suspiciously as she caught up with him. What did she want with him anyway? Other than music, she was far beyond him in the way girls are. When she wasn't crying about bombs, she was winning spelling bees.

"I told my mom how good you play," she said, "but she doesn't believe me."

"Naa," he said, torn by the flattery and challenge all in one line.

"Don't be a stuck-up."

"I'm not. I don't want to bother your mom."

"She'll like it if you play our piano. Mr. Tackett said I shouldn't feel bad if I don't learn as fast as you because you're a genius. I'm good, though. I have musical talent."

"Genius? He said that?" Phil, confused but proud, tried to compare himself to Albert Einstein, the only genius he could conjure. He couldn't think of anything he had in common with Dr. Einstein except that they both had bicycles.

But of course, Dr. Einstein could afford new inner tubes, which Phil couldn't. His bicycle had been in the garage for months.

"Uck," Katie said. "I have a pain in my tummy."

"I don't want your germs." Phil dodged away from her, scuffling in the gutter while she neatly stepped along the sidewalk, missing all the cracks. "Did he really say that?"

"Well . . ."

"Come on. Gotta tell."

"No, I don't."

"Tell me."

"Say please."

Phil walked in the gutter a few more paces, then stepped on the walk with one foot, staggering between the two levels with exaggerated stiff-legged monster steps. "Please," he finally said.

"He said it once because I cried when I couldn't play something."

Baby, he thought. He was hoping that she wouldn't ask him again to go home with her because then he would have to say no. He simply followed her as if he hadn't noticed that they had passed his turn. "So what did he say?"

"I *told* you. Where do you live?"

"Roosevelt Street," he answered.

"Oh. In a new house?"

"No. I've lived there all my life."

"My house is really old. One of the oldest in town. Dad says it's fifty years old. I have two big sisters. Do you have any brothers or sisters?"

"No." Phil stopped staggering and walked beside Katie. "We used to have a dog, but she ate some mouse poison."

"We can't have any pets. My sister's allergic." She adjusted her music folder in the crook of her arm. "Do you want to carry my book?"

"No."

"My neighbor broke her wrist yesterday. I saw it. It was bent like . . . like . . ." She held out her arms and crossed one over the other, which did nothing to help Phil visualize what she might have seen. He noticed that she was shuddering. Why are girls so sick? he wondered.

"Here's my house."

"Oh."

"Well, come on," she insisted when he paused.

Phil followed her in, sniffing out the new territory. Her house did seem old and had what his father would call a "mick" smell of cabbage, vinegar, scalded milk and beer. The furniture was deeply cushioned and covered with lace doilies. Katie pointed to the mirror over the mantel in the front room. "My Granny Byrne brought that all the way from Ireland."

Their piano was much like the one his grandmother had finally given him, a dark brown upright with chipped keys and a blistering veneer.

"Mom!" Katie shouted. "Guess what! Phil Benson is here."

Phil went to the piano and set up his music. He had begun to play a Chopin prelude to warm up when he saw a woman standing in the doorway that led into the hall he had only glimpsed. She was a tall and thin kind of mother, whereas his own was short and round, but in all other ways ordinary. Phil had thought she might look really different, having such a loony daughter. He stopped playing when she came in, wondering if she were going to tell him to stop making so much noise. He remembered his manners and said, "Hello."

"Would you like some lemonade, Phil?"

"Yes, Mrs. Doheney." He smiled, liking her. Relieved that he had found a sanctuary for the afternoon's practicing, he played on and tried to smooth out the wrinkles he had felt in the previous session with the prelude. He felt that in the middle of composing it Chopin must have received a letter with good news or had an exceptional bit of chocolate because the mood changed so much.

He found Katie companionable to play for. She didn't talk to him but sat in the room, reading. She spoke to him only between pieces and then didn't gush over him like his mother did but asked him interesting questions such as "How much time do you spend practicing?" or, "Do you still do scales?" An older sister, later introduced as Margie, came in and sat down and was as quiet as Katie. She just gave her whole attention and didn't even pick up anything to read. When he had flourished out a little Mozart rondo that he knew Katie had been laboring over a few weeks ago, Mrs. Doheney stopped at the door and told him that he played beautifully.

Phil thanked her and closed his music folder. He began to hammer out a Schubert song that he knew from memory, thinking that it would also impress Katie.

"Oh, Mom, I have a terrible stomach ache!" Katie said.

Phil heard her but didn't turn to look until she made a horrible noise that only girls can make, a particular moaning wail. He saw Katie standing with her hands behind her, face chalky. He frowned at the interruption by this kid and her tummy ache but then noticed the dribble of dark blood streaking down her skinny leg from her inner thigh.

"You're bleeding!" he shouted.

Mrs. Doheney did a mother-hustle on Katie, whisking

her through to the hallway. Phil saw a dark stain on the upholstery where Katie had been sitting.

"I'm dying!" Katie screamed. "I've got radiation poisoning!"

"Katherine Alice, settle down," Mrs. Doheney said. Her voice echoed up the hallway. "We talked about this. Do you remember?"

Phil looked at Margie who had been frozen on the sofa. "What's the matter with her?" he asked. "What is it?"

Margie blushed hard. "I don't know." She left the room quickly. Instead of seeing about her sister, though, she ran up the stairs.

Phil walked through the hall hesitantly. The bathroom door was shut, but he could hear Mrs. Doheney's voice soothing her daughter.

"Should I get a doctor?" he asked, thinking that he was the only one with a cool head.

"She's all right. Thank you, Phil." Mrs. Doheney's face appeared as she cracked the bathroom door slightly.

"What's the matter with her?"

"Well . . ." Now the mother was blushing, too. "It's just something that girls go through."

"Oh." Now Phil understood why everyone was turning red. He didn't know all the facts, but he knew enough to relate this event to a box of weird things that appeared in the bathroom of his own house every now and then. "Well, I'm going home now."

"Bye, Phil," Katie said meekly from within the bathroom.

"Bye." He felt a little sick during his walk home. It was frightening to see someone bleed like that—not just scary like someone being stabbed or shot, but it was something immense and unstoppable without a visible cause. It hadn't really been radiation poisoning but it might as well have. He remembered a time when Ronny brought one of those woman things to school with a bit of brown blood on it. So, Katie does that, too. But she's just a girl.

He walked listlessly, feeling peculiar tugs of tightness and giddiness. Now Katie seemed more superior and mysterious than ever.

I *can* play the piano better. He thought about how her mother and sister had listened to him, too. It had given him all the pleasure and none of the nervousness of a good recital. But that blood! He felt scornful, repelled, fascinated and protective toward the silly kid.

She wasn't sleeping. Dreams were different stuff from this. She lay in her bed, eyes shut, the bed softly folding around her as she drifted down near sleep.

There it was again.

First the siren, unlike police or fire, a more urgent single note.

Her teacher made her go under her desk, but she knew that wouldn't work. It comes through wood, it comes through glass and even steel. The only safe place is down, down deep under the ground. So as soon as the teacher was hiding, too, she got out.

Hurry!

She ran in the empty streets with the siren screaming. All the houses that stood behind their picket fences, windows open and curtains flapping, would soon be piles of rubble. She imagined the heaps of brick, clapboard, and shrunken stoves and fridges steaming with radiation. This was Wilson Street, within the fifty-mile circle around Cheyenne Mountain where soldiers in silos with missiles toggled switches and marked things on clipboards, grim-faced in the sounding of sirens.

She ran around the corner of Peach Street toward Second Avenue, heading for home. She saw Phil walking casually as if he couldn't hear the sirens.

"Come with me!" she shouted.

Together they ran for her house. Just as they reached her lawn, where she could see her mother's face watching for her behind the screen door, there was a brilliant flash.

Katie was swept up by the explosion, lifted high above the town. Unharmed, exhilarated by the ride, she could look down and see her street, then the next one; as she rose, all the streets in the town lay under her like a picture map. The cloud she rode was hot and smelled of steam and metal, but it didn't burn her. She was numb except for the lifting sensation.

Traveling at a fantastic speed she saw the town grow smaller and smaller. Then she could see from Castle Rock to Colorado Springs and could look across the top of Pike's Peak into the southwestern front range of the Colorado Rockies, which were pink and orange with reflecting snow.

Arms and legs, piano stools, and a little mewing grey cat spun and twirled with her as she rose even above the Rockies and could see from Kansas City to California, Mount Rushmore to the Rio Grande. And there was Hiroshima, too, in her dress, spinning and spinning.

"Good night, Katie," her mother said.

"Good night, Mom." Katie rolled over onto her side and pulled the blanket over her shoulder.

5

___

KATIE had always supposed that she wouldn't like sex, that it was something boys knew about and wanted to "get," like double-barreled carburetors or the right track shoes. She had thought that even if it wasn't downright disgusting, the most pleasure she would have from it would be the equivalent of listening with the patience of a girlfriend to boys talking about boy things.

But she lay in the bed of a cabin that belonged to a friend of a friend of Phil's, feeling delicious. Outside was a ghost town named Alice, which wasn't more than a few weather-beaten cabins and the smell of ice from St. Mary's Glacier and the pine. The wind in the trees sounded like a running mountain creek, but she knew that the creek was far below their steep mountainside. She still pulsed within, her skin alive and alert to the sheets, to Phil's palm on her ribs and his thigh against her. A creamy fish odor puffed out of the bedclothes with every movement.

Phil seemed spent and limp, but she was thinking that she would like to try it again. She wiggled her feet luxuriously, almost as happy to have the feeling of wanting it as to be having it. He gave a deeply contented sigh and turned on to his side, facing her, which pulled a draft of cold air under the covers. She snuggled closer, shivering.

"Well?" he asked.

"I love you. I never thought . . ."

"I love *you*."

"I'll never regret this."

"Why would you regret it?" he asked sleepily.

"Well . . ." Katie started forming the defense against what she knew people would say if they knew. It led to imagining her mother, teachers and girlfriends at school thinking her a slut for letting Phil have his way with her. She didn't want to think about it in that way, but the principle of keeping virginity until marriage was automatic in spite of Phil's arguments. The saints were probably crying at this very moment. The facts of what she had done and what might happen gave her a quick and profound depression. She began to cry.

"What's the matter?" He sounded alarmed.

"I'll . . . I'll never get married now. No one will have me."

"What are you talking about?" He peered at her through the darkness. "*I'm* going to marry you."

"Well, you've never asked me. Besides, you'll meet someone else when you're at college and I'll be an old maid. Or I'll get pregnant." She was in misery, certain that there were no happy solutions. Her future was damned. "If we have to get married, the Tacketts will never forgive me for ruining your career and my parents will be disgraced and your parents will disown you."

"Katie, I thought you said it was safe."

She rolled away from him, unable to look at his face any longer. In the night it was so pale and his eyes were eerily dark. His sandy hair was all awry; a cowlick stood sideways on his crown. She loved him so *much*, she knew that she couldn't possibly love anyone else. Thinking about what they had just done and how it was the best and closest they could be, she decided it didn't matter what happened. It was worth sacrificing her life to give It to Phil. She wouldn't regret it. This was what Love Was All About.

"Once you do it," she explained, now remembering a bit of girls' lavatory folk wisdom, "you go crazy for it. I won't be able to resist you any more. And then I won't be able to resist other boys when you've gone."

"Then why did you let me do it?" he asked, irritated.

"Because I wanted . . ." How could she explain it? All the other boys were yucky. She loved him. She wanted to give him the one thing she could only give once—the first and most meaningful time. "Because I love you."

"Who says we can't be married?" He sat up suddenly, which made his thigh and nothing else her entire view. She moved back but he gripped her shoulder. "If I can't have you I'm not going to marry anyone. So if no one will marry you because you're not a virgin, neither of us will be married. So why don't we get married? I can still go to the university. You can stay with your folks and we can be together at term breaks. Let's go get married now. If we drive to—"

"No."

"What do you mean 'no'? We love each other. I don't understand. Are you saying you don't want to be my wife?"

Katie rose in the bed. She reached up and touched his face, pleading. She wanted to restore things to the way they had been ten minutes ago.

His fingers tightened on her. "You're mine, old bony Doheney."

"I'm not yours. It's not like having a piano or a car."

"Oh-ho. I suppose you *want* to go out with other guys while I'm gone then. You're probably already crazy for them. You might not have resisted no matter what we did."

Katie was silent. She didn't know how to answer.

"Stop teasing me, Katherine. You wouldn't."

"Take me home." She threw the blankets back.

He grabbed her and began to tickle her. "Gotcha now."

"Oh, Phil."

He let her go. Without conversation they dressed and she smoothed out the bed. During that silence Katie thought about the Tacketts. She had always loved the Tacketts, but after Mrs. T took her aside and told her not to drag Phil down with marriage and babies, and that love could wait if it was strong enough, she had avoided their house. Somehow, she felt it was all true, that she would have to let go of him because he had something bigger to do than be her husband. He was a genius, not an ordinary man. No woman should possess him and hold him down.

As they prepared to leave the cabin Phil put his arms around her and gazed at her closely. "Listen," he said, "I love you, Katie, and I'll do anything in the world for you. Just remember that."

She began to cry. He soothed her and soon they were undressed again.

Katie picked up her mother's sewing scissors and clipped out the article from the local newspaper about Phil going away to college on a music scholarship. As she trimmed the edge, her mother leaned over her shoulder.

"Are you going to say good-bye to him?" Mrs. Doheney asked.

"I don't know." Katie stared forlornly at the name of the university in Missouri, which might as well be a million miles from home. She and Phil had not spoken more than a passing hello for about two months, since the night he tried to kidnap her and take her across the state line to elope. It had caused their most furious argument ever. When Katie discovered where Phil was intending to drive, she ordered him to stop the car and turn around. He had refused.

"I'm not going to marry you now!" she insisted.

"When will you then?" he had asked, angry at being commanded.

"Phil," she pleaded, "think how disappointed our families would be if we ran away to get married. They would want to be there."

"Well, *my* family, anyway," he said bitterly.

"What do you mean?"

"*Your* family must be dead set against it. You act like someone's turning you against me."

"My family loves you. You know that." Katie sighed in exasperation. "C'mon. Stop the car."

"Why don't you want me anymore?"

"I *do* want you! We're just not ready. You have to go to college first."

"Lots of people—"

"You aren't like lots of people!" she said, losing patience. It was hard to resist him. More than anything in the world, she wanted to share his dream of the two of them living in an apartment near campus, Katie working while Phil studied. Together. Together all the time. Wouldn't they be happy?

But Mrs. Tackett had squashed that. "You would argue about money. You wouldn't be happy. Phil wouldn't be able to concentrate on his music. He wouldn't be free to work hard, to be spontaneous. He couldn't practice and practice all night as some students do, because you would need your sleep for your job. You might be envious of him studying while you have some awful job as a waitress or something. What then? Let him go for a few years. He'll come back to you if you really love each other." Then Mrs. T paused and added the final words with which Katie couldn't battle. "Besides, if you really love someone, dear, you do what's best for them and not just what you want."

"Turn the car around, Phil," Katie said. "Take me home."

"I'll just do that. I can see how things are." They drove home in a thick brown silence.

The weekend after that had happened, she had heard that he had taken Annie Belton to the movies in Colorado Springs. She had cried so hard and so long that her eldest sister, Mary-Rose, had taken Katie home with her, fed her cups of chamomile tea and tried to distract her with the new baby. Playing with Mary-Rose's baby and seeing her sister and brother-in-law in what looked like complete domestic bliss only made Katie more unhappy.

She started having the pre-sleep dreams again.

Tomorrow, Phil would be gone and she might never see him again in her life. She was sure she would die an old maid, lonely and heartbroken because she couldn't ruin the life of the only man she would ever love.

"Oh, go see him," her mother said. "You can at least be friends, can't you?"

In the afternoon, she found the courage to go to his house, where his mother acted both glad and nervous to see her and told her that Phil had gone to the drugstore.

She found Phil there, receiving swats on his head and shoulders from well-wishers. She thought he seemed falsely hearty and wondered why he was putting up with it. It was unlike him to seek what he had always thought of as the phony attention of the townsfolk whenever anyone *did* anything, such as the time the good-for-nothing young Brown went off to Korea like a hero.

"Katie?"

They half-smiled at each other. At once Katie understood that he had been waiting for her.

"Come and have a Coke with me."

Trembling, Katie sat across the booth from him. The expression of wounded love on his face struck her to the core. She couldn't look at him. It was a relief when Bobby came and sat down beside Phil.

"Hey, hot shot," he said, "I always thought you'd get your name in the paper for running into a cow with that old wreck of yours."

Phil laughed. "Jerk." He only glanced at Bobby before staring across the table again.

Katie smiled. Phil put his foot on hers under the table. Just the touch gave her an extraordinary physical intoxication.

"Howya been, Doheney?"

"Not so good." She realized her mistake as soon as it

had slipped out. If she got mushy she would weaken. "I stubbed my toe on the back porch last week."

"Let me kiss it," he said with passion.

Katie couldn't control herself any more. Tears came even though she thought she had cried them all out.

Bobby tactfully left them. Phil moved around to her side of the booth and put his arm around her. "Katie, Katie."

She nodded, blowing her nose with a napkin.

"I'll come back. And if you ever, ever need me, just give me a call, OK?"

Katie nodded again.

The last of the summer crickets chirped in the faint moonlight. It was a crisply hot night; the sheets he sat on and the clothes strewn about the room, which were soon to be packed into three suitcases, smelled freshly ironed by the dry August heat. He stared, his mind alternately as vacant as the gaping drawers in the pine chest and as full and busy as the nightlife of the insect world in the garden.

He was lonely—the last man on a train to Nowhere.

Beyond his back fence were the houses that had been built on vacant land where once he had dug for buried treasure. And an irrigation ditch where he caught crawdads that had then been carelessly starved in cardboard shoe boxes. Beyond those houses were the flat mesas introducing the grander foothills and eventually the mountains. He had never grown tired of seeing the mountains; every day of his life he had turned his head when he first left the house to check— are they purple, blue or white today?

His room was a shambles from sorting and packing. The highly varnished knotty pine furniture was covered with mementos of his eighteen years: stacks of music books and scores, certificates and ribbons for his achievements, the Little League Baseball group photos, gifts that Katie had given him—a blue velvet pillow with a secret message embroidered inside, a cast-iron piano bank, a civil defense manual, her junior year photo. Yesterday he had started to take down the prints and sketches of composers on his wall, but his mother's trembling lip made him decide to leave them up. He would be back for visits anyway. It would make him happy to see the familiar Beethoven scowl when he returned.

In the front room his parents muttered to each other, probably about his bus schedule. They were filled with his plans, covering every detail and possible variation. After all the years of battling with his father's impatience about the music (the noise, the awful racket), now he was finally beginning to see that his father was a little proud of him. In his way. And his mother . . . He thought of her giving him all the money she could embezzle from the household budget for piano lessons until the day she simply said, "Dad, you've got to give me money for Phil's music." His father had been so surprised by her firmness that he assented without more than raised eyebrows and a wheezy sigh.

Phil was determined to make them proud. He could imagine his father standing in front of the hardware store with the other men, all of them wearing work shirts with wet patches under the arms and trousers with greasy thighs, drinking Grapettes and holding their cigarettes with a thumb and three fingers like tough film actors. Someone would say, "Hey, Benson, how's that kid of yours doing?" And his father would chuckle and say, "Oh, he's just won another of those darned piano competitions. Don't know where he gets it—must be his mother's side of the family."

Life to his father was just as he saw it; he had everything he needed or wanted except a little more pocket money. How easy that would be, too, except that he would have to give up Saturday morning puttering with the car or taking his wife down to the new discount department store just off the highway.

It was actually Mr. Tackett and Mrs. T whom Phil imagined sitting in the front row of the concert hall some day, watching him with all the pride in the world. Phil already missed the man who believed in him and had guided him, growing more wizened and tobacco-stained through the years.

He didn't want to go, but how could he make anyone proud if he stayed here in this arid, scrubby waste of Front Range culture? These people cared a lot more about square dancing than *real* music.

But he was afraid to go. Katie, Katie, he moaned. Every time he thought of her, a lion of uncertainty came alive, roaring and clawing, drowning out everything else that might be important in his life.

Resisting the impulse to slam the drawers, he quietly pushed them in and began to fold his shirts.

1962

6

H E rode the bus from Missouri to Colorado in his suit, the suit his parents had bought for him because they had an idea that he was going to a place like Oxford where the young men always wore jackets and the professors wore gowns. It was the first time he had worn it; his usual dress was khaki trousers and a cotton shirt. He found a five-dollar bill in his breast pocket where he should have had a handkerchief and imagined his father secretly putting it in there the day they had sent him off more than a year ago. He could have used that five a few times—no matter, he wouldn't have had it now for candy bars, potato chips and a ham sandwich if he had spent it then. He thought that it would have been useful if his father had also hidden a handkerchief in the pocket. Today, it's possible he would have to use it.

He changed buses in Denver, absently carrying the evening newspaper from Salina, Kansas with him. It was his first visit home since last Christmas. Having looked at the green hills of Missouri for so long, he was stunned by the ugliness of the reddish plateaus and barren scrubby hills that led to the mountains. All his life he had believed the motto: Colorful Colorado. But he found the eastern plain a wasteland. The mountains, at last, were a welcome sight, today deep blue, and reassuringly still magnificent. He had missed them.

The Salina crossword puzzle took him only fifteen minutes of the journey south from Denver and left him with grey smudges on his hands.

A deep feeling of apprehension twisted within him as the bus turned off the main highway, lumbered beside the creek, and rolled into town to stop at the courthouse. He was the only one leaving the bus and felt his suit, his small case, and the town gave other passengers a picture of him that he would never have a chance to correct.

He walked directly to the church.

"Oh, young Benson, hello, there." The pastor came toward him with hands outstretched.

"Hello." Phil put down his suitcase and shook his hand, acutely conscious of how dirty his hands were. He was the first one to arrive at the church, apart from the pastor, and was glad he had been able to duck through town without speaking to anyone.

"Well," the pastor said, looking into Phil's eyes. "It was very inventive of Mrs. Tackett to request you." By the emphasis on the word "inventive" Phil understood that the preacher didn't like the idea, not one bit. "I was wondering," he said neutrally, "if we could start the service out with something a little more traditional—a hymn, perhaps?"

"Yes, sir. Whatever you decide."

"Good, good." The pastor led him to the piano, which

stood opposite the choir benches. A battered book of hymns was opened. "Would you like to practice it?" the pastor asked, straining to look through Phil's eyes into his soul.

"No, I know it." Mr. Tackett had tortured him with it once long ago, and he certainly didn't feel like playing it more than once.

Carrying a dull silver coffin, three men entered the church. He recognized them as members of the Brown family, undertakers. They all nodded to him decorously.

"I would like to wash my hands," Phil said.

"Of course. Right through there." The pastor pointed and smiled sweetly.

Phil walked into the social wing of the church. Folding chairs and card tables stood against one wall, leaving the brown linoleum bare. The other side of the room had bulletin boards pinned with coloring book pages of Jesus holding a lamb, Jonah and the whale, Joseph's 64-Crayola-colored coat, and New England steepled churches made red and blue by children who probably likened them to the Tivoli Brewers tower in Denver. Phil glimpsed a toilet behind a narrow door.

He could hear the coffin thump in the other room. As he locked himself in the toilet, he hoped no one would come looking for him for a few minutes.

Sitting at the piano throughout the service, Phil could see Mr. Tackett in his coffin. Funny how old people get so small and dry. Mr. Tackett was dressed in his "recital" suit with a new hankie poking out three points from the pocket. His hands were folded across his chest. Those broad hands had been full of music once, reaching an octave and a note— like Rachmaninov. Now they appeared frail and brittle, his fingernails neatly pared and still yellowish. The tobacco stains on his right hand had nearly been scrubbed off. His shell-rimmed glasses were missing. He wouldn't need them in the grave, but without them the corpse didn't look like Mr. Tackett.

Phil had delayed his appearance with a walk and two cigarettes so that his parents, Mrs. T or anyone he knew wouldn't have a chance to speak to him beforehand. His own parents were just sitting down when he came in. His mother mouthed something like, "Where were you?" Phil shrugged with incomprehension. His father gave him a transparent glance as if he were seeing a photograph of Phil rather than the genuine son. Mrs. T gave him a smile when she came in surrounded by strangers, probably her relatives from out of town. Phil didn't spot any of his friends from school, but there were many faces he recognized as pupils who had visited Mr. Tackett's house weekly. Some were grown with families now; some were still children in school, having just begun when Phil went away.

Phil knew that most of the town regarded him as an oddity. Now he felt this was compounded by the college-boy image. If they only knew what that really means, he thought, falling into their expectations by remaining surly and distant. He stopped searching the congregation. The face he most wanted to see but dreaded seeing was not there.

It was hot for September, hot even for an Indian summer. The smell of gladioli and chrysanthemums and ladies' perfume in the damp warmth of the church smothered any hope for a clean breath of air. He could not have been more uncomfortable if he had been covered with boiling oil.

The pastor, who had probably spoken to Mr. Tackett three or four times in his life, droned on about how much he had meant to the community, to the youth, and about how much his music spread the goodness of man. Somehow he reduced everything in Mr. Tackett's life to the fine point of being better off dead in the arms of Jesus. Phil refrained from making faces, aware that he was on stage, too.

Finally, the latecomer arrived. Phil knew that her lateness was as deliberate as his delay had been. Katie looked at him quickly, then away again as if to pretend she hadn't seen him. But her cheeks flamed. She had her husband with her— Perry, the new young fire chief. Phil's mother had written to him about the marriage cautiously and with some bewilderment. He understood that his mother, a woman of a basically generous nature, didn't like Perry. Now he saw why. He was tall and red-faced, with a belly that one could imagine falling outward a little more with each beer-drinking baseball season. Perry wore an unpleasant expression and guided Katie into the pew as if she were his responsibility, not his lover.

Phil could imagine only one thing that would have let Katie Dohency fall into the clutches of such a beefy prole. He had a bomb shelter.

They stood in prayer; then the pastor gave Phil his cue. Phil stiffened for a fleeting second of stage fright. He had to get it right. Old Mr. Tackett deserved at least that.

First, Debussy's "Clair de Lune."

"Have I told you the story," Mr. Tackett once said, "about the man who was so moved by this piece that when he decided to end his life he sat by the record player and, at the last note, shot himself?"

"Yes, sir. I hate that story."

"Oh, don't you be depressed, Phil. I only see it as an example of how important music can be to people. Would he have done it anyway? I think so, but it makes one wonder what else could give a man a final moment like that. Surely not a painting, for there are no moments in visual art. Not prose or poetry or dramatic arts because those are too social and interactive. No. Understand that music pours into a man's heart unfiltered, pure and abstract."

"I'll remember that if I ever choose a moment." Phil had been old enough for cynicism but not nuance.

"Yes, well, you can choose music for a moment of life as well—like weddings or graduations." (And funerals, Phil thought now.) "Ah, but you have such a life ahead of you, my Paderewski, my Horowitz, my Chopin."

Then, Phil played Beethoven's "Für Elise."

On a quiet day not too long before Phil left for Missouri, Mr. Tackett had sat, smoking and silent, his elbow propped on a stack of scores on the lamp table. He was not commenting on the composition Phil had finally brought out of hiding. Phil swung his legs around and faced his teacher. "Well?"

Mr. Tackett seemed reluctant to answer. "Before I criticize that aggravating concoction you've just played, let me tell you that simplicity is not a fault of the unsophisticated. Simplicity is elegance. Isn't 'Für Elise' a breathtaking piece of music with a simple melody?"

No one applauded at the end of the peculiar funeral music, nor did Phil expect them to. They sat woodenly in the pews, blinking, slapping at an occasional fly. Probably relieved that the esoteric racket was over, they waited for the pastor to give the signal that they could return to a Saturday afternoon of washing the car, listening to the radio, painting the garage, playing croquet. They may have thought it inconsiderate of Mrs. T to insist on a Saturday service so the young ones wouldn't have to miss school. Phil imagined he could hear whispered conferences about whether to go to Sally's diner or just home for hot dogs.

Phil watched across the coffin as a file of mourners passed. Mrs. T turned her head toward him, refocused her eyes, and smiled. Just a little. Just enough.

She probably still believed what Mr. Tackett had said. "Some day, Phil, people are going to ask you who your teacher was. If you mention my name, that will be the achievement of my life."

Awkward young Philip Benson carried the sum of another man's life in his fingers. His hands became so heavy with this knowledge that he could not lift them out of the self-conscious tangle on his lap.

"Hello, Mother." Phil leaned over and kissed her. She looked ever the same, unremarkable, mother-shaped and slightly distracted. Phil shook hands with his father, who gave him that same transparent gaze and called him "boy" with more affection than he ever had done before. His father was not a children's man. Phil suddenly saw this, coming back from the distance. He and his father might get along all right if they talked man-stuff to each other.

Phil stood with his parents as Mrs. T climbed out of the limousine and came across the grass to the grave. She was still beset with relatives to whom she seemed indifferent. She gave the suddenly shy music students longing looks, apparently hoping for rescue. Phil had just made a step toward her when he saw Katie and Perry arrive. He became inert.

Her slim black dress made her look thinner than ever. A pillbox hat à la Jacqueline Kennedy perched on her hair, which was twisted into a French roll and stapled with hairpins. She was still gawky but had more of the look of a young wife than the girl he had known.

Had known.

It hurt him to think he didn't really know her any longer. In fact, dressed and coiffed as she was, he might have passed her on the street without knowing it. He didn't know what to do as he watched them come nearer—say hello? Pretend we're just friends? Pretend we're virtually strangers?

The first Christmas he had returned home from Missouri had gone so wrong that he should have known he was losing her. After riding hours on the bus, he had dropped his bags, hugged his mother and dashed over to the Doheneys'.

Katie was at a party.

By the time he saw her the next day, he was beyond anger and well-steeped in hurt and bewilderment. She pointed out that he hadn't told her exactly when he would be home. Besides, when she stayed at home too much she always began to brood. Phil knew what that meant. Katie didn't just brood about little things like love or money or the color of her hair like other girls might—she fretted about missile silos and what should happen if a country like Brazil got the Bomb.

In the end, he realized later, that because of her neurotic fears, she needed constant attention, company, and someone to play the survival game with. Her family was too offhand and easygoing to take her seriously. Her letters to him became infrequent and vague, full of news but not much affection. His mother gave him gentle warnings that Katie was being seen with this boy or that—information which chilled Phil to the bone. Following long days and nights of worrying about her, he got a letter that said, "I think it would best for both of us if we didn't stick to promises made when we were so young. We both need to grow up."

Phil sat, head in hands, on his bed in the dorm recalling her, analyzing her. Eventually he realized that he had abandoned a fragile woman. He wrote to her that he would come home and they could be together again.

"No," she had said, "don't do that." No. Don't come home.

Six months later, he heard about the wedding. He had spent the summer in Missouri rather than come back and be in the same town with her. There had been time enough to put it in the past, but . . . Katie had been his forever. How could she possibly be someone else's wife?

To his amazement she walked toward him rapidly with an expression of determination. Perry sauntered behind her. "Hi," she said quickly. "Hello, Mrs. Benson. How are you?"

"Fine, dear." Phil's mother grew a worried face. She turned to look for her husband, who had wandered a few feet away to talk to a neighbor. "Excuse me."

"How are you?" Katie asked Phil. She sounded brusque, hurried.

"I'm all right," Phil said, uncertain about what he wanted to express to her.

"This is my husband, Perry Davis. Perry, this is Phil."

"Hi." Perry seemed to know exactly who Phil was from the tone of his voice.

They shook hands.

"How long are you going to be in town?" Katie asked.

"Leaving tomorrow."

"Oh. I thought you might drop by for a beer some time."

"Sorry, can't. Between my parents and Mrs. T . . ." Phil

noticed that she was trembling. Good. And he noticed that Perry had stopped smiling and squinted, as if he couldn't believe what his wife was saying. Phil understood that Katie would be trouble for a man like that. He hoped that Perry wasn't as mean as he looked. Might be a big old puppy, Phil thought lamely.

"Well, maybe we'll see you sometime then," she said, moving away with Perry.

The entourage had arranged itself around the graveside; the services were about to begin. Phil followed his parents and sat on a chair under the canopy, wishing that he had never come home. Katie was weeping. His old wounds were bleeding.

7

K A T I E discovered that she felt better as soon as Perry had gone. If only he wouldn't say "Don't be stupid" over and over again as if she were really stupid and not just scared out of her mind. There was plenty of knowledge, plenty of reason.

She sat on the couch with her knees drawn to her chest, trying to decide whether to turn on the radio or to sit in silence and ignorance. She wanted to know exactly what was happening; she didn't want to know anything about it. It was already past time for the news, and her favorite station would be playing music again as if there were nothing to be concerned about.

Standing at the window now, she saw a pregnant woman strolling down the sidewalk with a small child in hand. How could people take walks? Up and down the streets, houses had cardboard witches and cheerful ghosts and jack-o'-lanterns stuck on front windows and doors. At the moment it was bright and mild, a perfect Indian summer moment with golden sunlight on red, brown and yellow leaves, which only made the terror within her more sinister.

It's finally happening.

All her life she had known this time would come, yet life around her was carrying on with a perverse normality. Could it be that she, President Kennedy, Defense Secretary McNamara and a few others with worried faces were the only ones to understand the trouble? Russian ships steamed toward Cuba, hurrying to finish the terrible missiles. Kennedy had the area blockaded—or quarantined as they were calling it. But Katie knew what it really was. It was the end of the Cold War and the beginning of the complete and utter destruction of civilization.

Everyone else is stupid, she thought. She didn't care what Perry said about Americans having balls and guts and backbone or anything about the Commie menace. All she knew was that they were really, really starting it with the full knowledge of what was to happen. Some miles down the road at Cheyenne Mountain, the missiles were humming, ready to go. They didn't care about her family. They didn't care about what life would be like afterward. All the important people would sit it out in shelters and think they were wise enough to put the pieces together afterward.

She leaned her forehead against the glass, cool in spite of the golden sunshine, and began to cry again. She had never in her life felt so helpless and abandoned by the entire world.

Twice that day Katie was startled by sirens but realized that they were only fire engines. She knew that somewhere

Perry was probably putting out a grease fire in a kitchen or prying a boy out of a storm drain.

When they were first married, Perry had given her a police radio and instructed her on how to find out what he was doing. She had only listened to it once   it alternated between being boring and nerve-wracking. He was hurt when she told him that she didn't *want* to know what he was doing, that it was better for him to come home where she could see him and tell her about it.

Not that she really feared for him. She didn't think much about him in that sense when he was gone. Perry had always been a sort of big teddy bear to her until they were married. He was the kind of man who sent flowers and candy and told her endlessly about his adoration at every step of the courtship. She had been overwhelmed by his gushing affection, which disappeared soon after the wedding. Once her husband, he was as imperious as he had been romantic and expected her to toe the line for him in all matters of house-keeping and wifery. Many anxious afternoons passed with Katie on the phone to her mother for advice on cooking, getting stains out, repairing scratches in furniture, or trying to stem the growth of his general grumpiness. The day her mother broke down as Katie agonized over Perry's criticism of her cooking, Katie realized that she had made a very big mistake.

She had known it all along anyway, though didn't want to think about it. She didn't really love Perry. He had the prospect of being a workable husband who would give her the chance of an ordinary life. That lack of love ate away at them both. Katie suspected that he knew all along and thought marriage would make her all his. She felt sorry for him sometimes.

She turned on the evening news about an hour before Perry was due to arrive home. Castro was preparing for war. NORAD was on full alert. The Free World was standing behind President Kennedy. Katie paced in front of the television, seeing the end of the world approaching. She felt sick to her stomach and ached to do something to alleviate the grief.

For most of her nineteen years she had been terrorized by this moment. During most of that terror she had also assumed that she would have Phil with her. Now that comfort was gone. The Bomb and Phil were tangling together in her mind as she watched the bald-headed man with thick glasses read the news report with his usual calm but concerned voice. I am going crazy, she thought. Shivers with the force of earth tremors started in her legs, spasmed through her back and neck. I am going crazy I am going crazy I can't listen to this I can't go on another minute without falling apart and screaming going crazy.

Later, after she had done it, she was amazed at her nerve. But in that moment she couldn't think what it might mean, what would happen to her life if she did it. She only knew that in a short time the rules wouldn't apply anyway. The earth was heaving and making her dizzy.

"Phil," she said into the crackling long-distance line. "I need you."

8

P H I L crept into town guiltily. He did exactly as Katie had instructed. Fearing what Perry might do if he caught them, he was willing to do whatever she asked. His upper mind repeated over and over, "She's my oldest friend. She needs me." His deeper thoughts came popping through the cool reasoning every now and then with, "She still loves me."

Since he had seen her a month ago at the funeral, he had been obsessed with memories and sorrow for his lost love.

He had composed a sonata in his wretched state, thrown it away but was tormented in sleepless nights by its sad glissandi. He found his fingers wandering to it between practice pieces. It haunted him, but he refused to write it down, convinced that it was only his mood that made it sound good.

He stepped off the bus and checked the street, hoping no one would recognize him. A Mexican family got off with him, shuffling their battered suitcases and looking lost, speaking softly in Spanish, both parents caressing the dark hair of their children's heads. The basement lights of the courthouse were on, casting sinister jail bars of light across the dry lawn. A middle-aged couple walked by, he in carpet slippers as if they had gone to a neighbor's for their nightly Ovaltine. The woman was speaking softly. Phil heard the word "crisis," but everything else seemed normal.

He walked across and down the street and watched through the pool hall window for a moment. He recognized no one, though some of the young kids had vaguely familiar faces. The guy behind the counter was about his own age, but Phil didn't know him at all. When he was a child, he had known just about everyone in town. How times had changed. Even this one-horse town had strangers now.

He found a pay phone in a corner of the pool hall and dropped a dime in. After paying for his bus ticket, he had had about forty-five cents left over and had made the long journey across Missouri and Kansas on one Coke and a distressingly small chunk of beef jerky. If Katie answered the phone the first time, he might be able to spend a remaining dime on another Coke. He looked longingly across the room at the low red machine with its silver lid, praying that he would hear her voice.

The phone rang twice. Soothingly familiar, the voice said, "Hello?" He had been dreading what sort of silly sound he might make if Perry answered and he didn't hang up in time.

"Is that you?"

"No, it's the King of Siam."

"Please, Phil, don't be that way with me."

"Look, Katie, I don't have the slightest idea what *way* you want me to be with you."

She paused then whispered, "Perry's home."

"Well, what do you want me to do then? He lives there,

doesn't he? If I were married to you I would be at home, too." He knew he was sounding cross but couldn't stop it. "I can get back on a bus if you're going to play cat and mouse. What do you want me to do?"

"Please don't be angry with me." She sounded as if she might cry. "Why don't you just come over?"

"Just sort of drop in from Missouri for a little chat?"

"Yes."

"What are you going to tell your old man?"

"I'll tell him that you're visiting your family. I did invite you over for a beer right in front of him, didn't I?"

"Katie, before I see you, I want to know what you intend to do. What am I getting into?"

"I'm scared. All I know is that I couldn't stand going through this without you. It's worse than ever today. Now Russia is getting ready for war. There are more than twenty ships headed for Cuba. When they get there . . ."

"They might not . . ." But that didn't sound good, either. He was afraid, himself. Some of the guys in the dorm had taken off with their girlfriends for the deepest Ozarks, hoping to get away from military targets. Classroom attendance had fallen as students from surrounding towns had gone home after Kennedy's speech on Monday evening. There was gloom everywhere on campus. Even those who carried on as usual found their conversations and laughter ringing out like child's play in church. The pall itself was frightening.

And here I am, he thought. I've come straight to the foot of Cheyenne Mountain, which we've always boasted was one of the prime targets.

"Please come over," she said. "I never imagined I would have to face this without you. I'm sorry about everything in the world, Phil."

He knew then that she still loved him and that things had accidentally gone awry. She was still his Katie, the only thing that mattered to him. If this really was to be the end, he wanted to have her with him.

"I'll see you in a few minutes."

9

WHEN Phil arrived, Katie swung the door open. For a moment, he thought that she had forgotten him somehow. She said, "Philip!" in a surprised voice. Then he realized that she was acting for Perry. He hadn't known that she was such a good actress.

"I was just . . . I'm just visiting and I thought I would take you up on that beer. 'lo, Perry," he said as amiably as he could, coming into the front room. He didn't think his performance could match Katie's.

"Hiya." He was sitting in an overstuffed chair (Phil could imagine that it was "his" chair) and got to his feet with reluctant slowness to greet Phil. He clicked off the television set, which had been filled with a senator's face.

"Perry, I wanted to hear that."

"Give it a rest, Kath. We have company."

Kath? Phil saw that Katie had twisted a strand of her hair out of the French roll that apparently had become her usual hairstyle. He remembered that she constantly fidgeted with her hair. As he looked at her now, however, she wore a dead expression and her hands hung straight down at her sides.

"A rest?" she said. "We'll all have a permanent rest."

"Like heck." Perry rolled his eyes. He had obviously grown weary of her nervousness. "Offer your *old friend* a beer, huh?" He walked out of the room and down a hall, where he shut a door just short of a slam.

"What would you like to drink?" Katie asked in an eerily even voice.

"Uhm, I don't know, Katie. What do you have? I could do with something stronger than beer." He found himself imitating her flatness, but inside he was being torn to pieces between her presence and Perry's unfriendliness. He watched her move, studying the prettiness of the loose hair dangling to her shoulder, the gingham dress, and thinking how good it was to be with her, how much he missed her, and how awful it had been to lose her. The gravity of what was happening in the outside world lessened.

"Jack Daniels?"

"Yes, fine."

She poured out a measure with shaking hands. He wanted to hold her but thought of the big guy down the hall. Instead, he returned to the front room and tossed his jacket over the arm of the sofa. Apart from the big chair, their furniture was nearly new, modern and sleek in hard stylishness. Phil realized that he had always assumed a grown-up Katie would imitate the old, cozy and casual style of her family house, a house in which he had always felt at home. Like her hairstyle, it unbalanced him.

No artwork hung on the walls, only a row of framed photos—Katie as a child (that one had been in the front room at the Doheneys'), Perry's graduation portrait, and two wedding photos. Phil only glanced at them. (How could she? he thought again.)

Katie brought his drink and a beer for herself. He sat on the sofa. She sat on a hassock and lit a cigarette from the pack on the Formica-topped coffee table. "Would you like one?"

"Sure." He lit hers first. "When did you start smoking?"

"Oh, I just do it every now and then." But her motions were practiced. She glanced around the room quickly but absently, as if to make sure some particular thing *wasn't* in the room. "I'm so glad you're here," she whispered. "I was going crazy with you so far away during all this."

Phil felt he was glimpsing his Katie again, she had that familiar anxiousness in her eyes.

It had been one of their games when they were young to plan out what they would do and where they would go should the attack begin. Sometimes they would start from the drugstore, or from the irrigation ditch south of the high school, or from her house or his. A chill ran through him. The newspaper lay on the floor with the bold headline, "JFK Grips Cuba in Blockade," subheaded with "Orders U.S. Armed Forces to Prepare for 'Any Eventualities.'"

"My God, Katie . . ."

All the years of threats and counter-threats, wrangling and banging shoes, and Us vs. Them—that terrible alien race who loved nothing but potatoes and authority—here it was, right from a morning in the New Mexico desert, Hiroshima, Nagasaki, Sputnik, dogs burning up in space, Gary Powers and spy planes, the Berlin Wall . . . Like one who fears a dread disease then has the doctor confirm the diagnosis, Phil felt sickened relief and fear.

The toilet flushed down the hall and Perry came back.

Phil could hardly move with Perry in the room. He didn't know where or how to look. The burly young fire chief appeared as calm as any day. Or was he just better at hiding it?

"Perry," Katie asked, "do you think we should take some more water down to the shelter?"

"Let's change the subject, huh?" He lowered himself into his chair with an enormous sigh. Phil got the impression that he had just relieved himself of days and days worth of constipation or that he was simply a man who enjoyed a good shit. "Get me a beer, too, will ya, Kath?"

Katie jumped to fetch it for him.

Perry turned his head toward Phil but didn't actually look at him. "So you were one of the old man's piano players, too, huh?"

"Old man? Oh, you mean Mr. Tackett?"

"Yeah. Tackett. Katherine dragged me to the nursing home where they put him after his stroke. I didn't know him. I just about tossed my cookies in the place. Not because of him, but those rest homes are rotten. I see a lota bad stuff in my job but those places . . . We got to this one on a call once where about five of 'em had burnt to a crisp. They were so feeble they didn't even know what smoke meant. Just lay in their beds and burnt up."

Phil took a deep drink. Katie brought Perry's beer. He drank from it and belched softly.

"Sit down, missus," he said, pointing to the floor in front of him.

"Perry, not now." Katie frowned.

"Come on, come on." He made an insistent rolling gesture to his lap.

Katie shrugged and settled on the floor with her back to him. He rubbed her shoulders. Phil was revolted by the way he touched her—she was a woman to be caressed, not kneaded. Phil wanted to play his fingers across her throat, to kiss her softly. *He* knew what she liked. Phil saw Perry grinning to himself and realized that this was all a show for him. Perry was simply telling him that Katie was his territory.

They exchanged a quick glance. In just a few seconds, they silently indicated how much they hated each other. Katie was most of it, but they also hated each other's kind and would have never been in the same room drinking together if it weren't for a third person.

"Why don't you run along and fix us some sandwiches," Perry suggested. "I'm starved and I'll bet your old friend Phil is, too."

Phil squirmed. His hunger had disappeared completely.

If they decide to drop the Bomb right now and I'm sitting in this man's house, Phil wondered, would he share his bomb shelter with me? I doubt it. Phil imagined being outdoors and seeing the flash coming from behind Pike's Peak, tasting the ash and fallout, and dying over a period of days of radiation sickness. It could be preferable to sitting in a hole in the ground with Perry for a couple of weeks.

It's actually possible, Phil thought, losing his concentration on the other two. Katie moving into the kitchen and Perry sipping his beer were like a dream. The whole situation seemed grandly stupid.

He reread the headlines. Tomorrow the world could be in cinders, reeking of immediate and pending death. But then—it might *not* happen. Maybe the politicians would resolve it somehow. They were always posturing and backing down, weren't they?

He studied the line drawings of the U.S. ships around Cuba and the X that marked the end of the island where the missiles were preparing to point at the top of Katie and Perry's house.

Perry slammed his beer bottle down on the coffee table. Phil jumped.

Perry laughed. He gave Phil a sideways look. "So what are you going to do when you get out of college?"

"I don't know." Phil couldn't think about the future. Even if there was one to be had, he wasn't sure what to say to Perry, who asked questions in the same way as parents did.

"You got a girl, Benson?"

"Nothing steady," Phil said politically, hoping Katie didn't hear. In fact, he had been on a few dates during this autumn term, but college girls were either silly or threatening. There weren't too many ordinary women who weren't already taken.

"Well, you can't have my wife, you know."

Hot with embarrassment and guilt, Phil tried to appear nonchalant. "What makes you think I want her? I came to see her because she's one of my oldest friends."

"The hell you don't want her." Perry's voice was menacingly low and snarling. "I see these looks going back and forth." He belched loudly.

Just at that moment, Katie came in from the kitchen. "Perry, please try to have some manners." She seemed unaware of the words but had heard her husband's belch. One hand was dripping with sudsy water, the other held a spatula.

"My manners are good enough for you when Mr. Coat-and-Tails isn't around," he said.

Katie's expression changed. "What's going on here?"

"I think I had better go." Suddenly Katie's company didn't

outweigh the prospect of things to come. Phil picked up his jacket and headed for the front door.

"PHIL!" she screamed. "You can't leave me at a time like this!" She ran across the room and threw her soapy hand one way and the one with spatula the other way over his shoulders in a hug. "Please don't go!"

"*I'll* go," Perry said, rising from his chair. As he walked toward them, he pointed his finger at Katie, who looked startled to see that he still existed. "Don't think you aren't going to pay for this, little lady. I've had just about enough of being fucked around." The photos rattled against the wall as Perry slammed out.

"I hate you!" she screamed at the closed door. She lunged at it and beat it with her fists. "I hate you, you pig, you . . ."

Phil leaned against the wall, stunned. He went to the coffee table, swiped another cigarette and took another long drink.

Katie cried for a moment then came to the sofa, still sniffling. When she lifted her head again she had a pleading look.

Phil shook his head. "God damn, Katie . . . what the hell have you gotten yourself into?"

"It's your fault!" She began to cry, but the only words Phil could make out from the terrible noise she made were "no one else would have me."

"I don't understand why you had to have someone else anyway," he said. He was hurt and out of sympathy. Had she deliberately married this jerk to prove she could have another man? Why? Phil had, until a few moments ago, thought there might be some inscrutable quality in Perry that he just couldn't see because he was a rival—that there was a chance Katie might be happy. He genuinely wanted to

believe Katie did things for a good reason. This was just a
mess.

"I have to turn on the radio!" she said suddenly.

She ran to the black cabinet in the corner and lifted the
lid. The red light at the bottom came on and distant crackling
from KOMA in Oklahoma City hissed through the fabric
front. She twiddled the dial, passing the rock-and-roll stations, which only had news on the hour. It was twenty to.
The radio said "oo-wee," then homed in on the song
"Patches." Phil hated that song. Maybe if she would leave
the damned thing alone they would play Marty Robbins or
the Four Seasons.

He had suddenly ceased to believe in the end of the world.
It was too full of shit to burn; it would just have to molder
on forever.

Katie stopped crying after a few moments. She knew that
Phil was annoyed with her, which made her too angry to
cry. Didn't he understand how *awful* her situation was? Didn't
he have any sympathy for her at all? Worst of all, she was
suddenly afraid of saying anything to him—he had crossed
his arms and was brooding into his empty whiskey glass
with a distinctly unapproachable expression.

"Would you like another?" she asked, sniffing.

"Yes, as a matter of fact, I think I need another."

She poured him more whiskey and got a second beer for
herself. When she returned, he was sitting in exactly the
same position and didn't look up at her.

"Thank you," he said.

"Are you angry with me?"

He straightened up, stretching his arms upward as if to
work kinks out of the muscles. "No, I don't suppose it's

anger, Katie. I'm disgusted. Really disgusted with the way everything has turned out."

Although she knew she shouldn't, she lit another cigarette. Too much smoking these past few days was making her throat raw. Perry sometimes complained that she looked like a whore when she smoked even though he was the one who had encouraged her to try it one night, long ago, when they were drunk together. It had started as a joke, but now she always checked the top of the fridge to count the packs before she went to the grocery store.

"Well, what—" she began.

"Let's not talk about it right now."

Frustrated, she made a sort of squawking sound, but it didn't budge him. Katie knew well enough that when Phil was this silent he would only snap at her if she tried to work on him. "How's college?" she asked.

She thought it would cheer him up to tell her about his courses. The last letters he had written to her before they stopped corresponding had sounded so full of excitement and were all about the things he was learning. That had been so long ago. Katie remembered how much she had looked forward to finding letters on her chest of drawers when she came home in the afternoons. It hurt to look at him now and think about all the things he hadn't told her, things she would never know about, changes that had happened, bits of conversations, little observations about his professors and other students.

She had never felt that giving him up was the right thing to do, though it hurt so much she knew it *must* be. She had decided this after one particularly lonely letter from him in which he said he missed her so much that he was thinking about coming home, giving it up.

Now he sat with her, still familiar, still Phil, and yet a strange and distant person with experiences about which she would never know.

"College," he repeated. "I don't feel like talking about it right now. It's all right, I guess." He shrugged.

"Oh." Katie felt shut out.

"It just doesn't seem to matter right now, does it?"

Katie shook her head. The only sounds for a long time were their inhalations and exhalations of smoke and the rustling of clothes as they moved their cigarettes to and from the ashtray on the table.

"What's that?" Katie said. "It sounds like someone in the backyard."

Phil seemed to be listening, but his eyes were on the front door. "Maybe it's Perry."

"Shh." Katie held up one hand. She pulled her legs up onto the chair and tucked them under her dress, like a child expecting the bogeyman to leap out from under the furniture. She had chills running up and down her arms and legs as she listened. Was that the creaking of the shelter door? Was someone walking around the house? "In the back," she whispered.

Just as he had done all through their lives together, Phil became the brave one and got up to investigate. But Katie noticed how stiffly and uncertainly he approached the back door. She got up and followed him but stayed at the edge of the kitchen. He turned out the light and parted the curtain, peering outward. "I can't see anything," he murmured against the glass.

Katie reached out and turned on the back porch light, then stepped back again.

Phil stood for a moment more. "Nothing there. Just the wind or something."

They returned to the living room and sat down. Phil still looked remote and stubborn. Katie glanced at him and lit another cigarette, still listening. She thought she heard Perry's car drive by the house but convinced herself that he had probably gone down to Duffy's for a beer. What would happen if he came back? How long would he probably be? What would he do to her—or Phil? Then her mind switched gears. What's happening in Washington and Moscow at the moment?

Finally, Katie said, "Would you hold me?"

He glanced at the door. "What if Perry comes back?"

"What if he does?"

They stared at each other for a few seconds; then Phil looked away. Katie fought as hard as she could to keep away tears. She was sick of crying, sick of wanting to cry. She wanted to be pretty and happy and fun—it had been so long since she had felt that way. She rose and went to the kitchen with half her mind on washing the dishes.

She picked up the dishrag. Suddenly Phil was behind her, squeezing her with a force just short of strangulation. "Katie, Katie, I miss you."

As they had through a lot of their teenage years, they curled together on the sofa and cuddled and kissed and whispered. Phil felt such relief to have her back. Even though he couldn't quite make her say it and he feared pressing her, he did feel that she was his girl again. He understood from the rather confused things she said that she had been misguided into thinking that she was bad for him. She wouldn't tell him more, but it was enough to know that she still loved him and always had. It restored his faith in the hope that she would love him all through the future, too.

"What's that?" Katie bolted up from the sofa.

Phil's first thought was of Perry; then he heard a distant sound. It made him heavy, almost sleepy, with deep dread. The moment had come. It had really, really come.

The power went down. The lights blinked out, the radio faded, the refrigerator died, clocks ceased to hum. At the top of Rattlesnake Mesa overlooking town, the siren held a steady note.

Katie screamed. Phil groped for her to comfort her and be comforted.

"The shelter," she said.

"What?"

"Let's go to the shelter."

"What's happening?" he asked stupidly, knowing it was stupid.

"Come on, come on." She pulled his arm. He got to his feet, still pulled along, and followed her. She kicked something in the darkness and said, "Damn," and immediately Phil stubbed his toe on the same thing. He couldn't swear. His mouth was stuck together with fear. He could only move because Katie tugged at him.

"Come on!" she said impatiently.

They made it through the back door. Outside, it was easier to see. Phil hazily heard screen doors banging softly at the backs of other houses and curious voices filled the neighborhood. A distant dog had started howling with the siren and closer dogs joined in. Katie dragged him by the hand as he staggered over the lawn. She was sure-footed. They passed the incinerator, which had the fragrance of burnt orange peel, brown paper bags and melted cellophane wrappings.

Katie let go of his hand. She gripped something in the ground and swung up a door like a tornado storm door. He helped her hold it up; then she slipped quietly into the earth.

He followed.

10

THEY clung to each other, listening, staring at the door she had sealed safely above them. They both trembled as uncontrollably as if they were standing naked in a blizzard. In the shelter, the light was dim, coming from a single bare bulb behind the ladder. It felt and smelled damp and stale inside.

"Can you hear anything?" she asked.

"No."

They listened a little longer. Then Phil glanced around curiously. The shelter was only about six by six feet and curved inward on the sides. It was like being inside a giant septic tank. Along one side was a shelf of canned goods and below that ten cider jugs filled with water. On the wall a white box marked First Aid hung by a wire handle. By the opposite wall were two folded camp cots, a fat roll of sleeping bags, a transistor radio, a flashlight, a toolbox with a few tools, and a white cardboard box, which looked new and unopened, with Chemical Toilet printed in small black letters.

Phil's mind was unproductively busy. He saw things, thought things, and yet had to look and think all over again. First, they would have to stay here God knows how long and when they got out—what then? In his mind, he saw the burnt-out cinders of his hometown against a grey sky and pictured the two of them stumbling along without catching a single glimpse of another human being. Or perhaps the town wouldn't be cinders; it wasn't a target itself. So it might be intact but irradiated. Would they be able to eat anything? Drink water? Live? What would they do after leaving the shelter? These things he had considered only lightly in his life—getting to the shelter and finding what the shelter would have in it had always been something of interest, similar to other kids' interest in tree houses.

When would the bomb drop? Uselessly, he strained to hear the siren. How would they know when it had actually happened? How would they know if it was clear?

He saw the radio again and grabbed it. "Here we go," he said, satisfied that the little plastic box would have the answers. He switched it on. Nothing. Not even a bit of static. He twisted the tuning dial. Nothing. "Jesus H. Christ, Katie."

She took the radio from him and opened the battery slot. There were no batteries in it. She rummaged in the toolbox with its few odd screwdrivers, pliers and a claw hammer. Behind it were a hatchet, a folding army surplus shovel, a coil of rope. "The flashlight!" she said.

Phil knew as soon as he picked it up that it was too light. He unscrewed the bottom and the bare contact stared back at him. He threw it on the floor.

"Hey." Katie picked it up and examined the bulb. "We might need this."

"What good is it?"

"We might find some batteries somewhere." She gazed around. There weren't many places to find things.

He leaned his hands against the slanted wall and hung his head. He felt like weeping. Everything short of the bleakest possibilities seemed too hopeful to him. At his feet was a tidy row of beans and corned beef hash in cans. How long was that going to last?

Would there be any pianos left in the world? Would there be any symphonies, any radio broadcasts from Chicago, or even anyone who might miss these things? What about his parents, what about Mrs. T, what about his music theory professor, what about daffodils and coffee and women's perfume in a restaurant . . . what about . . .

"Katie," he said hoarsely. "Let's get out of here."

She stared at him. "What?"

"I'd rather have the Bomb hit me on the head than stay down here and go back to nothing."

"But, Phil, it's the *Bomb*. It's safe here." Her voice rose an octave and she began to look very frightened.

"For one thing, we don't have enough food. How long do we have to stay in here anyway—two weeks? We have as much food as I can eat in two days."

Katie clutched him. "Please, please, don't make me go out there."

"We'll just die slowly, painfully. Don't you see?"

Katie screamed. Then she sank to the floor. He had never seen such a hollow look on her face in all the years he had known her, all the hysterical episodes he had witnessed. "Katie," he said, but she didn't move. He prodded her shoulder with his finger. "Doheney, stop playing around. Talk to me. Katie."

She had fled from him somehow, leaving only her body for him to look after.

"Shit." For good measure, he picked up the radio and slammed it against the wall, shattering its case and exposing a colorful but silent card of soldered wires.

He unfolded the cots, then unrolled the sleeping bags. There were two zipped together which he separated and draped over each of the two cots. It was already too warm in the shelter; the armpits of his shirt were soaked. He wondered if it might get cold at night. There were no pillows.

He scooped up Katie with a grunt and put her on the cot near the wall. She seemed to be sleeping soundly. He moved her tenderly, not because he felt tenderness—he was angry with her somehow—but because he was a man with the woman he loved in his arms.

As Katie slept on, he sat on the cot, studying the details of the shelter. He counted the cans of food and the jugs of water. He noticed the two rolls of toilet paper and a pair of garden shears on the shelf as well. Garden shears? No one would think to put them into a shelter deliberately. He imagined Katie out with her rose bushes one day deciding to take a peek at her precious shelter. He was aware that at any other time it would be amusing, but at the moment it wasn't.

This was a game they had played over and over in their lives, but Phil now saw that he had never taken it seriously. He never really believed this would happen. Everything about it had the unreality of practice and expectation combined with dreaminess.

Katie had always been obsessed with the Bomb. Her father, a renegade nonpracticing Catholic who had led the family to skepticism of the Church, said once at supper that Katie had replaced God with Peace, the Devil with the Bomb, and said her prayers to a lovely Saint Hiroshima. It had tickled Phil at the time, partly because he usually liked whatever Mr. Doheney said. A hint of brogue in his voice, coming down hard on r's and pronouncing his t's sharply, Katie's father inspired Phil with his passion for home and family. It was as strong as Mr. Tackett's cerebral influence in many ways. But, also, Phil knew he had his own father's practical and dull approach to things. Like Katie's obsession with the Bomb—he could see the reason for worrying about it, he knew it was a problem, and yet he had never worried about it with Katie's faith.

She had affected his life with it so that he was surprised to meet people who didn't have a thought about it. They might never have heard of Robert Oppenheimer or Bertrand Russell; they didn't think about looking for the nearest civil defense shelter in public buildings before going to a meeting, concert or lecture. They didn't care about half-life or the safety behind lead.

Other people had been perfectly content to carry on their lives as if there were no threats of mushroom clouds or death to come. But Katie knew—she had always been certain of it. He thought back to the way she had towed him into the shelter like a mother fetching a child out of the rain.

Some individuals contracted terrible diseases, had maiming accidents in cars, got into desperate financial troubles, or had other personal calamities that seemed tailor-made to their lives and attitudes. The Bomb was Katie's calamity. Trouble was, she had dragged the whole world along with her, hadn't she?

Was it possible . . . ? Phil had an eerie feeling that this wouldn't have happened to him if he had never met his odd little Katie.

———

They both sat straight up out of their sleep when the explosion came. Dust floated down as the earth around their shelter groaned. Phil stared at Katie, stunned. He waited for more sound—it must have been the shock wave flattening the town. He couldn't hear the wind. They were too well insulated.

"Phil," she said, reaching for his hand.

They squeezed each other's fingers, listening for more.

"It must have been close," he said. Then he thought his voice and words were so banal in the face of the end of the world that he never wanted to speak again.

Katie began to weep. Phil found breathing painful in his cramped throat. He thought of his poor mother and father, surprised and taken, innocent as they were.

11

—

"WE have enough food for about eight days," he said, squatting by the shelf of cans. "The water—I don't know. I don't know how much we use in a day, but there's probably a better supply of it than of food."

She sighed, wishing he would hold still, stop organizing and pacing. What she really wanted was for him to give her a big comforting hug, but he managed to stay busy in the tiny room with counting, rearranging, assembling and reckoning. "So what do we do?" she asked.

"Well, when the food runs out there's no point in staying down here, is there?"

"But . . ."

He lifted his hand to stop her protest. "I know—we're supposed to stay for about two weeks, but what's the difference? We starve to death down here or we go up and die of radiation poisoning. There's a chance, Katie"—he pivoted on his heel and took her hand—"that things might not be so bad in this area. The bomb may have dropped far enough away . . ."

"Yes." But she heard the hopelessness in both of their voices. She ran her fingers through her hair, which was becoming stringy and oily from lack of shampooing. She tried not to start thinking again about her parents, her sisters, her nephew—where were they, would she see them again outside, were they dead or hiding in a hole somewhere else in town? These worries made her writhe with pain, so she thought about her hair and how filthy it was already.

Phil suddenly came to the end of his activity and sat down on the end of the cot. She put her hand on his back, hoping for a response. He remained as he was. She began to cry again, which made him sigh deeply.

She couldn't stay awake. Phil was usually silent, staring at the ceiling. A lot of the time, his eyes were closed, too. Hazily, she looked at him and drifted into sleep again.

"What's that?"
"Sounds like a dog scratching at the door or something."
"What if it's someone wanting in?"
"Well, we can't let them in, can we? They're radioactive."
"What if . . ."
"Go back to sleep."
"I can't sleep any more. How long have we been in here?"
"I think it's two days now."
"Are you hungry?"
"Starved."
"Me, too. Let's eat the can of new potatoes."

———

He heard her crying again but felt completely cold toward her tears. He was numb, sick to death of this room, sick to death of Katie's blubbering. He had read the first aid manual and the instruction leaflet that had come with the toilet so many times that he could recite long passages from them to himself. The signs of shock. The application of a tourniquet to the femoral artery. Assembly of the disposal unit. Keeping the airway clear of foreign objects. He longed for a newspaper, a book, a dictionary . . . anything.

"What's up now?" he finally asked.

She only cried more audibly.

"For God's sake, Katie."

"I can't remember Chopin's 'Minute Waltz,' " she sobbed.

He turned on his cot and touched her shoulder, trying to mix the surge of love, guilt and laughter that choked him. What a civilized and courageous woman, what a beautiful girl. He sang the tune of the waltz into her ear. "La, la . . ."

She rolled over toward him, her eyes shining with halted tears. She laughed and joined him, picking up the tune.

They sang it through to the finish in about two-and-a-half minutes.

He put his arm across her stomach affectionately. "There's no one in the world I would rather be stuck with than you, Doheney." He leaned over to kiss her; the wooden frame of the cot jabbed his ribs.

"Let's put the sleeping bags on the floor," she suggested.

They zipped them together.

She was embarrassed when she farted; not only was it horribly loud, but it also had a rich diarrheal odor.

"Do you want me to go outside while you do number two?" he asked.

"I'm sorry. I . . ."

"Don't be sorry, goose. I'll sit over here with my back to you. I'm constipated to the gills myself. Wish I could go."

"Phil . . ."

"Look, if we're going to sit in this hole together for weeks you've got to get used to it. I don't have any place to go to leave you alone, do I?"

Katie knew she had to. She could hardly blink without thinking about moving her bowels. "You're right." Gingerly, she sat up on the cot.

Phil turned his cot diagonally across the room and sat with his back to her, head hanging. She sat down on the chemical toilet and let go with pleasurable abandon.

"Wish I could take a bath now," she said, trying to decide whether her job was worth four or five squares of toilet paper rather than the two allowed for a pee.

"Wish I could go swimming in a glacial pool in the mountains. And eat hot dogs and watermelon and drink Coke." He paused. "We'll probably never eat watermelon again."

"Don't think about it."

"What do you mean, don't think about it?" His voice was curt. The shirt across his back became taut as he strained further forward. "All I can think about is how happy I am *now* compared with how I'll feel out there."

Katie dropped her dress back down around her knees. "You can turn around now."

But he didn't. Not for hours.

He sat on the floor idly drumming the top of the toolbox in waltz time with a screwdriver and pliers.

"Stop it," she said.

He stopped. He tossed the tools down with a clatter, pleased with the noise that made, too, but knowing he had better not do it again. Katie had been getting more and more ragged in the past days. They had talked each other out and stopped when they discovered each had a variant version of everything that had happened to them together. Since the argument about the color of the roses he had given her for her sixteenth birthday they had not said much.

He wanted to hear sounds, sounds with patterns and tones and textures.

Bored, he looked at his arms, which appeared to have paled in the days that they had been underground. It was absurd to think that the lack of ordinary sunlight could already be affecting him so. He glanced up at Katie and saw that she, too, looked pasty. Perhaps it was the light bulb. If the light bulb in the shelter blew, they would be thrown into darkness, since it was the only one. At first, Phil switched it on and off conscientiously to save electricity but then decided it might be more work for the generator to handle the switch than the forty-watt steady glow. He remembered hearing about a bulb Edison had made, still alight, constantly burning.

Last summer I was tan, he thought, studying his arms carefully. It was last summer that he had met Charlie, who had taught him how to tune pianos.

Phil had worked in the piano factory (trying to forget Katie by staying away from Colorado for the summer job), doing a little bit of everything there—sawing, sanding, carrying timber, pulling and cutting piano wire, screwing in bolts. It had made him muscled and vigorous, something new to him, as he had never concentrated on physical activity.

He first saw Charlie sitting at one of the finished pianos and playing scales, up and down, up and down, then the tune from the movie *Bridge on the River Kwai*, which Phil had learned to play a few years before. Any other time, Phil would have found that kind of piano playing tedious listening. But the chubby man sitting there in the July heat and sweating over the keyboard of a walnut baby grand had the definite air of an expert. He wasn't a great musician, but he knew about pianos. He had dismantled the keyboard, put it into his lap, and tinkered for more than an hour. His hands touched the hammers and strings with the same deftness that Phil might use to scratch his own nose.

Phil watched him surreptitiously, finding excuses to do some of his duties in that part of the factory or passing back and forth in feigned busyness. When his lunch break came he picked up his sandwich and Pepsi and sat on an unfinished bench near the piano tuner.

The man casually nodded over his shoulder as if he had expected the audience.

"Hi." Phil nonchalantly took another bite of his sandwich and gazed outside the warehouse doors where the paved lot shimmered with heat waves. "Hot one, isn't it?"

"You betcha." The man wore baggy brown trousers, which looked as if they might have belonged to a Sunday suit a long time ago, and a white shirt with the sleeves rolled. "You ain't worked here long," he said.

Phil didn't know whether that was a question or a statement. "Not long," he answered in the same noncommittal tone. He wiped his forehead with his arm.

The piano tuner picked up his crooked tool and leaned into the piano, making a twanging noise quickly and repetitively. His voice came from within, a working man's tenor, resonating with the strings in his range. "Working off the summer? Going to college?"

"Yeah."

"My daughter just graduated high school last year, too. Maybe you know her—Charlene—"

"I didn't go to high school here. I come from Colorado."

"Oh. Never been there. Good trout fishing, I hear." He stood and patted his face with the blue bandanna that he kept in one of his back pockets. "Lordy, it's hot today."

"Yeah." Phil's clothes were sticking to him and sweat was rolling down from his scalp, tickling his face and neck. He drank the remainder of his Pepsi, but its sweetness left him thirstier than before. He was too oppressed by the heat to walk across the factory and get another from the machine. And he wanted to stick around and watch this man who seemed to have such wisdom about pianos. He sounded like a simple-minded guy, not like his teachers at college, but he was so adept with the instrument itself. Phil wondered how this could be. "You play the piano?" he asked.

"Huh? Oh, I used to. Now I just tune 'em up. Doesn't do much good after all. Soon as they put these babies on the truck it knocks 'em right out again. But they're closer than before. Close enough to sell, I s'pose."

"I'm studying music. I'm going to play with the symphony."

"Oh?" The piano tuner smiled. "Which symphony is that?"

"I don't know. I want to play with a big one, maybe New York or Philadelphia or Chicago."

"Well, you gotta be pretty good for that, don't you?" The man sounded distracted again, punching A over and over, staring at the piano.

Phil was silent, suddenly chilled by the tuner's skepticism.

He wanted to slide onto the bench and play Grieg's concerto, but he kept in mind Mr. Tackett's warning—never, never play merely to show off. It corrupts talent. With the superior inner wisdom of his genius, he didn't answer the man.

"Yep." The bandanna came out again. "Now violins and horns—orchestras always need lots of those. They don't need too many piano players at a time. You gotta have a crackerjack agent or connections with somebody important."

"Have you tried it?" Phil was impatient with the man's paternal tone.

"Well, not a symphony orchestra." He looked up at Phil and grinned, then dived under the lid of the piano again. "I was more of a honky-tonker, to tell you the truth. Tried out for Lawrence Welk's show, though. A long time ago. They gave me a tryout and it woulda been for their summer tours." More plucking came from within; then he stood up straight again. "Might not have been good enough." He sounded a tiny bit wistful but also as if it were so long ago it didn't matter any more.

Phil ate the rest of his sandwich as the tuner worked. He balled up his waxed paper and set it next to the Pepsi bottle. His heart was pounding with a new thought—what if I don't make it?

But of course he would. Mr. Tackett had said he was a genius.

The piano tuner stood up straight and stretched a little as if his back hurt. "This is a good job," he said to Phil, shaking the tuning key at him. "You can take the toolbox anywhere. During the Depression, I used to go door to door in the rich parts of town and tune pianos for a meal. Be surprised how glad people were just to feed you so they could play their pianos without it hurting their ears. In them days you had to make your own fun—folks didn't have the nickel to spend on going to a dance, so they'd roll the rugs back and have a dance at home. Nowadays people don't play their pianos anymore—they listen to the radio or watch television. The kids take lessons and forget it once their mothers stop nagging them. But there's lots of pianos in America, kid. Lots of pianos."

Phil studied the man's toolbox; apart from the L-shaped tuning key with interchangeable heads, he carried a tuning fork, a pitch pipe, a felt strip that wove into the strings as a damper, wedge-shaped mutes, a metronome, and other items that Phil couldn't identify. His box was well-worn and resembled a ladies' overnight case.

"Yeah, I'll bet there are," Phil said thoughtfully.

"Whoa and how!" The man laughed inside the piano, which resonated a laugh with him. "Every mother's daughter has to have piano lessons these days."

"Bet you can make a living at it then."

The piano tuner emerged and wiped his face. "Yeah, not bad if you're just looking after yourself. Me, I have myself five kids, though. Got another factory job five days, tune pianos weekends and when I'm working graveyard in the other job."

Phil hesitated. He wanted badly to have the knowledge, the secret lore of his beloved instrument. "Where'd you learn it?" he asked.

"From another tuner."

Phil watched the man work with increasing interest. Every flex of his wrist made the piano tuner money. "I'll bet you're thirsty," Phil said. "Would you like a Pepsi?"

———

Phil sat in the shelter, glanced over his shoulder at her—she was sleeping again—and wondered what sort of perverse design had led him to spend last summer learning how to care for pianos and forget Katie. Now he had Katie and only God knew if he would ever see another piano in his life.

12

"THERE she is," Katie said, seeing the woman in a dress climb through a hole in the ceiling. Katie wondered why it had taken her so long to get here. "She's come to see you play, Phil." Somehow Katie knew it, even though it had been years since Hiroshima had been able to visit like this.

"Doheney, wake up."

Katie sat up. Phil was sniffing down the throat of one of the water jugs. She stared at him. "Was I asleep?"

"Does it make a difference?" He screwed the cap back on. "I think the water's going bad. I don't know. I just can't tell any more, but it looks cloudy and smells like pond water."

"I have to go again." Katie hurried from her sleeping bag to the toilet.

"Don't hog it," he warned.

They gave each other a tentatively frightened look. Katie didn't want to say anything about it, but she suddenly saw that Phil was worried, too. They had both been having terrible diarrhea and were no longer hungry. Katie ached all over whenever she moved and had a constant headache. She knew that they were dying of radiation poisoning, that it had come down into the shelter, that it wasn't a perfectly invulnerable place after all.

She wiped herself gingerly and returned to the cot. Her bottom was sore, itchy and bleeding. Everything seemed to hurt—even her fingertips could hardly stand the pressure of picking things up. Yesterday, or perhaps just several hours ago, she had dropped the hatchet on her foot while holding it for Phil. It still hurt.

She wanted to lift her leg to look at her wounded foot but couldn't sustain the effort of holding her leg up.

"I think the water's going bad," Phil said, as if he were saying it for the first time. "It's cloudy and looks like pond water."

Shut up, she thought. Shut up, shut up.

If I die, she thought, he won't be able to boss me around any more. No more holding heavy hatchets or doing this and doing that for him. He's always bossed me around. She remembered the time when she was about fifteen and he had left his good shoes with her to polish before going to a concert at the Air Force Academy. He had something "more important" to do, and when she had forgotten to do them he sat through her apologies tight-lipped and stern. In the car, he told her that if she was to be his woman she would have to take care of him.

Why didn't he ask his mother to do them? Katie wondered, four years older now and less subject to the pride of being someone's girlfriend.

He never thought I was important. He's always assumed I would just be there to polish his shoes and iron his shirts and dust the piano. A few days ago, Katie had had a lonely insight. She and Phil had been through a lot together, they lived in the same town, did the same things, had the same friends, the same teachers, and knew each other's parents almost as well as their own. Yet their lives seemed to be as different as strangers'.

Just as it had been with Perry. Just as it was with her sisters, her parents, her friends. No matter how closely people revolve around you, Katie decided, they never really see you or understand you. They forget the things that are important to you or tread on them carelessly.

I hate everyone, she thought. No, it's not hate—I just wish I had a *real* companion, someone who understood me.

She suddenly pictured her family, dead in various rooms of the Doheney house. Just as well. People are miserable creatures, and none of us ever cares about each other, so we're better off dead this way. This is how the Bomb came about in the first place. If Phil and I were countries, we'd be at war. We'd build bombs and, with the first bad argument, it would all be over.

The first times they had made love in the shelter it had been a comfort and reunion, the very thing that Katie had wanted and needed. But now he was endlessly on top of her, pumping away for lack of anything better to do. All the pleasure seemed to be his, however, because he no longer kissed her or caressed her or called her sweet names.

And the sex came between arguments about what food to open and when. He wanted to eat all the substantial food first—the hash, the cream of chicken soup—which would leave them with green beans and consommé at the end. She understood that he was hungry, but it made her feel old and matronly to have to argue with his boyish appetite and lack of common sense. She saw him so differently now. Once her lover, protector, and the genius, now he just seemed selfish, moody and immature.

She lay on her back, took a deep breath, and thought it would be nice if she couldn't think or see or feel . . . What I want, she decided, is to be dead without being dead.

I don't care about making music any more. Phil rolled the shiny can without a label toward the wall, where it bounced and returned to him. He rolled it again. Soon Katie would tell him to stop it, so he treasured each motion with defiance. His fingers had itched to play the first few days, but he now wondered if he would ever want to play again, even if provided with the opportunity.

He couldn't get that first day with Charlie, the piano tuner, out of his mind. For some reason it rolled back at him just like the empty soup can propelling back from the wall of the bomb shelter. That skepticism, which never entirely disappeared even after Charlie heard Phil play but which Phil discounted as the man's lack of sophistication, wormed into his mind. He also thought of his earnest classmates at college, all of whom were as dedicated as he was to the goal of being famous musicians, expecting admiration and remuneration. He had always felt a cut above them—wasn't he a genius as certified by Mr. Tackett, who knew a genius when he saw one?

Phil suspected that some of the students he knew were more practiced or better at certain composers or worked the teachers' pet system and therefore got more attention. It had made him work harder and more silently, but he had never doubted.

Never doubted until everything was taken away and the

music drained away from his fingers by the sucking vacuum of the End of Everything.

It had occurred to him in a flash one day as he was reading the first aid manual again that everyone probably felt the same way as he had, with their own personal variations. Why would they all be so single-minded if they didn't have their own mothers or Mr. Tacketts back home egging them on? Why would they spend hours and hours a day practicing and studying if they didn't believe in themselves? He did see some that didn't have the faith, but they fooled around and eventually failed or dropped out.

We couldn't *all* have done it, he realized.

In this reflection, Phil knew exactly which of the musicians he knew "had it" and would probably make it in a big way. He also recognized that he wasn't one of them. He had been deceived by someone else's innocent hopes for him. The final touches and polish of his so-called genius had always been just around the corner, just beyond a few more intense practice sessions. Now he could see that they would always be around the corner. If he hadn't achieved it by now with all his experience and work, then he simply didn't have the ability.

Oh, he was good in his way. Good enough to teach or somehow make a living in the music business. But the vision of himself onstage in New York, Paris, London and Moscow vanished like an unsustained note.

He pitched the can against the wall.

"Why do you TORMENT me?" Katie screamed.

"Sorry, ma'am," he said and stopped.

His head cushioned by the back of the still-shiny camp shovel, Phil stretched out on the floor. He was as light as an autumn leaf—everything had been thrown off. Mr. Tackett, whom he had loved so much, whose expectations had been strangling him even beyond death, was naive, sentimental and mistaken. Phil no longer had to perform or dread or hope. He was free.

She remembered the first time she had ever held her own (rented) violin in her hands. It was a beauty, varnished and frail, mysteriously self-musical under the curly F-holes. She peered over the balsa bridge, down the strings, then into the hole where a maker's tag, an old yellowed piece of paper, was handwritten in old-world calligraphy. At the scrolled end were the pegs that groaned and squeaked when she forced the strings into tune. It was months before she stopped wincing while tuning, and when she finally relaxed, the feared event happened—the A-string popped and stung her across one eyebrow.

A piano was a piece of family furniture. Anyone could bang out "Chopsticks" or "Heart and Soul." The violin was hers, in her bedroom on the seldom-opened toy chest. Trinkets came with a violin; the case was covered with black leather and upholstered inside with red velvet. A little compartment opened at the end with the tug of a ribbon, and there was the extra bridge, four packets of crisp translucent paper with the spare strings, and the blue box of rosin, lettered in red and black, which looked as if it should contain exotic foreign sweets.

At first she could only make hoarse whining sounds with the instrument. It embarrassed her so much, after having learned the piano to level four, that she took her violin away on her bicycle to Santa Blanca pond. There she fought ants, mosquitos, horseflies and sun-glare on her scores until she could make clear notes.

After that it was forward motion—learning double stopping, second position, vibrato, pizzicato, and how to follow a conductor. Such joy in doing something, something important, doing it well and with pleasure.

Katie turned her head slightly toward the new sound. Phil was vomiting into the toilet.

The violin, she thought, was the only thing I ever loved.

Her sense of smell was gone. The shelter had once reeked with their armpit, excretory and sex smells—with an underlying whiff of something like tomato soup corroding in a tin can. But the smells were gone most of the time now.

Her back and face were sore with pimples. But her foot was the worst problem. She couldn't even remember how or when she had hurt it. All she knew was that it was a constant nagging pain and her toes had gone to sleep or something. He must have cut my foot. He was hungry and took a chunk out of my foot and ate it, she thought.

Phil pressed a huge erection against her thigh. She moved slightly, and suddenly could smell again, briefly. She rolled away from him and the smell stopped.

The light bulb had gone out days ago and neither had said anything about it. Phil didn't know if he could speak anyway—his tongue was swollen and sore. It seemed that they had been in the silent darkness forever. Sometimes Katie snored a little, but her own noise woke her and she would turn onto her side.

I suppose we could leave now, he thought once. But he couldn't summon the effort to open his mouth and ask Katie if she was ready to go. He didn't even know if she wanted to leave. Or if he did. It could wait a little longer . . .

After the light was gone, Katie saw a lot more of Hiroshima. Always wearing the same flowered dress she had died in, she sometimes appeared dismembered on the floor beside Phil's cot. Once, just her head sat on the floor, like in the comedy routines where actors would stick their heads through holes in the stage. Her eyes looked back and forth between Katie and Phil.

Or Katie would see the dress, empty, swirling in the air above her, the skirt rippling out in regular scallops like an inverted rose vase.

Katie's mother had told her about the ordinary woman that had been killed in a car crash when Katie was little; she knew about the Japanese city that had been destroyed. These things had been explained.

But the Hiroshima in a flowered dress meant something. She returned time after time whether Katie wanted her or not. She didn't know if Hiroshima was a warning or evil or good, but there she was.

I have escaped her fate, Katie thought.

Phil heard something scraping at the door. Then there was a terrible pounding and wrenching sound. He moaned and covered his eyes as a flood of yellow-green light filled the room. He smelled something fresh and cool and forgotten and heard a voice that he thought he should know.

"Katie? Katie, are you down there?"

Someone came down into the room, but he couldn't see anything. He felt Katie stir next to him.

"Oh, Mother Mary."

It sounded like Katie's father. What a vivid dream, Phil thought, still unable to pull his hand away from his eyes.

"They're alive, but that's about all you can say," another voice said.

"I'll have that Perry dragged by the balls down Main Street," said Mr. Doheney's voice. "Katie, honey?"

Katie made the only sound that either of them had been able to make since their tongues had swollen. Her father reached over Phil and scooped her up.

It's real.

"Maybe we should call an ambulance."

"No, let's just take 'em down ourselves. There's room in your car, isn't there?"

Phil was helped to sit by the other man, but when he tried to stand his legs wobbled badly. He felt his shoulders gripped by incredibly strong hands that propelled him up the ladder.

It wasn't until days later that Phil made sense of what he saw above ground again. They stood in an overgrown yard staring at the back of Katie and Perry's house. The kitchen had been flung outward, dynamited. Charred clapboard, wallboard and pipes dangled out through the broken house. Glass and roof tiles littered the yard. The rest of the neighborhood was a normal drizzling November morning.

Mr. Doheney leaned over the back of his seat in the car, Katie slumped against his chest. He looked at Phil directly and parentally with his clear blue eyes. "I know how you must feel, son, but you've got to have a Christian attitude. Perry told us you'd run off together, but then his conscience got the better of him and he told us where to find you."

Phil turned his head. Through the car window he saw an old black and tan mongrel on a lawn, nipping at its back.

A woman stood at her picture window and watched them pass. The blue-flanneled postman turned the corner of the block with a wad of letters in his hand. A pregnant woman led her toddler for a walk down the street.

Oh.

It was a mistake.

Oh.

1965

13

———

KATIE stopped typing to look out of the window. She couldn't concentrate with all the noise that the visiting auditor was making as he showed Marjorie a magic trick with paper clips.

His name was Louis, not Louie but Louis, and he had a harelip so he talked through his nose. He was many things that Katie couldn't put together—all the harelips she had ever known were shy with sorrowful eyes as if they couldn't recover from wondering why they had been born that way. Louis was funny and even a little flirtatious with everyone except her. Accountants were supposed to be dry and conservative, but he wore his hair with a Beatlish fringe combed forward, which Katie thought silly no matter how stylish.

All morning he had been sitting in Mr. Wood's office and joking with Marjorie on his way back and forth from the men's room or the percolator in the kitchen, making it hard for Katie to concentrate on the tedious details of the insurance contracts she was supposed to type perfectly. The forms were numbered; Katie made such a botch of one that she didn't even want to turn it into the stack of discards that had to be accounted for. Let them wonder what happened to number 5683; she didn't care. Planning to throw it away later in privacy, she folded it into a thick square and stuffed it in her handbag.

At noon she picked up her crutch and her packed lunch and made her way outside to sit on the brick wall that surrounded a small juniper garden under the insurance office's front windows. She had only taken out the apple when Louis came down the steps, apparently in a big hurry, with his tie and jacket flapping. He stopped abruptly.

"Hi," he said. "Isn't it a little chilly to be eating out here?"

"Sun's warm," she said, fussing with her lunch so that she wouldn't have to look at him. It made her nervous to talk with a strange man like this.

He sat down on the wall beside her. "Do you eat here every day?"

"Yeah."

He kicked his feet against the wall, staring across the parking lot, squinting into the winter sun. "Too bad about Churchill, isn't it?"

"Who?"

"Winston Churchill."

"Oh." Katie couldn't summon up anything for Churchill. He was an old man; everything he had done that she knew about was long ago and far away.

"I saw some of the funeral on the TV. Did you?"

"No."

"They took his body down the Thames on a boat with

guns booming. What a send-off. I'd like to have a send-off like that, wouldn't you?"

Katie shrugged, wondering why Louis was talking to her now. He had completely ignored her inside, flirting with Marjorie instead. What was this—Be Kind to Katie Hour? It made her angry to have people be nice to her just to be nice.

"I'd like to visit England someday and see the Thames. Do you like the Beatles?"

"Don't know. Don't listen to the radio much."

"Oh, you should!" Louis sounded so enthusiastic that it made Katie wonder why he wasn't sitting in his car with the radio on right at that moment. He was quiet for a few seconds more, then asked, "What happened to your foot?"

Katie, with a mouthful of sandwich, took a long time to swallow and think of an answer. "Someone ate it."

"Come on." He laughed.

Katie wanted to scream. "Will you just leave me alone?" she finally said. She hated the way she sounded, but that was the last straw. What a wretched day—I should have stayed home, she thought.

"Oh. I'm sorry." He was quiet and stopped bouncing his heels against the wall. Only his tie moved in the wind.

Katie was getting cold and thought about going in to her desk. Most days she'd rather be cold than stuck inside, but at least there was a window there. She had insisted upon having a window when being interviewed for the job. Mr. Wood understood, knew "all about" her.

"You see," Louis said in a quiet voice, "I always feel a kinship with other cripples."

"I'm not . . ." Katie was infuriated with him and felt close to tears. "I just don't have a foot, that's all. Please, would you . . ."

"Look, Katie, I didn't mean to make you mad at me. In fact, I wanted to ask you to have dinner with me sometime." He jumped down from the wall and stood in front of her, but not facing her. Instead, he seemed to be studying the paving.

"Dinner!" Katie was astonished. "Are you kidding?"

"*Touché.*" He hurried across the parking lot to his car and drove away quickly, unlike an accountant.

The life seemed to have gone out of the office that afternoon. Louis said little, even around Marjorie, and stuck to the books in Mr. Wood's office. Marjorie left early to collect her daughter, who had developed a fever at school. Katie kept her head down and worked hard, typing better that afternoon than she ever had before.

He likes me, but he likes me because I'm a cripple. She was relieved that he didn't try to talk to her again. At five, everyone left but Katie. She had to wait for her mother since Marjorie, her usual ride, had left.

Katie had *thought* everyone was gone, but as she sat on the wall pulling her coat around her, she noticed that Louis was sitting in his car. She didn't know what he was doing. After a few minutes, he got out and came across to her.

"Need a lift?"

"My mother's coming. Thank you anyway."

He sat down beside her, just as he had at lunch. "Ever hear about the man named Mark walking through the graveyard?"

Katie shook her head. Is this a joke? she wondered.

"He kept hearing someone calling to him—'Mark, Mark.'

But he couldn't see anyone. It was dark and quiet as he walked along the headstones, trying to hurry home. 'Mark, Mark,' someone said again." Louis gestured like a man swimming through eerie muck, peering left and right for the voice.

Katie smiled at his acting.

"He came to a fence. And there he saw something move. Not a human, but something covered with hair crouched down. It called to him again, 'Mark! Mark!' He ran to the graveyard fence and the beast ran behind him. Mark was so scared he couldn't open the gate." Louis held out his hands and rattled an imaginary wrought-iron gate in a spooky cemetery. "And then the creature caught up with him and shouted, 'MARK! MARK!' So Mark turned around very slowly to face up and fight. And there"—Louis pointed down to the ground—"was a harelipped dog."

Katie laughed but stopped short, realizing who was telling the joke. "Oh!" she said, surprised.

"It's all right. It's a funny joke." He chuckled to himself.

Katie was confused. Why would *he* go around telling jokes like that?

Louis put his hands in his pockets and whistled a few notes. "You know," he said, "I never heard the word 'harelip' until I was about ten because people would only say it behind my back. Then I met a boy from another school during a science fair one spring who had a cleft lip and palate, and he told me all sorts of jokes and names that we're called. I thought through the Mark-Mark joke and decided it was funny. So I told it to my parents. They just sat there in a rigid silence and, after a discussion, sent me to bed for telling it."

"Oh." Katie didn't want to make a judgment about someone else's parents, but it didn't seem like the right thing to do. She wondered how he had kept his apparent good nature.

"Well, that taught me a lesson," he said. He stared right into Katie's eyes. "Taught me to take everything personally."

Something about the way he said it made her feel she would have to think about what he had just said.

After a moment, he continued, "I asked my mother for a hare for Easter one year. She didn't make the connection and they were happy that I wanted to look after a pet. So when I got the hare—well, actually, they got me a rabbit—I saw that it had a cute little symmetrical face. Couldn't reconcile it with the scars I had all over my lip and my nose." He touched his upper lip tentatively, where the scars had faded to white lines but still visibly criss-crossed below his squashed nose.

Katie noticed her mother's car approaching.

"Well, what I—" he began.

Katie's mother tooted the horn. Katie waved and stood.

Louis stood with her, glancing at the car. "Oh, well, I'm sorry about getting sensitive this afternoon."

"No, I . . ." Katie thought it would take years to explain. Louis was walking her toward her mother's car, which would end their conversation. Even at her hobbling pace there weren't enough steps.

"See you," Louis said, passing her.

Katie got into her mother's car with the usual ordeal of sitting sideways then throwing the crutch in the back. "Hey, big boy!" she said, kissing the head of the little boy sitting beside her mother. He grinned back and held up the toy elephant in his hand.

Katie looked over to Louis as they drove out of the lot. He seemed to be singing along with the radio in his car.

———

Katie was puzzled at how distant Louis seemed the next day. He *had* smiled at her when he came in, but throughout the rest of the day he was merely the visiting auditor and she was one of the typists.

In fact, she hadn't thought much about him after leaving work the evening before. Gordon had been irritable with a new tooth, her mother was in an unusually menopausal mood, and her father remained in front of the television where Katie eventually joined him out of boredom.

When she saw Louis again in the morning, she thought, Oh, yeah, him, with a certain hazy fondness for the joke and story he had told her. Her mind had been elsewhere since then. At least he apparently had thought better of asking her out again and had cooled off.

At the end of the day she was struggling to get her jacket and handbag and crutch coordinated as Marjorie waited with a thinly disguised impatience when Louis came out with Mr. Wood from his office. Mr. Wood said, "Well, I'll follow up on that item."

They paused to shake hands. Louis said, "Been nice working with you. You also have a nice staff." He glanced her way then gave a sort of salute without actually touching the fringe of dark hair on his brow and walked briskly away.

Something about Louis's leaving made her feel even lonelier than usual.

More than a week after Louis had come and gone, Katie had to take her lunch at her desk because of the blindingly white blizzard outside. The office was empty, as usual, though Katie couldn't understand why her coworkers would want to go out in the awful weather. From her window she could see cars grinding slowly across the slippery roads, whining when they lost their traction. Although it was warm enough inside, she could smell the cold seeping through the window; it smelled like frozen putty.

Katie heard the door and felt a sweep of cold air around her ankles. It was Louis, bundled in a coat, muffler and leather cap with furry ear flaps.

Katie amazed herself at how pleased she was at the sight of him.

"Hi, Katie." He came forward and sat down in Marjorie's chair, staring over the typewriter at her, pulling his cap off and unbuttoning his coat. "You're not sledding to the local hot dog stand?"

"I don't sled to anything any more."

Cold and red, his nose looked even more deformed, but his eyes were bright and a little shy. "I'm on another job in the neighborhood and saw the lights on. Thought I'd stop for a cup of tea."

"Tea? I don't know . . ."

"Just a figure of speech. I would like some coffee, though. Would you like a cup?" He rose and headed for the kitchen.

"Oh, yeah, sounds good."

Two coins clanked in the coffee kitty and Louis reappeared with coffee. He put hers on her desk. "It's hot. Be careful." Then he sat on the corner of her desk.

"Thank you." She was glad she didn't have to pick it up—her hands were trembling. There wasn't much doubt as to why he had picked this time to drop in.

"So . . ." he said, "tell me about yourself."

The snorting laugh that came out of her was unladylike, she knew, but genuine. "There's far too much to tell."

"Well, start with your son. How old is he?"

Katie was startled. "You know about my son?"

Staring into his coffee mug, he said, "I asked Wood about you the first morning I worked here. He told me, 'She's divorced, has a son, lives with her parents, hometown girl, hard worker, lost her toes in some damn fool thing to do with a fallout shelter.'" Louis had managed to capture Mr. Wood's way of speaking in spite of his own speech difficulty.

Katie's face warmed up. It was strange to hear an encapsulated account of herself. Some damn fool thing . . .

"Katie, let me take you to dinner."

She winced. "It's not that I don't like you, but . . ."

"Yes, yes, all right," he said, cutting her short. "You're a nice man, Louis, but." Now he seemed to be mocking a long string of women.

"It's not what you think." Katie was at the edge of being angry with him for misinterpreting. "I don't date, I am not in love with anyone, nor do I wish to start up anything like that."

He looked at her sideways. "Easy, girl. I haven't asked you to marry me yet. I just want an evening's conversation with you, all right? How about if we don't call it a date but"—he searched for a phrase—"dinner with a new friend? Make it simple. No candles, no wine, no violins—as if you could find a joint like that around here anyway. I'll meet you for a hamburger and, if you like, call you a taxi or you can have someone pick you up."

"All right." She didn't see any harm in it as long as he understood that she wasn't interested in more. She could hold him off with that. Maybe it would be good to make a new friend. Between work and her home life, she didn't really have any social life. All her old school friends were married and interested in their own lives. Besides, she had somehow taken on a bit of a stigma since the damn fool shelter thing.

"Saturday?"

"OK."

"See you at the coffee shop at the junction around six?"

"Six-thirty."

"Right." He drank down his coffee and stood. "Well, I'm miles from the job I'm doing this week. Better hit the road."

She laughed, remembering his tall tale about being "in the neighborhood."

As he left, he pointed a finger at her. "Six-thirty."

With regret, Katie noticed that Pearl was wiping down the red Formica tabletops with water and vinegar, refilling the sugar jars and napkin holders. One man sat at the far end of the counter with his pie and coffee, but the other booths were empty.

Louis had been quiet for a moment. He had just told her a funny story about his father and a Christmas tree. After she laughed the conversation seemed to have fallen. "Look," he said, "I feel like there's this great big thing sort of hanging over you. Do you mind if I ask you about it? We can get it all over with and then talk about other things."

Katie shrugged. She knew what it was. It was the thing that other people said about her but never mentioned to her face. It was so embarrassing and, from other people's point of view, too silly to talk about. "I don't know. It makes me feel like a fool."

Pearl came around with the coffee pot. "Fill 'er up?" she asked.

"Do we have time?" Louis asked, already pushing his mug toward her.

"Just one more," Pearl said, "then we all got to git, OK?"

Katie sighed, relieved and terrified that there was more conversation to come.

"Well, do you want to tell me what happened? Sometimes things make sense when you hear it straight from the fool's mouth."

Katie glanced up quickly.

Louis smiled. "Gotcha. You don't really think you're a fool, do you?"

"I don't know." She took a deep breath. "You remember the Cuban Missile Crisis, right? It just seemed like everything was going to end. All our lives, we'd been training for the moment the Bomb would fall. I was so scared. I was married to Perry then and he just . . . he wasn't . . . he wasn't enough comfort. So I called my old boyfriend, Phil—you know, childhood sweetheart and all that." Katie stretched her hands out on the table. "I wish I had a cigarette."

Louis looked up. "Pearl, you smoke?" he called out.

"Menthol."

Katie smiled. "No, I don't want to start that again."

"Never mind. Thanks."

"Anytime, Lou." And as if it reminded her, Pearl took a crumpled pack out of her apron pocket and lit up a cigarette. She leaned against the tray full of mugs and chatted quietly with the man who had finished his pie with a great moan of satisfaction.

"Well, Perry got really jealous. He was the fire chief then, so he could blow the air-raid whistle, you know? So, he blew it, knowing that I would run for the shelter."

"With Phil."

"Well . . . yeah. I thought I loved him."

"Why did you stay down there, though? Weren't you

down there a long time?" His tone was curious, not judgmental.

"Perry took the batteries for the radio. So we didn't know
what was happening. And then he blew up the kitchen with
dynamite and we thought that was the Bomb dropping."

"Oh." Louis tapped his fingers once, across, like a run
on piano keys. "So why do you feel foolish? You had a good
reason; you had no better information. For instance, what
did your neighbors do?"

Something returned to Katie; when she had been in the
hospital her father had told her about a neighbor, Mrs. Dodge,
who had hidden in the basement during the whole crisis,
except that her husband kept dragging her back upstairs to
cook him dinner. At the time her father told her, she couldn't
put it into perspective at all. But now it made her smile. "I
guess everyone was scared."

"You bet. I was in Denver then, just after business college
and in my first job. I took off for the mountains. It was
freezing cold up there, but I just sat by a campfire and listened
to the transistor radio until it seemed safe to go back. I wanted
to beat the traffic jams of people heading for the hills."

Katie smiled.

"But I had a radio. If I hadn't . . ." He gestured as if to
say he might have frozen or starved to death himself.

"Yeah. It would have made all the difference. I'd still
have my foot if . . ."

"What happened to your foot?"

"Well, Phil said I dropped a hatchet on it. By the time
they found us I was, uhm, septic or whatever they call it. I
was crazy with fever. I thought Phil was eating me, bit by
bit. We were obsessed with food for a long time and I . . ."

Louis didn't urge her any further.

The man at the counter was paying his bill. Pearl yawned as she watched him go.

"We'd better go," he said.

Katie managed to slide out of the booth and lean on her crutch while Louis paid, but he helped her on with her coat. They didn't say any more until they were outside the diner. Pearl turned out all but the light over the cash register and the kitchen light. Katie stuffed her hands into her coat pockets. Strangely, she felt much as she had when she was younger and out with friends—not Phil, but her own friends—full of talk and cheeseburger and reluctant to go home. She looked up at the sky, which was clear, black and cold; the stars were so vivid that they looked like tiny balls rather than points.

"There's Orion," Louis said, following her study.

"Which one is that?"

"It's like that." He drew in the sky. "See, the belt, the sword, his top and bottom."

"Oh. I don't know constellations."

"I used to have a telescope. When I was a kid."

Katie nodded. "I used to be scared of the stars. I hated it when my parents dragged me out to see Sputnik, then Echo. I hated looking at the sky. I used to associate it with war and missiles and planes dropping bombs."

"You *were* scared, I guess," he said, searching the sky, then gazing at her.

"You know what's weird," she said. "I've never said this before. But I'm not scared anymore. I mean, I'm not even when I should be. When awful things come on the television or are in the newspaper, I just feel cold about it all. I can't believe in the Bomb anymore. It's like . . ."

"Not believing in God?" he asked after her hesitation.

She shrugged. "I don't know." Then she nodded. "Yeah, maybe. I still *think* it might happen, but . . . I used to believe in it. Now I just don't care."

They were quiet again. Katie studied Louis as he pointed out another constellation. "Pleiades. Seven Sisters."

She tried again, as she had through the meal and endless coffees afterwards, to imagine Louis as a kid. It shouldn't have been that difficult because as a man he was full of fun and good humor and hope, but she had learned from their conversation that he hadn't been so happy as a child.

"I wish we could go for a walk," he said wistfully.

"Well, why not? I don't mind if you don't mind taking baby steps with me."

"All right."

They started down the road that led to the highway south to Pueblo, Trinidad and, eventually, Taos, New Mexico. Even at this late hour, it was bright with rainbows of neon motel signs, filling station lights, and the headlights of cars and trailer trucks roaring through the flat mountain valley. Katie found her stride after a few steps and they moved at almost normal walking speed.

"Katie," he said, "there's something I should tell you, I suppose. Before I ask you if you would want to do this again next Saturday."

She glanced up at him.

"Well, this business of just being friends, you know?"

"Yeah."

"Well, it's one-sided," he said.

"Yeah, I thought so. It's all right with me, Louis. Just don't . . ."

"No, I won't. I just thought you'd like to know."

"OK." Katie felt strange inside, strange and young. She

did like his company. Would it be bad to spend more time with him? Where would she draw the line? Too much time? An attempt at a kiss? Words? But as long as they both knew how things were, there couldn't be any harm in it.

"So will you let me buy you another cheeseburger next Saturday?"

"Sure. Sure, be glad to."

They stopped and sat down on a bus bench and he taught her some of the constellations.

14

"O H , Katie, will you please calm down," her mother said, hands in the air as if she were about to pull her hair out. "You're not the only person in this house with a life to live."

"Let's not start that again." Katie, after having found the right color of thread, the needles and pins, settled down by the window to hem hurriedly the only dress she felt she could wear. "I found them. I'm sorry."

"Every Saturday night . . ."

"Mother," Katie said with false patience, "whenever you want a Saturday night out just let me know. I don't know why you should start now, though. You and Dad have stayed in and watched television or played cards all my life."

"Well, maybe we would like to play cards in peace and quiet again. Between you and your sisters . . ."

Katie listened with enough attention to answer a question if one should be asked. Why am I, a grown woman, letting my mother rail at me for going out for a meal? Why don't

I make more money at the office so I can afford a sitter? Why does every dress have to be mended before I put it on? Why can't my life be like that of the wives and mothers in *McCall's* magazine?

It was once, she suddenly remembered. With Perry.

That's why it's not—I hated it.

She finished the hem and took the dress to her room. It was wrinkled again, but not so much so that she wanted to get the iron out. As she slipped it over her head, she heard the doorbell, then her mother's voice, which had reverted to the sweet soprano of Katie's childhood.

"Hello, Louis. Would you like some coffee?"

Please, Louis, say no. Be in a hurry.

"I'd like that very much, Mrs. Doheney. Thank you."

Katie sank down on the bed, head in hands. He had a knack—her mother was always nice to her for a few days after Louis visited, as if she saw Katie as a little more worthy of consideration if that nice Louis liked her. But Katie wanted to get away. Going out with Louis had become the only bearable part of the week other than the few moments with Gordon when he was well-behaved.

Katie sighed and brushed her hair languidly. No reason to hurry now. She should have caught him at the door and signaled somehow. In answer to a small voice in the hall, Louis said, "Hiya, big guy!" It made her smile. Big Guy or Big Boy. She called him that herself, her family had picked it up, with variations—sometimes her father said Big Shit when he thought Katie couldn't hear—and now Louis. Perhaps she should go on a campaign to have everyone call poor Gordon by his name.

When she arrived in the front room, she found Louis being run over mercilessly by Gordon's wooden truck. Louis took it patiently, even when Gordon jumped the road block—Louis's hand—and landed dangerously near Louis's crotch.

"Gordon, don't do that," she said. "Play on the floor."

"It's all right." Louis tousled the kid's hair. Then he winked a hello at Katie.

Gordon compromised by running his truck on the empty sofa space beside Louis, driving near but not on the forbidden trousers. Katie's mother brought in the coffee on a tray. Her father followed, looking sleepy, tucking in his shirttail by shoving one hand down the back of his jeans.

"Hello, there, Louis!"

"Evening."

Katie sat down on the piano bench and watched her family settle around Louis. Her father picked up Gordon with one arm and carried him to the big chair. Her mother sat next to Louis and handed him his coffee. Katie gritted her teeth, holding back from telling Louis that they must leave or she would scream. He liked this family life. It's my curse to have likable parents, she thought, recalling that all through the years her boyfriends had gravitated towards the casual Doheney house rather than the coffee shops.

But Louis is not my boyfriend; he's just a friend. She watched his eyes shine as her son wriggled out of Grandpa's lap and crept back toward Louis.

Gordon, after making his way hand over hand across the expanse of sofa, clung to Louis's knees. The two grinned at each other. Suddenly, Louis leaned forward and picked up the boy with his hands wrapped under the small arms and halfway around his back, sweeping Gordon high into the air. Then he lowered him to eye level, making play engine sounds while Gordon laughed like mad, and then kissed his forehead.

Katie fled. She wobbled on the crutch to her bedroom and flung herself onto the bed. She wept into the pillow, a descendant of the many pillows she had cried into during her life.

She knew the timid knock wasn't her mother at the door. "Katie?"

She sat up, wiping her eyes, certain that her mascara made streaks. "Just a minute." She found a tissue and tried to mop up the damage. "Come in."

Louis came in hesitantly, glancing around at her things, then came over to her. He sat down on the bed beside her, his hands on his knees. "Have I done something wrong?" he asked.

"No." Katie laughed. "I just realized that you love my son more than I do."

"I don't believe that." He smiled gently, looking down at the violin case just inches from the brown leather of his shoes. "I do love him, though," he admitted. "Almost as much as I love you." It was the first time he had said so. "Almost. I don't think I have much more room without dying of love."

Katie squeezed the tissue in her hand with the force of a woman in labor. She bore the words that had been planted as an infinitesimally small seed and had been growing in her for months. "If you want me, I'm yours."

"Katie." Louis only moved his hand, which he placed over hers. They sat for a moment, neither able to add to what had been said and done. Finally, Louis turned his face toward her, his eyes especially shiny.

"Cheeseburger?" he asked.

———

Katie didn't know if Louis was still awake. He was breathing slowly but quietly. She tried to keep her eyes shut but could not.

I hope he understands that it wasn't him, she thought, not daring to move, even though Louis's hand was squashed uncomfortably near her shoulder. He's a nice lover, just as he is a nice man.

Katie's mind wandered to the sea, or rather the bay, which was the most water she had ever seen in her life. And there, just like the picture postcards, was the Golden Gate Bridge —if she could only climb out of bed and stare out the window at it again. They had only had time for a meal down by the pretty little boats, staring across at Alcatraz, then a stroll to Ghirardelli's for some chocolate before dark. San Francisco was beautiful, but neither of them had anticipated the difference between fifty-five degrees of damp chill and fifty-five degrees of dry air at home. They were at the edge of being cold. A waitress had told them that the weather was almost always like this.

I like him very, very much, she thought. Finally, she rolled, as if in sleep, off his hand. He didn't move.

It was just being smothered by a man on top of me. Katie shut her eyes tightly in regret for having pushed him away. Smothered. And the smell, that horrible rotten smell of the shelter. At least I didn't scream and I could talk to him about it. I can talk to him. He seems to understand. I hope he does. He's such a nice man. I like him so very much.

Poor Louis. He will pay a thousand times over for loving me. He's only just discovering.

She didn't regret the marriage. Even the wedding just that morning had been a relaxed, friendly affair, unlike her wedding to Perry, which had pulled somber faces from family and friends. She didn't regret Louis. She didn't regret a honeymoon without Gordon.

She only regretted that such a good person loved her and that she would inadvertently make him suffer for it.

He had asked her as they made wedding plans, "Where in the whole world do you want to go?"

"Japan," Katie had said so carelessly. She knew that Louis had a special fondness for Britain, had a cousin with whom he had been corresponding for years, yet she couldn't help but say Japan. He didn't ask her why, and when she realized his disappointment and tried to change it, he wouldn't hear of it. "If you want Japan, you have it, my love. We can go to England later, when Gordon is old enough to appreciate it."

As she lay in her honeymoon bed, Katie winced at all the things she had done wrong thus far. And yet, she was going on a pilgrimage.

In a few days, I will walk in Hiroshima, a brand-new city, where the other survivors walk.

15

P H I L made sure that he had cigarettes, ashtray, a fresh cup of coffee, and pencil and paper before dialing the phone.

"Katie, is that you?" he asked, hearing her voice.

"Phil?"

"Hi." He didn't know where to go from there, even though he thought he had a million things to say to her. "My mother gave me your new phone number."

"Yeah, oh, Phil, where are you?"

"I'm in Jackson."

"Jackson?"

"Jackson, Mississippi. I've been playing piano for Miss Abbie's Ballet School for Girls for a few months."

Katie laughed. "Sounds like a good job."

Phil laughed, too, loving the familiarity of her voice. "You sound good. Are things better this time?"

"You mean with Louis?"

Louis. Phil tried to store the name permanently. "Yeah. I mean, no slug-like fire chief this time."

"Oh, Phil, if I could only tell you . . . I'm really, really happy. He's a good man. You'll have to come and visit us sometime. He took me to Japan for our honeymoon and I fell in love with him there."

"Japan! You've been to Japan?" Phil was amazed. His little provincial Katie in such an exotic place. But, of course, Japan. Then he thought about the rest of her sentence. "You fell in love on your honeymoon?"

"Well, yeah. It's a long story. I liked him—it wasn't like before. I knew I would always like him. But he chased a lot of ghosts out."

Phil cleared his throat, then lit a cigarette. "I suppose I was a ghost."

"I suppose so."

The hesitation between them was painful, so Phil jumped into the next painful thing. "How's Gordon? Like his new daddy?" He tried to sound casual and bland but somehow a slightly strangled sound touched his voice.

"Oh, he's terrific. Really shooting up."

"Yeah. My mother told me."

"Your mother is really good with Gordon. She says he's an independent little cuss just like you were."

"Yeah." Phil knew that he was failing. All the cheeriness that he had managed before was seeping away. Katie sounded good, happy. She loved her husband, her family. She sounded *cured*, as if he had always known someone not quite functional who had been put right. He felt excluded, even though he wouldn't actually want to step into Louis's shoes. He just wanted to still be a part of Katie's life somehow.

"How long have you been in Jackson?"

"Just a couple of months. I was in Los Angeles and did a couple of film scores."

"Film scores!"

Phil laughed at how impressed she sounded. "Yeah, well, I don't know if you'll ever want to take your kids to those movies. I just happened to meet a man who was making a couple of monster movies on a shoestring budget, and I was just the composer for him. A matter of being at the right party at the right moment. I tossed around for something a little more serious and couldn't make any headway."

"Must have been exciting, though."

"Tell you the truth, Katie, I hated it. California's pretty, but—"

"I know," she said with a hint of dreaminess.

"—I came running to the opposite end of the country to get it out of my system."

"Yeah, Jackson must be different all right."

"I like it. Miss Abbie is a genteel old Southern belle. I've never known anyone who seemed so aristocratic by nature. She's got some funny ideas though. She had my piano turned around and put a screen across the mirror so that I can't watch the girls dancing."

Katie laughed.

Phil stared out the window. He could see only branches of trees and a bit of a window of a huge white clapboard house across the street. It was hot and sticky. "How's your foot?" he asked.

"Louis bought me a set of toes. They don't wiggle but I have my balance back and just have a cane. I might give up the cane, too."

"That's good. That's really good, Katie."

"How's your claustrophobia?"

"Oh, you know that's not anything much." He shrugged for her even though she couldn't see. "I just take a lot of walks. I'm healthy anyway."

"Good."

Phil knew they had run out of things to say. "Well, I can't afford to talk much longer. Say hello to . . . the family. Glad you're happy, Katie. I really am."

"I know. Take care of yourself?"

"Sure."

After he put the phone down, he went to the window and pressed against the screen. But it wasn't enough. The room on the third floor of the boarding house stifled him, so he went for a walk.

He liked to walk in what he knew was the "wrong" part of town. In Colorado and in Missouri, he had seen the shabbier parts of towns and cities, but he found the absolute poverty of the southern states fascinating. It was like walking through Walker Evans and Dorthea Lange photos of the Depression, just with more modern fridges and stoves rusting on the porches of the badly weathered clapboard houses. The children stared at him from their mothers' laps as the families sat on the porches trying to cool themselves on heavy, humid evenings. He wanted to tell them that he was sorry about the state of things, that he wished everyone had enough to eat and electric fans and good record players and a car to go places in. He wanted to tell them that he supported President Johnson's War on Poverty as well as programs to get these kids educated so that they could make something of themselves. But if he ever imagined actually saying these things, his imaginary self became a mealymouthed liberal from the city talking about things that just didn't have anything to do with their daily lives.

So he strolled, a white man walking where a white man shouldn't.

Down a little street was a row of shops—a florist; a small drugstore that also sold bread, milk and newspapers; a barbecue joint with a column of hickory smoke rising from the back; and a grimy filling station on the corner. Phil paused in front of the screen door of the barbecue, peering inside at the voices, faces, cigarette smoke and empty platters still covered with dredges of sauce. Although the old black upright was silent at the moment, an old man with grizzled white whiskers sat at it, grinning as he spoke to a woman about his age at a nearby table.

Phil opened the door and walked in.

"Hey, hey, Philip, what's that you got all over yo' skin?" the piano player asked, filling in the pause in the café caused by Phil's presence.

"Mama's flour," Phil said, grinning. He could never quite understand whether this was a joke at his expense or a friendly maneuver, but he played along with it. It was his ticket.

And the return was Tom's honky-tonk, ragtime, blues piano and a plate of Aunt Shirley's best ribs with a chunk of cornbread and a cereal bowl of black-eyed peas.

Phil always had to take an Alka-Seltzer after one of these meals, but there were few meals he had eaten in his life that he had enjoyed more. He loved the smell of the greasy old furniture, the hickory smoke, and the faint whiff of illegal whiskey poured from jacket pockets into Aunt's coffee. With the piano boogie-woogie, the people around him rocked side to side, clapping in time and whooping out an appreciation at each tune's end.

This time, as was often the case, a young girl of about seven or eight danced in the kitchen. The way she moved her undeveloped stick frame had such grace and ease that Phil always glanced toward the door into the kitchen, hoping he would see her moving across the floor, pirouetting with outstretched arms as well as and perhaps better than the girls in Miss Abbie's studio. As at Miss Abbie's, Phil kept his observation surreptitious. He had no interest in the little girls because they were girls, only an intellectual interest since he was now "in the business." But he was aware of the suspicions an outsider could arouse.

Phil ate as quietly as he would in a white restaurant in downtown Jackson and sat for two cups of coffee and two cigarettes.

The South is a seductive place, he thought. He loved the warm climate, something he had grown accustomed to in California; the magnolias and honeysuckle in the semi-tropical night air; the graciousness of the old homes with rambling gardens; the deep-fried catfish, homegrown tomatoes and peaches; the politeness and gentle pace of speech (he found himself adopting it, saying "thaink yew, ma'yem" to Miss Abbie); the eternal youth of women who, spinster, married, or widowed, were "Miss" until death. But most of all he loved this—the music and language and real-life bluesy world of the Negroes, or blacks as they called them "up north" in California.

Phil reluctantly decided to go. He refrained from over-tipping Aunt Shirley and saluted Tom, still banging away, as he left.

He headed for home, filled with bits of a secret culture

that seemed to him more real than anything he'd ever known, half wishing that he, too, was the great-grandson of a slave.

Near his boarding house, Phil crossed paths with a white man completely unfamiliar to him. As they passed, he thought he heard the man say quietly, "Nigger lover."

Later, lying on his bed and thinking about the man's voice, he decided that it had been impossible. But even if he had heard correctly, so what?

Miss Abbie came to the door, wiping her brow with the back of her hand. "Well, Phil, what brings you around? Hot one, isn't it?" She smiled and opened the door for him. Though fifty-odd, she spoke with a high, flirtatious voice and wore a frilly calico housedress. It was easy to imagine that she had been the belle of belles thirty years before. Now widowed, she had a beau who called on her Thursday evenings and Sunday afternoons.

"Hi, Miss Abbie." Phil stepped into the house, where it was not much cooler but at least didn't feel as if the heat were a tight hat.

"Lemonade?"

"Oh, yes, ma'am, that sounds good."

While she was in the kitchen, he peered at the photographs on the curved corner shelf. Her ancestors posed in white clothes and hats on the porch steps of this same house, or in the rocker that was a few feet from where Phil stood. The house was still filled with the furniture of those days— a dark sideboard and dining room set, a lamp table covered with a tasseled velvet cloth.

Miss Abbie brought the lemonade on a silver tray. "There we are." She sat on the sofa and held one of the glasses to Phil as if he were sitting in the rocker. He took his cue and sat down there. "Now you haven't come to tell me that you're leaving me, have you?"

"Oh, no. Not at all." Phil didn't know exactly how to broach the subject. "Well, you see, I've just come to ask you about something. It's sort of political, you see."

"Political?" Miss Abbie's eyebrows raised. "I'm not much on politics, Phil."

"Well, it's not exactly that. It's nothing to do with Democrats or Republicans. It's just . . . well, you see, a few years ago—remember the Cuban Missile Crisis?"

Miss Abbie nodded. She was leaning forward and had her left ear turned toward him intently.

"I was with, uhm, a friend, and we were tricked into thinking that the country was being attacked. So we spent more than two weeks in a fallout shelter."

"Oh, my goodness," she said. "Goodness me. What an ordeal."

Phil warmed up with her sympathetic response. She's easy to talk to, he thought, I'm glad I came. "Yes, well, you see, during that time I learned what is *really* important."

Miss Abbie's eyes widened.

"Nothing."

"Nothing?" she said, obviously disappointed.

"Well, at first I thought about all the things I would miss—music, fun, my parents and friends. Then after a while they didn't matter any more; we were just thinking about the food and water we had and how rotten we felt. And I was worried about what would be outside when we left the shelter. Then I started thinking, 'Well, it just might be a brand-new start.' Because there would be nothing."

Miss Abbie nodded very, very slightly, still watching him with interest.

"Eventually, I couldn't think at all. I can't really describe it to you, but it was like being sort of asleep when you know you're cold or thirsty or have to go to the bathroom and you can't wake up enough to do it. It was like that—too dead to be alive and too alive to be dead and unable to move."

"How awful it must have been," Miss Abbie said breathlessly.

Phil realized that the lemonade glass in his hand was sweating and dripping condensation all over him. He drank half of it and set it on the tray. "After I was out again and realized that nothing was different, that it was the same terrible old world, I started thinking that the only things wrong with it are the problems that people make."

Miss Abbie nodded, waiting.

"There's nothing wrong with sunshine or flowers or birds and rabbits." Phil waved his arms to encompass the natural world. "The problem is *people*."

Miss Abbie clapped her palms together. "You're so right, Phil. You're absolutely right! What a fascinating story." Her eyes were Sunday-sermon bright. "I've often said that very thing myself. If only people could look deep into their good Christian souls we wouldn't have all these goings-on."

"Yes," he said uncertainly. He wouldn't have phrased it quite that way. "I've always thought that I had a purpose in life. I mean, everyone feels that, I guess. What I mean is, I have to do something *important*."

"Yes?" Miss Abbie took this moment to sip her lemonade but she only glanced at the glass quickly, to let Phil know that her attention was still with him.

"I used to think it was music."

"Oh, you're a talented pianist, Phil. You really understand what music means, how it fills out life." She made an arc with her arms similar to the movements she taught her beginning class. "My girls get so much out of hearing real music instead of that old hi-fi."

Phil smiled reflexively. "Well, thank you, Miss Abbie, but I don't think music is what I was put on earth for. After I came out of the shelter, I realized that what I had to do was try to fix things that are not quite right. Try to say to people, 'Hey, life can be good if we only make it better. It's really up to us.' I tried to write a book when I lived in California, but it all just sounded stupid and silly. I can't write. So I want to just do my best until I find the way. Do you understand?"

Miss Abbie nodded. "I am inspired by your story, Phil. Why don't you come to church with me on Sunday and I'll introduce you to the preacher. Maybe . . ."

"Well, in fact, Miss Abbie, I had something a little more concrete in mind. Something you could help me with."

"Me?" She touched the calico ruffles at her throat and sat up straight with surprise. "What can I do?"

"Well, one of the biggest problems in the world after the atom bomb and war is racism."

Miss Abbie's color faded.

"I was wondering if you could take a girl into your class. She has a natural talent for dancing—"

"That's impossible."

Phil opened his mouth to ask why, but he knew why. How else to convince her? Where had her sparkle and inspiration gone so suddenly?

"You Yankees," she said, "come down here and y'all just don't understand a single thing, do you?" She glanced over at the clock on the wall. "Well, Phil," she said in her former sweet voice, "it was *so* nice of you to come by and visit me.

I've never before met anyone who's been in one of those bomb shelters. My goodness."

They both stood and moved toward the door—Phil confused, Miss Abbie shepherding.

"Would you think about it?" Phil asked desperately.

"Morning, Phil," she said, holding the door open for him.

Phil stepped back out into the hot sun, sorry and embarrassed. "Morning, ma'am."

May Day, Phil thought, his hands in his pockets and head down. Aren't there supposed to be children dancing around maypoles and baskets of flowers and kissing and springtime things?

Instead, it was almost unbearably hot and quiet in the streets of Jackson. He thought about the few dollars in his wallet, the small amount in the bank and felt vaguely guilty about heading to Aunt Shirley's for a plate of ribs. It would be cheaper if he ate at the boarding house, and there would be less to explain to Mrs. Withers, who always wanted to know why he missed meals.

It was something of an uncelebration, though. To uncelebrate losing his job. Miss Abbie had cooled off to near silence for three days before finally telling him that she could no longer afford him and would have to resort to the old hi-fi again. She almost convinced him with her head-shaking and tongue-clucking that she didn't want to let him go.

But Phil had plainly botched it.

He had gone over their conversation a million times, remembering how excited she had become by his words, how they had come to a moment of passionate understanding—leaning forward, expressions alive and suddenly—zip! She was gone. How could he have done it differently?

"Where you goin', boy?"

Phil lifted his head. He was about three streets over and one up from the ribs and Tom's piano playing, just on the wrong side of the avenue that was an understood dividing line between poor white Jackson and black Jackson.

Three white men stood by the post of a traffic light. One wore a suit, the other two work clothes. They didn't look like three men who would usually be together, but all of them were staring at him.

"What's it to you?" Phil said and walked on.

"Hey, boy, we're talking to you."

He ignored them and crossed over. Shaken, he tried not to change his pace. Nor did he look over his shoulder until he was only a block from the barbecue. The cracked sidewalks were empty, the tumbledown houses and shops quiet.

Too quiet. Phil wondered what was happening.

When he reached the door, there was no music and the place was dark. Over the Rainbo bread advertisement on the screen door a sign said "Gone to the park for Emancipation Day."

Phil stared at the sign for a long while. Even if he had known which park, he wouldn't have gone. He wasn't included. He hadn't been emancipated.

He took a circuitous route back to the boarding house. After packing his belongings into a suitcase and a box, he wrote out checks for his bills and stuffed an envelope under Mrs. Withers's study door and walked down to the bus station.

At the bus station Phil noticed two black soldiers playing a pinball machine while waiting for their bus. He considered asking them if they realized they were defending a country full of jerks who would be just as happy never to see their kind except in the kitchen or the fields. But he didn't really like military people all that much, so he let it go.

The first bus was to Memphis. From there, through St. Louis, he found another bus that went to Hannibal, where he trudged through Mark Twain's home, stared at the Mississippi River for a few hours, and spent some of his last change on a riverboat charm for a bracelet that he eventually gave to Holly, in Madison, Wisconsin.

1985–1986

16

THE sleaziness of the theater appealed to Phil. It had once been a luxurious cinema—in its heyday parents would have brought their children to see a Disney movie or a big Western in it. He could imagine James Stewart's face where now hung balding curtains. Phil had been told by the taxi driver that this Mr. Glass had rescued it in 1982 from dollar-night fourth runs and midnight Kung Fu films before turning it into a dramatic theater. Someone had also done the same with the Fabulous Fox but with a bigger budget.

"Thought it wouldn't last a month," the cabby had said, almost wistfully, "but he's got patrons up the wazoo."

Phil tried to imagine the patrons here, feeling charitable as they sidled into their stiff seats. The concrete floor had been painted ruby red but was chipping like a careless girl's fingernail polish.

Restlessly, he returned to the lobby to see if Mr. Glass's

door had opened yet. The secretary who had allowed him in had disappeared. Phil leaned against the counter where popcorn and Coke used to move; it was now outfitted for California wines and imported beer for the upmarket St. Louis crowd. The industrial pile carpet was fairly new, which made Phil wonder what the old one had looked like for carpeting to be a priority purchase in this place.

Glass's door finally opened. A man with an oily head paused as if seeing Phil reminded him of forgotten business. He was too small and wizened to be handsome and yet not aged and ugly enough to be interesting. His shoulders bent at a twenty-degree angle in the forward direction, giving him a more dynamic appearance than his speed merited.

"Hello. Phil Benson, right?"

"Right. Glad to meet you, Mr. Glass." Phil reached out and shook Glass's hand.

"Have you ever played for a theater before?"

"No."

"Well, understandable. Not too many people do it, do they?" The comment was inner-directed; Glass was already headed for the auditorium. "Come on, let's hear you."

Phil followed Glass down the aisle to the baby grand tucked into the curve of stage left.

"The scores vary a lot," Glass said, picking up a sheaf of papers separated by jumbo paper clips.

"I'm versatile." Phil wondered if he would like working for this man. The theater itself had a sleazy kind of charm, but to have a sleazy boss might be a little too much. He sat down at the piano bench.

Glass thumbed through the scores. Phil noticed a movement behind the curtains. Probably that secretary or a janitor. But then he heard a soft sound, like bare feet dancing.

"Here." Glass handed him a score that was soft and smudged with handling. Phil glanced through it. Pages thick with triplets and arpeggios. It would look difficult to someone who was not an adept musician, but well-practiced hands could play it lazily.

He set it up, then felt out the piano, chording from low C to high. "Your piano is slightly out of tune."

"Just had it done a few months ago."

"Change in the weather," Phil said. When Glass frowned, Phil realized that he sounded as if he were making excuses for his audition ahead of time. Christ, I'm not just talking to some Joe in a piano bar, he thought, and made a note to be careful.

The piece was terrible—influenced by Gershwin and Stravinsky all in one without magic or finesse. Pretentious off-off-Broadway. Good God, could I even *listen* to this four days a week and twice on Sunday? He winced a few times at the deliberate dissonances crammed into the pop melody. Ya-da da, Susie's gone, ennui, ennui . . .

He ended without going back for the coda. When he turned back toward Glass, he could see that the man knew nothing whatsoever about music.

"Do you drink?" Glass asked as he leaned over and replaced the score with another.

Phil's mind blanked for a moment. It seemed too early in the day even to discuss drinking. Then he understood that there was something very important about the question. "Occasionally," he said, "at parties."

"Occasionally," Glass repeated. He had a schoolmaster's sternness. An arthritic finger pointed at the new score.

Phil played. Although the second piece was better, it didn't win by much. It was a variation on Chopin's

"Raindrop" that faded into "Les Sylphides," and suddenly he realized that it was a mishmash medley of Chopin phrases. He couldn't imagine it as an accompaniment to a play. Perhaps they danced, too.

"Softly," Glass said. "You can't go above the actors' voices. You have to be an undertone."

Phil touched the keys of the piano lightly. It sounded a bit less like piped-in supermarket music that way. He finished with a shudder, partly because the auditorium was drafty and partly because he had a sinking feeling that he was going to be playing this stuff for a few months until a better job came along.

"Look, I have some original compositions. If you like I'll play you one of mine."

After an annoyed pause, Glass nodded curtly.

Phil dredged out of his memory a piece he had written years ago, while living in Absecon, New Jersey. He had been inspired by the mixture of sweet-smelling woods and the seediness of the Atlantic City area, where airplanes that sounded like bombers flew overhead continuously. He had enjoyed his months living there, eating in a café with two huge, usually empty dining rooms and a good-natured waitress who apologized for everything. In that café he had copied out the final score from notes, incorporating the sound of his waitress reading out her horoscope to the cook and the rhythm of her breakfast sausage calls to the kitchen—two quarter beats for patty, one quarter note for link.

It had been months since he had played the composition. As he launched into it, he realized with horror that he had been as guilty of the same sort of thing as the composer of the first piece he had played for Glass. Only he had mixed Thelonius Monk with Field. He played it softly, secretly ashamed, hoping that Glass had a taste for "pretty" jazz.

In the periphery of his vision, Phil saw a figure carry a tall stool onto the stage, just ten feet away and above him. The hem of a flowered skirt was all he saw in a quick sideways glance. She put the stool down with a loud thump as if it were a prop at the beginning of a play, meant to signify something. In another situation Phil would have turned his head to look at her. But he suspected that she might be part of a test that Glass had set up for him.

He ended the piece dramatically and turned deliberately to Glass.

Glass's apparent nervous habit was that of standing stock still. He stared absently at the woman onstage rather than at Phil as he spoke. "I need reliable employees here. I won't tolerate missing even a rehearsal. No alcohol, no drugs while you work for me."

A wail of laughter came from the woman onstage. Halfsung, it filled the auditorium and made it clear that she was an actress or singer. Phil had never heard such beautiful and chillingly empty laughter. He allowed himself a look at the woman.

She was probably less than thirty, pale-skinned, dark eyed, with black hair in a long, spiky do. Far too modern for Phil— he had discovered in his last town that he was at an age of being frightened by some young women.

Glass made an irritable face, then merely rubbed at his lower lip with his thumb. "I will hire you on a two-week probation since you have such sketchy references. Even if you had a reference from Leonard Bernstein, though, you might not work out with the audience and the actors. We'll see how you do. However, being late, absent or intoxicated will get you fired even if you've been here twenty years."

You won't catch me still here in twenty years, Phil thought.

The woman tumbled off the stool in a heap. Glass tensed and narrowed his eyes at her, but she simply stayed where she was, silently.

Phil gazed into the piano keys, wondering if he was happy about this job. Having already been threatened twice with losing it during the interview made Phil worry that he would go badly wrong sooner or later. The only alternatives he could see at the moment were working in a music shop or a piano bar or hustling hard with tuning. He was tired; he wanted a job that was interesting and regular. Besides all that, he hoped that Glass was the kind of boss about whom people would say, "Oh, he's not so bad once you get to know him." Perhaps under all that coldness, Glass had been a little impressed with the original composition. Phil saw an intriguing possibility of writing scores for plays.

"May I practice here?" he asked.

"I suppose. I'll give you a rehearsal schedule. I'd like you here at noon tomorrow."

"Thanks, Mr. Glass. Happy to join up."

Glass gave Phil a thorny look. He seemed acutely aware of all acting in human nature.

The woman rose from the floor, picked up the stool, and walked simply and gracefully offstage.

"Who's that?" Phil asked as casually as he could.

"Pam," Glass said flatly. "I would advise you—don't."

"Don't?"

"Never mind." Glass started up the aisle. Phil followed and waited at the office door. Glass opened an filing cabinet and pulled out a sheet of paper. He had a tidy office. The schedule he handed to Phil was for a seven-day week, color-

coded for rehearsals, auditions, read-throughs and performances.

"Noon," Glass said.

"Noon," Phil repeated.

Phil didn't take his jacket off when he got back to his
apartment. It was chilly inside, and he hadn't yet worked out
how to tamper with the steam heater to boost the temper-
ature. It seemed that the manager was under orders to keep
the costs down, and that meant anyone on the third or fourth
floor had to freeze. At the bank of mailboxes in the foyer, a
woman who lived in the basement level told him that they
were too warm down there, with all the hot water pipes
exposed in the ceiling doing a better job than his steam heater.

Didn't matter. He didn't mind keeping more clothes on
if it meant he could be higher off the ground. As he stood
at the curtainless window, he could see cars in clumps of
three or four moving down the street, racing to one traffic
light, idling, then racing to the next. Across the road was a
convenience store and next to that a modern apartment com-
plex that towered six more floors above Phil's shabby old
building. Down the street were dark patches of trees alternating with spotlit parking lots of small businesses shut for
the night. At the end of the block was an all-night café, a
square white stucco box with a blinking neon sign. It seemed
to have been untouched for decades. Even the waitresses in
there looked outmoded. He liked that. He thought about
going down for boysenberry pie and coffee, but inertia won;
he watched the traffic.

There were many things he could do—he had already
taken a long walk in the city park after the interview with
Glass. So with a clear conscience he could do something

quiet, like listen to the little radio beside his narrow bed. Or eat the pork chop in the fridge. Or read the paperback biography of John Lennon that he had picked up in the supermarket.

Instead, he just stood, looking at all the lights that strung across St. Louis, mostly blue with yellow, red and green dots. He wasn't sure why he had come here. In college, he had spent a few days kicking around St. Louis, besides the many times he had been through it on the way to somewhere else. It had always seemed to be a good city, as cities go—lots of trees, the best river in the country, old gracious neighborhoods, and all the modern things of cities these days. He hadn't spent many of his years in big places, preferring the small towns where he could actually get a feel for the people who lived there, have them recognize his face, trust him— and eventually he would be tuning their pianos and playing for weddings and tutoring.

Also, he had found that people in small towns would let him talk about the important things. They didn't agree with him for the most part, but he felt he had a chance to say his bit about nuclear armament and power, racial relations, social justice, economic madness. It actually seemed to Phil that people in cities were less tolerant—they traveled in their own little circles and chose their friends carefully—while people in small towns at least listened. Maybe it was because they *had* to deal with everyone in one way or another, from mayors to village idiots.

But in the past years, something had started to happen all over the country. Everyone had a cause, but the causes were getting smaller and smaller and more fervently held. No one worried about the Bomb because they felt white sugar was the enemy of western civilization—or perhaps abortion or lack of women's rights or aluminum in the water supply. He had encountered a man who was active in the campaign to save whales and dolphins but was all for U.S. military strength and intervention in places like El Salvador, where human beings were being slaughtered every day. He had also once had a frustrating discussion with a woman who was adamant about having nonsexist education for her two children but sent them to the private academy because the local school "had too many blacks and Hispanics to be any good."

It was hard to sustain a conversation about good and evil when someone might be so certain about evil being personified by those who smoke cigarettes. Phil found people looking at their feet, thinking about their pet anger, when he talked about the world situation or morality in general. Ethical frameworks, whole world views integrating peace, healthful living, and positive attitudes had disappeared—as outmoded as long hair and beads. A "position" on an issue became a fashion accessory, not a total look.

He pushed the window open and leaned out to look at the sky, which was a brownish glow of the city on clouds. Yes, he thought, white sugar will be the death of us because everyone will have their heads in the sugar bowls when the president finally presses his old finger on the button.

He slammed the window shut again and went into the kitchen. From a small box on the counter, he retrieved a cigar. He didn't smoke them often. Wasn't tonight a night to celebrate?

Dear Gordon, he mentally wrote as he lit his cigar, *I got a new job today in a palatial, old-fashioned theater that has only the most experimental repertoire. I saw Dustin Hoffman coming out as I was going in—he was just visiting. It's in a classy part of town, so I've had to put a down payment on a black suit for the performances. My new boss gave me a smuggled Havana cigar, which I am smoking at the moment . . .*

Phil smiled wryly. He wondered if Gordon was too old for that stuff now anyway.

He heard a thin siren far away and hurried to the window. It seemed to be coming right out of the heart of the city. He saw the flashing lights of a police car about four blocks away. He returned to the kitchen table, blinking in the bright fluorescent light of his modernized kitchen.

Dear Katie, Tonight I have the blues again.

17
———

T H E transformation of the actors during rehearsals fascinated him. He didn't know them well offstage, yet, since they
still remained aloof. But when the shabby little stage became
a window into the lives of Yvonne, Charles, Mimi and
Wayne, he felt that he knew them intimately. He knew what
they would say and do, and could anticipate the trouble they
would go through and how it would affect their lives. All
the while he underscored the turbulence of a two-hour view
into these imaginary people with his piano. Glass gave him
terse but wise direction. It wasn't like playing for drunks in
a bar or for twelve-year-olds in Danskins and tap shoes. It
required a kind of invisibility and subtlety that he found
challenging. He felt himself suited for it.

He began to think of himself as part of the play, and his
notes as part of both dialogue and scenery. But when the
actors stepped out of their roles and became Pam, Chester,

Karen and Dennis, they obviously didn't have the same notion. He obviously was not one of *them* (and they had definite ideas about who *they* were), but neither was he just a stagehand. By opening night they had condescended to greet him by name when they encountered him for the first time each day. Except for Pam, the eerie one who had watched his audition.

He participated with the most interest when she was onstage. Though she never spoke to him offstage, sometimes he felt that she was speaking to him while she was acting in the play.

On opening night, he thought this was especially true. At one point she always walked to his end of the stage, turning her back on her lover and staring down at the top of the piano. He could see the texture of her stockings, smell her perfume, hear her take a breath.

"There's that beggar again," she said, peering out of a pretended window. "Do you know, Charles..." Here, where she usually turned to face "Charles," she chose this time to gaze steadfastly at Phil. "I could probably love you if you became a beggar."

Phil got gooseflesh at the quality of her voice. She delivered that particular line with the intonation of a pentatonic scale, making it sound like Scottish folk music. In rehearsal it had always sounded stagy, belted out for the last rows. But she said it quietly and personally that night, as if to him.

He was baffled. Was she acting within acting or sending him a message, or was he just in her line of sight or what?

He was in love with her voice. It was a sweet instrument. Once he had heard her singing a Bruce Springsteen song to herself as she waited for shifting scenery. He found himself humming the tune for two days but was unable to catch the music of her in his own throat.

She swept back to center stage with a great shout of frustration at Charles. Phil waited for his cue to accent, *pianissimo*, the last words of the play.

When the applause came, he listened with a touch of melancholy. None of those eyes were upon him; no one had come to hear the piano player, even though it was a gimmick of Glass Productions. And I may be, as mediocre as I am, a better musician than they are actors, he thought bitterly. With the exception of Pamela Rust.

He decided to stop wanting what he couldn't have and watched with cold appreciation as they took their bows. Then he quickly got his coat and left the theater rather than join the others backstage.

He liked the city now that he was getting to know his way around. At first it was a mess of unfamiliar streets, awkwardly rebuilt areas, shabby spots, and the huge city park, which was most notable for having been the site of a world's fair — the same one where in the old movie Judy Garland wanted to meet someone. The streets were becoming his territory; the landmarks he could see from his apartment window were things he knew from the ground, too.

The theater was near the park, behind the Chase Park Hotel, in an area that seemed to have been redone with all the new wealth that people suddenly seemed to have in the last few years. The bars were called pubs, and the shops sold things that Phil couldn't afford but didn't want anyway.

After the performance, he walked out of the stage door. A warm front had come through during the evening. It was warmer at ten than it had been at four; the air had a hint of the humidity that was a killer in the summer but made for balmy days in the spring, with promises of greener grass and budding trees.

He had walked about two blocks when he saw a phone booth. Feeling as expansive outside as he had felt oppressed inside during the applause, his head was finally clear of the play. He dug in his pocket for change and found enough for a short hello to Katie and the family. She might be moderately impressed with the job, and it had been—God, how long? —since he had phoned her. What was the time in Colorado? But Katie would never reproach him for phoning too late.

He searched through his wallet for the number, pausing to stare at the creased photograph of a slim, bespectacled girl. He flipped it over for the new number. As he recited the digits to the operator, he sorted the quarters, dimes and nickels into stacks on the narrow metal shelf. Damn modern phone booths, he thought. In the old days you could set a coffee and sandwich on those shelves. Now—

"Hello?" said someone at the other end.

"Louis? Louis, this is Phil."

"Oh, hello, Phil. Haven't heard from you in a year of Sundays. Did you want to talk to Katie?"

Phil imagined Louis at home, perhaps in his bathrobe now, his hair thinner on top each year, the moustache calculated to cover the scars on his lip growing greyer. The first time he had met Louis, he was struck with how differently again Katie had chosen. Louis was nothing like Perry, and neither of them was like Phil. The woman had varied taste in men. Phil had thought Louis stuffy, mainly because of his job. "Where did you find *him?*" he had asked her, which was one of the many times he had hurt Katie's feelings. "He's a nice man," she said angrily. After that, Phil saw Louis differently. He might wear his business suit straight through until after the ten o'clock news and read the *Wall Street Journal* carefully, but he took good care of the family. Even later, Phil discovered that Louis was funny and good-natured and kept Katie buoyed up. He had given in to the idea, with some contained jealousy, that Louis would be Gordon's father and probably a good one at that. Phil and Gordon always found time alone together awkward and difficult; Phil knew this was his own fault, due to the long absences from the home town. No encouragement came from any quarter, either, for the two of them to be closer. Only a look of faded disappointment on Phil's mother's face occasionally signaled a wish for things to be different. Feeling like an outsider, he kept his feelings to himself. Though unstated, it had been clear to him from the day he had visited after Gordon's birth and asked Katie to marry him, that if he couldn't have Katie he also couldn't have the boy.

"How is everyone?" Phil asked Louis, trying not to sound anxious to get to Katie.

"Oh, Katie's getting fat, Josie's in college. And, uh, Gordon got married last year."

"Married! He's only . . ." Phil ticked off the years in his mind. Gordon was indeed old enough to marry. Had it been so long since Phil had seen them all? He couldn't believe it. Without his knowing. A year.

"Your mother has some wedding pictures for you when she gets an address."

"Yeah, OK, I owe everyone a letter." Phil was still digesting the news when Louis said he would get Katie. There was a muffled shout, then the bonk of the receiver being put on a table. Come on, come on, I don't have many quarters. He dropped in another to ensure the connection.

A lone woman turned the corner at the top of the block and walked down the sidewalk in his direction. Phil felt another surge of affection for the city at seeing this brisk female coming down the boulevard late at night. Definitely not New York. This city also goes on twenty-four hours a day—cars moving, cafés grilling hamburgers and bacon, people alive and active—yet a woman can still walk down the street.

My heart is a peach, he thought, watching the woman come closer down the sidewalk. Ripe, rosy and juicy. Doesn't she have a nice shape?

Then he recognized her. Pam Rust. He turned closer into the shelter of the phone.

Katie, dammit, get your crippled self to the phone. He tensed, realizing that not only was Pam behind him but also that she had stopped there.

"Hello, Phil?" Katie said.

Pam tapped him on the shoulder. "Just a sec." He turned, surprised, and made a sound like "huh" when he saw a small revolver pointed at his nose.

"Hang up, fucker, or I'll blow your head off," said that beautiful voice. Behind the revolver was the wondrously made woman, her hair changed from the conventional style of her character back to the spikes he had seen the first day. Her eyes were shining with angry passion.

"What?"

"No, I'm going to blow your hands off. Hang up the telephone," she said slowly.

"Hello?" the telephone said in a distant tinny voice.

"It's a toy, isn't it?" Phil put the receiver on the hook over his shoulder without taking his eyes off Pam. He had always sensed that she might be psychotic. It was probably a toy, but . . .

"Glass fired me because I don't get along with people. He says you were a test." Her hand trembled as she held the gun to his face. "You don't like me, and he's fucking fired me on opening night because you don't like me."

"Christ." What a quirky turn. It sounded so completely absurd that it must be true. How like Glass. She's so upset that she says hands and keeps pointing at my head. She's going to kill me. She's crazy. I knew she was crazy from that first day. Christ, she's going to kill me.

As if reading his mind, she lowered the barrel of the gun to point at his right hand. "I'm going to sizzle your fingers, honky-tonker."

Phil's skin went cold. He was shaking as if a sudden northern wind had peeled him naked. He felt nauseated when he tried to swallow. As he stood absolutely still, it occurred to him that perhaps she would only take him hostage and a SWAT team would rescue him with sharpshooters and tear gas canisters. That's television, though, isn't it? "Pam, listen, I don't know where he got that idea. I never said . . ."

She looked startled. "You mean you like me?"

"Well, I thought so," he said, confused. What was the right thing to say now?

"You think I'm pretty?"

"Very. Oh, yes, *very* attractive."

"What do you like the most? My face? My tits?"

"Great tits," he said. A car passed through the intersection at the top of the street. Damn. "Terrific legs, Pam."

Pam smiled slowly. So slowly that it seemed an illusion

at first until a crease appeared at the corner of her mouth. "You're lying." Her hand contracted on the gun.

Phil jerked as the gun spat out an innocuous click.

They stared at each other for several seconds. His arms and legs went weak, his heart was hammering.

"What's a girl gotta do?" she asked, tucking the revolver into her belt so that the handle pressed against her ribs. "You gay or something? Got a wife?"

He thought about smashing the phone receiver into her face. He hated her.

"Scared the piss outa you, didn't I?" she said happily.

Shaking with anger, he crossed his arms over his chest and walked away from her, back up the street.

"Hey, I thought you liked me." She ran to catch up with him. "I just can't resist sometimes. I was just showing off. Phil? Listen. Glass says I'll get myself killed someday playing around like I do. You think so?"

He stopped. "Impressive performance, kid. Now fuck off."

"I'm sorry," she whispered. "I just wanted you to remember forever our first real conversation."

"I'm sure I will." He wished she would stop following him, stop talking to him. She had played the game so closely that all the usual signals between people were nothing—no tone of voice, no posture, no cold shoulder could throw her off.

She skipped around in front of him and stood with the toes of her shoes against his. "Hi."

As he dug his fingers into her shoulders he was aware that he had lost a lot of self-control. He pushed her against the brick wall of a dry-cleaning shop. She yelped and covered her head with her arms, as if expecting hard blows.

He shoved his hands into his pockets and walked on. I can't believe it; what a silly bitch. What a silly dangerous bitch.

By the time he reached the intersection he had calmed down. He could hear her sobbing. The gesture she had made of defending her head against a beating made his stomach turn with disgust for himself. She had just been playing. Actress. Actress with punk hair. She probably plays all the time. No sense of reality.

He looked over his shoulder. In the darkness he couldn't see her face but knew that she was watching for him to look back at her. He shrugged and stood facing her.

Her soft-soled shoes barely made a sound on the sidewalk as she ran. Like a cat, he thought. She stood close again but without touching him, her head bowed. "I'm sorry, Phil."

Stupid, talented thing. Damn.

"Why aren't you going to the cast party?" she asked.

"I don't know." He came close to telling her that he felt he didn't belong but stopped himself. He wasn't really in the mood for confiding insecurities to her.

She put her hand through the crook of his arm and drew close. "Would you do something for me? I've been dying to ask you but you're so standoffish . . ."

"Me? Standoffish!"

She laughed. "Come on. You know you are. Would you do something for me? Do you forgive me enough to do me a favor?"

"What's that?" He was still suspicious of her, but now she seemed like just a friendly, silly kid. Even though his knees were still a bit shaky from her attack, he felt himself calming down. Eventually he might forget that he had been rough—he hoped so. That was a heretofore untapped reaction, and he wondered how she had brought it out.

"Would you accompany me on the piano while I sing a few songs? My voice is going rusty and harsh because I can only practice with the radio or records."

He considered. Should he charge her his usual hourly fee? Was this once or was she offering him a job? "I suppose, but . . ."

"Good! Oh, good." She sounded relieved and squeezed his arm just a bit. "Let's go to a piano right now. Your place?"

"I don't have a piano."

She stepped back. "I don't believe you."

"I've been on the road. Had to leave my last piano behind in Wisconsin."

"Wisconsin," she said slowly, as if weighing the distance or the value of the place. "Well, let's go back to the theater then."

"Mm. OK, I guess." She was running the show at the moment. He was thirsty, so as they walked back he bought a liter bottle of cola from a liquor store. She chided him for rotting his teeth.

When they got to the theater, she took a key out of her bag and opened a side door that Phil had never noticed before. He said nothing but wondered how she had the privilege of a key. They entered by way of the janitor's room, which was lit by an overhead fluorescent bulb and had a concrete floor smelling strongly of the disinfectant that was swabbed across the red-painted auditorium. He followed Pam steadily, uneasy in the small room filled with brooms, paint cans and stacks of toilet rolls. He suddenly found his lungs demanding more air; his hands and scalp became sweaty. The walls were closing in on him, but he fought the desperate feelings silently.

"Are you from Wisconsin?" she asked, taking his hand and pulling him through toward the auditorium.

"No. Colorado." Uneasily, he kept a hold on her hand in the dark passage. He took a couple of deep breaths quietly.

"Oh. Mountains. Do you ski?"

"No. Can't you turn on a light?" he asked, hoping he didn't sound too nervous.

"Don't worry. Last year I played the lead in *Wait Until Dark* and I walked through this place with a blindfold every day for two weeks to get the feel of not seeing. Have you ever tried that?"

"No, thanks."

"Do you know Joan Collins?"

"Why would I know Joan Collins?"

"You know, she's in *Dynasty*. That's in Denver, isn't it? Have you ever seen her?"

"No. I don't pay much attention to TV stars. Besides, I haven't lived in Colorado for years and I didn't live in Denver and I doubt that Joan Collins has ever been there longer than a night at the Brown Palace Hotel."

"My, my. You know a lot."

"Sorry. I'm a little irritable. I almost got killed tonight."

She stopped and threw some switches on the wall. The house lights came on, then she whirled around, her eyes wide with concern. "Killed? What happened?"

"Some idiot woman pulled a gun on me," he said.

She belted out a great gust of laughter that moderated down to a giggle into her hand. She seemed embarrassed.

Phil couldn't help it; he laughed a bit, too. He was also feeling freed by the lights and the great expanse of auditorium around him. It had been a long while since he'd been caught in a claustrophobic situation. Each time he was surprised at the power of the past to grip him with irrational fear of dark, enclosed spaces.

They moved toward the piano. "What do you want to sing?" Phil shuffled through the scores in the bench although he could have recited the titles without looking.

"Something like, uh, 'New York, New York.' "

"All right." He settled down at the piano and began to play the dum-dum-*dum*-de-de until she managed to collect herself enough to sing. She obviously hadn't expected that he would know things by heart. She didn't know about Mr. Tackett's insistence that he learn to reproduce things by ear. "Mozart did it as a tiny boy—you know music. Play it! Play it from where it comes from!" Mr. Tackett would say, tapping his chest.

The real truth was that Phil had played in enough piano bars to know every tune that had ever been sung by Sinatra, Streisand or Bennett. The hard part was to pay attention to what he was doing. Mr. Tackett would be appalled to see me playing this song in this way for this woman in this situation, Phil thought. But it was the sort of thought he had so often that it no longer hurt and was merely a casual sense of failure.

She had a good voice that sounded as if it had been trained for strength and timing, but he hated the way she used it. She bent her knees and dipped with the beat and spread her palms out in the air, probably as she had been doing for years, imitating singers on television variety shows. He could imagine her a few years ago, probably pushed by a stage mother, in sequined costumes and cardboard top hats, doing Liza Minelli for a school show. Her hair, standing out all over her head, was incongruous with her motions. She would have looked more natural with a bit of heavy metal head-banging.

She danced around to face him and sang to his face. Her slick routine confused him and made him self-conscious; he watched the reflection of his fingers in the dark wood above the keyboard.

She is me, he suddenly realized, sick with recognition of the hard edges of ambition. She's been pushed and prodded—you're the best, you're a genius, you'll be a star, Pamela. He could hear her voice coach, her mother, her home town, all proud and pleased with her and expecting great things. And here stood this poor young woman in tight black trousers and a baggy shirt, her hair stiff with mousse, too much make-up on a pretty face, dimestore bangles clanging as she sang her way to stardom in the same crummy dive he had fallen into almost by accident.

But she's never taken the time to think about it. Not everyone gets the chance I had.

Cynically, he added a few chords at the end that would please any guest on the *Tonight Show*.

"Well," she said, not a bit breathless, but expectant.

"You've got a very good voice," he said.

She narrowed her eyes at him, then suddenly made motions as if pushing someone or something away from her. "Down, boy! Down!" Then she laughed, heartily and defensively. "Good thing I'm not *auditioning* for you," she said.

"Hey. I *said* you have a good voice. I mean it."

"All right. What would you like to hear? Special request?"

"Mmm. Something with a bit more bite. Do you know 'St. James Infirmary Blues'?"

She smiled at the back row of the auditorium, a smile so

automatic and fleeting that he understood it was merely a pause for thought. "I might forget a few words. Used to know it."

He began to play it. She made a gesture and he began again in another key.

She sang it with only a little less glitz than the previous song, but half-heartedly. After one verse and chorus she stopped. "Oh, come on, you're playing it so slow!"

Phil dropped his hands to his lap and stared at her. "Not your kind of music, I take it."

"Well, I *like* it, but it just doesn't sound right." She sounded genuinely unhappy and leaned against the piano limply. "I don't know what's wrong." She covered her face with one hand.

"Pam?"

"What?" she whispered.

"Look, let's try something else." He was suddenly sorry, and also worried that he was going to be asked again for an opinion. He didn't want to get into it. A matter of taste, he thought, rehearsing what he might say: you've got a good voice, terrific range, timing . . .

She lifted her face. "You won't get far in this business, you know."

Phil's heart suddenly pounded at her certainty. He felt something awful coming. Some awful truth about himself as seen from a beautiful young woman's mind. He reached for a cigarette from his jacket pocket. "Oh?"

"No. You've got such an honest face. You have to learn how to suck up to people, how to make them feel good. Like Chester. If you ever hear Chester praise you to your face, you *believe* it. But he never says what you think he says. 'That was splendid, just fantastic,' " she said, making her shoulders broad and her posture hearty in imitation of the big, bluff actor. Her voice didn't sound like his but took on some of his character. " 'I've never heard such an original interpretation, my dear. All these years I thought Lady Macbeth was insane. You're so original.' " Pam laughed at her own performance.

Phil smiled a bit. "Well, maybe I'm not the one . . ."

"No!" she shouted, as if it were a stage line. Her finger pointed at him like a gun. "You're exactly what I want."

He shrugged. "Darling, you were astounding," he said in a high-pitched minciness. "It was like hearing Joan Sutherland sing Chicago blues."

Pam stiffened with outrage. "You bastard," she said. But before she had finished the word she was relaxed, dropping next to him on the piano bench. Out came the laughter again. She tried to speak but couldn't even catch her breath.

Phil, pleased to see he could make her laugh so easily, chuckled with her. He liked women who could laugh, especially like this—so deeply, so uncontrollably. She had as good a voice for laughter as for speaking and singing. Without hacking or whispering or shouting, she laughed out the notes of a unique little tune.

She punched his shoulder. "You bastard!"

He waited while she calmed down. When she was quiet, smiling and absently rubbing at the edge of the piano, he said, "I have a tape of Louis Armstrong singing 'St. James Infirmary Blues' if you want to borrow it. One of my favorite songs."

"Is it?" She didn't look at him, but her long fingers stroked the wood of the piano. "Where is the tape now?"

"At home." After a silence, he added, "We can go listen to it if you like."

She tucked her hair behind her ear slowly as if considering his words carefully. The black hoop of earring dangled against her jawbone as she bowed her head. Then she turned her face to his, an innocent and trusting expression in the shape of her eyes but not within her eyes. "OK."

Katie shuffled down the hallway and crawled back in bed. The sheets had grown a little chilly in the moments she had stood at the phone, hearing Phil's voice but not understanding why he wasn't speaking to her. When the dial tone returned, she had replaced the phone and waited for a few moments, staring at the receiver, ready to pick it up when it rang again.

It didn't.

Louis moaned and sighed when she sidled closer to his warm back.

"Louis, you awake? What did he say to you?"

"Just small talk. Why?"

"Well . . . I don't know. It was weird. He was talking to someone else, the operator came on and asked for more money, and then the connection went. I just hope he's not in trouble."

"Phil? He could be in a vat of boiling oil and somehow wish himself out of it."

"Louis." She didn't know what he meant by that, but it was another of his occasional disapproving remarks that made her edgy on the subject of Phil.

"It's true." Louis turned his head and shoulders on the pillow to talk. "I've never met such a slippery *honest* man."

Katie laughed. That did sound right. She moved back as Louis rolled onto his back. She took his hand where it lay on his chest. "I just hope he wasn't being mugged or something. I couldn't hear what he was saying. It's like a movie where the phone hangs off the hook."

"Oh, he's all right. Probably giving his spare change to Greenpeace."

"Yeah."

"You sound worried."

"I do worry about him . . . sometimes."

"Do you?"

Katie felt Louis's heartbeat pick up pace under her knuckles. "You know."

"Yeah." Now Louis sounded vaguely worried.

"He's just an old friend."

"And father of our son," Louis said. His heart was pounding just a little faster still.

Katie didn't know whether to ask or not, but a thought came that had never occurred to her in all these years—that Louis might be seriously jealous of Phil. She thought it had always been obvious that any romantic notions were long gone. Didn't he know that? Didn't he know after all these years of marriage to her that she had no regrets at all? Louis was the man of her choice without a doubt. She still felt that he was an angel fallen out of the sky.

"Katie?"

"Yeah?"

"Can I ask you about something?"

"I love you," she said.

"No, listen. Do you remember one time when Phil came down with that big horsey woman—Holly? The time they dragged us off to Denver for some demonstration or other?"

"Yeah," she said slowly, trying to sort out that time from the other two times he had brought Holly home with him.

"Do you remember how the two of you played music together for about an hour and a half while Holly and I sat on the sofa?"

Katie tried to see Louis's face in the dark. She couldn't. Only the darkness of his profile as it stood out from the paler bedroom wall. "You weren't jealous, were you?"

"Did you . . . did it even sort of *remotely* come into your mind that you still loved him?"

"No. Not at all. It was just fun to play the violin again."

"Oh."

"Have you been saving that up all these years?"

"It was one of the worst hours of my life."

"Oh, Louis." Under the covers, she moved close again and gave him an awkward sort of hug. "I'm sorry."

"Holly, too."

"Holly? She didn't look like she had a jealous bone in her body. Seemed that she wouldn't have *let* Phil have stray thoughts."

Louis didn't respond to that at all. Katie waited, then thought he may have gone to sleep. She tickled his earlobe. "Hey."

"I know it's silly. It's just . . . well, when you were pregnant with Josie . . . well, it just seemed to happen right about the time Phil was visiting . . ."

"Louis!" Katie sat up and switched on her reading light.

Her husband, blinded by the light, his face weak-eyed without his glasses, put his hand over his face and moaned. "Bitch."

She laughed. "You're joking with me, aren't you?"

He peeked at her through his fingers. "As soon as I saw Josie I knew she was mine."

"Of course."

"Of course." He smiled a little and sat up. "I mean, besides the harelip. She looks like me, doesn't she?"

Katie shook her head. "She had a much better plastic surgeon. And she doesn't sound like you." Katie spoke the last sentence through her nose, exaggerating Louis's nasal voice.

He put his spectacles on and smiled across the bed at her. "Bitch," he said again.

"I love you."

"I love you, too, you fat old one-legged lady."

"Fat? Just womanly and one-legged, like Sarah Bernhardt. Only *I* can play the violin, too."

As she mimed the violin he caught her hand and squeezed it. She settled back against the pillows, and they sat in the bed as if watching television, but instead stared at the three sets of toes propping up the bedcovers. "Now, what I mean to say," Louis started again, "is that Phil has this sort of romantic, wandering gypsy appeal and I feel like such an *accountant* next to him."

Considering Phil's qualities, Katie shook her head. "I can see why you would think that, but Phil . . . well, you know how it is when you're young and idealistic—you feel that if you can just explain your point of view clearly enough to people, and they listen to what you're saying, they will agree with you. Phil's still like that. And he listens to you, too, and thinks about what you say. It's a good thing, I suppose, but sometimes he seems so naive that it's embarrassing. You—you're so much tougher inside. In fact, it makes you more tolerant because you don't feel so betrayed when people disagree. You expect it. You might think that he's romantic because he looks kind of dreamy when you're talking to him, but it's just . . ."

"Sounds like you feel more motherly than anything."

"Well, I feel like his big sister now. That's really how it is. Even his son is more like a nephew to him. Gordon is your son. I can't *imagine* that you thought Josie . . . It never even crossed my mind that you were worried. Besides," she smiled across the corners of their pillows at him, "I can still remember the night we made Josie."

Louis raised his eyebrows, grinning. "You can?"

"Yeah. Gordon was staying with Grandma Benson. Now that you mention it, I suppose it was because Phil was visiting. We were sitting out in our new lawn chairs looking at constellations when we first moved in here, remember?"

Louis furrowed his brow.

"And you said, 'This privacy fence is really private.' "

The furrow disappeared with a big laugh. "I remember. Mmm. I remember that evening. Grass stains on my elbows. So that was Josie's night, huh?"

Katie grinned. "Men. They don't know nothing about how it works." She turned out the light.

"We know enough," he said.

18

I N the morning Phil felt Pam curled against his back. From the sound of her breathing he could tell she was still asleep. He wallowed in the bedclothes and finally opened his eyes. Somehow they had both squeezed onto his narrow bed. Pam was gorgeous even with her mouth slack and her lashes gummed with a few hours of hard sleeping.

"Hey," he said, caressing her throat with his knuckles.

She stirred a little and opened one eye carefully. "Mm," she said and rolled over, taking a lot of the blanket to her side.

He put his hand under the blanket and stroked the smooth skin of her thighs and buttocks, hoping she would respond. More eager than ever, remembering the night just gone, he wished that his bed was wide and hard. The older he got, the more he enjoyed morning sex, but it was more difficult now to find women who could or would spend the night with him. They either had jobs, children, husbands or all three to start their days. He knew from women that men preferred one side of the day or the other as they aged, but he felt that Pam could work her spell on him any time. He slid down close against her back and held her, kissing the back of her neck and between her shoulders.

"All right," she said, muffled by the bedclothes and the wall, "but no French kissing. My mouth is horrible."

"Stay where you are." He rubbed his nose on her neck and in her hair, luxuriating in what was to come. She smelled like herbal shampoo or hair conditioner. The way she received him convinced him that she was as ready as he. They started out cozily, but soon part of his attention was diverted to worrying about the safety of the bed.

Eventually they lay tangled, joined and still. She opened her eyes and looked at him over her shoulder. "Morning."

"Good morning."

"I've never been to bed before with a graduate of a music conservatory."

"Still haven't." He leaned over the edge of the bed and found the towel, which was stiff from last night. He refolded it and stuffed it gently between her legs.

"Oh," she said sleepily. "Thought you said . . ." She never finished.

He was now wide-awake and feeling frisky, wondering how long she would hang around. *I should at least offer her breakfast,* he thought. She slept on again. He got out of bed and, while the coffee was brewing, discovered there wasn't enough food around to make a breakfast. In his wallet, he found just enough for two breakfasts at the café down the street.

He suddenly thought of the possibility of reviews and ran down to the newspaper rack outside his building. When he let himself back into the apartment, Pam was still dozing in the same position. Plays hard, sleeps hard—she's young. He sat at the kitchen table only a few feet from the bed, flipping the pages of the newspaper with as much crackling and rustling as possible, hoping she would stir.

There were no reviews. Perhaps tomorrow. Perhaps in the free weekly arts and entertainment paper.

He poured her a cup of coffee, black, uncertain about putting milk or sugar in it, and took it to the bed. "Pam. Coffee. Yoo-hoo. Wake up."

She turned and moaned, making a long slow journey upward from sleep.

Why didn't she go to the cast party? he wondered. Had she been acting so long that she would rather chase the piano player down the street than go and be toasted as the terrific leading lady?

Phil was too detached himself—he doubted anyone would have noticed his presence. But Pam . . . she wasn't just part of it, she was the best of it. He admired her acting, her voice, her looks and, now that he knew it went beyond appearance, her sexiness.

It suddenly occurred to him that her aloofness from *them* could be their distance from *her*. He recalled Glass's warning that first day, a simple "Don't." But whatever, he had enjoyed the hours over coffee and Boston cream pie at the café and the good time in bed.

Curious, he went to the kitchen counter and picked up the gun, which he had made her put out of sight. He hadn't wanted any practical jokes during the night. A long time ago, his girlfriend Holly had been a regular at the pistol range. He had never felt much interest in guns; most of the time that boys usually spend playing gangsters or cowboys he had spent at Mr. Tackett's knee. Holly had taught him the care and cleaning of guns ("Philip, a man's gotta know how to hold and unload a piece—minimum," was Holly's firm statement) for his own protection. Women and guns, he didn't understand it. Anyone and guns.

Pam's was real enough, not just some tin prop. He aimed it out of the window as he studied it. Wasn't very wise to carry this sort of thing around, even as a joke or a prop. Somewhere he had read that most murders were committed upon victims who knew the murderer, and the chances were that if there hadn't been a gun handy, there wouldn't have been a murder. The lover, friend, parent, spouse or child would only be bruised or cut rather than shot dead.

Perhaps it isn't really Pam's anyway. Just something she picked up at the theater.

He opened the barrel. Chilled, he saw that out of the six chambers every other one held a bullet.

19

PHIL stopped playing when he heard footsteps in the auditorium. He was on edge, anxious not to find himself alone with Pam. In spite of her attractiveness, modernness and air of casual affluence he had decided her gun was too much trouble. It disturbed him.

"Good God, it's freezing in here!" Chester hurried down the aisle, rubbing his hands together.

"Yes, it is a little chilly." But Phil hadn't noticed before. He had just come in and sat at the piano without taking his jacket off. He put his hands back on the keyboard, but Chester stood by the piano as if interested in conversation. This was an unusual friendliness; Phil had never been alone with any of the actors other than Pam. He glanced up at Chester. He was a big guy, ruddy-cheeked and handsome in a broad, theatrical way but roughly cut at close range. With that face, and the booming voice, he walked and talked the life of an actor every day.

"You watch the shuttle launch?"

Phil shook his head. "I used to watch them. They're pretty routine now. Shame, isn't it? Going into space being boring, I mean."

"Hey, I'm glad we're getting out there. Better us than . . ."

Phil knew that his sudden sharp look had thrown Chester off. He couldn't help it. It was now reflexive of him to show immediate disagreement with a glance when others had a certain sound in their voices—the people who might always call the U.S. "America," ignoring the fact that the Americas extended from the Northwest Territories of Canada to Tierra del Fuego, because they listened to politicians too much.

". . . Libyans," Chester finished.

"Libyans!" Phil laughed and Chester laughed with him just a bit nervously.

"Yeah," Chester said, warming up to his comic substitution, "I'll bet the Libyans don't know how to put twenty-four cats, two squirrel monkeys, and a senator into space."

Phil shrugged. "What's the big deal about Libya?" He made an A-minor sweep of the keyboard that he hoped would be punctuation to their conversation. He didn't feel like talking politics to Chester. It would only lead to a heated discussion about missiles in Europe, submarines, ratios of death. Like a New Year's resolution, he had decided to make a St. Louis resolution to keep his mouth shut. After Jackson, after Holly, after falling out with his agent, Thayer, and after a complete social shutout by the crowd in New Jersey, he was beginning to see the wisdom of keeping one's opinions to oneself.

Chester thumped the piano as if it were a friend's back. "Catch you later, Phil."

"Yeah."

He played for another fifteen minutes before he heard the second set of footsteps, which he knew for certain were Pam's. His hands went sweaty, knowing that she was approaching. He tried to think of how he was going to manage this brush-off. He had played in a bar for several months in Santa Fe where the barkeeper had warned him off a waitress. "Don't get your meat where you get your bread, son." Crudely put, but not bad advice for either sex. Now why didn't I think of it last week?

She walked behind him, up the steps at the side of the stage, onto the stage, and then back into the wings without a word.

Well, I'll be damned, he thought. She ignored me, the little bitch. He didn't like that, not one bit. He had planned the first snub and somehow she had taken the initiative.

They hadn't parted on the most affectionate terms the morning after their romp. After having looked at the gun, he kept quiet about it through breakfast. Finally, in his car as he took her home, he said, "Your gun is loaded, isn't it?"

"Do you think I'm the kind of woman who would carry a toy around?" she asked, smiling.

"No, but perhaps I would prefer that kind of woman."

The only exchange after that was her directions. "Here!" she had said suddenly and got out of the car at the park, near the zoo. He understood that she didn't want him to know where she lived.

He stared at the stage sulkily. Or perhaps she lives in the zoo.

Through that evening's performance she never looked into what Phil thought of as his "piano pit." The lines about the beggar were delivered straight through the clear panes of the imaginary window. As on opening night, Phil left the theater immediately and went home.

He was warming tamales from a can when Pam came to his door. She was still wearing Yvonne—the make-up, clothes and hairstyle. Though onstage Yvonne looked natural, in ordinary surroundings Pam appeared gaudily done as an upper-middle-class housewife dressed for a club meeting. She smelled strongly of night air as if she had been walking.

"Hello," she said tentatively. "May I come in?"

"I'm just about to eat dinner." His voice didn't invite her to join him.

She moved past him and leaned over the counter and peered into the narrow galley. "Oh, tamales. I love tamales. My mother used to let us eat them on Saturdays."

"I have a lot of work to do this evening."

"Work? What kind of work do you do here? Drugs? Addressing envelopes?" She sat down on the bed and checked out the room, looking for his work. "You're angry with me about that stupid gun, aren't you?"

"Not angry. Just wary of you, lady." He went around to his kitchen and tore off a chunk of French bread then set it on the counter.

"I was just playing. It's my life. Playing. The gun was filled with blanks. I even took out the *blank* for you."

He stared at her, not knowing whether to believe her. Playing, and playing when? Then, now?

She watched him like a hungry child as he heaped his plate and sat down at the kitchen table. "Will you please let me apologize again? I'll cook you dinner some night at my place."

Phil couldn't decide how rude to be—should he dig into the tamales or dismiss her first? When he lifted his head and saw her, he softened. She really did seem to be trying. And she probably wasn't a murderess after all, was she? I'm being hasty and judgmental, he thought—and doesn't she have a nice, smooth neck?

"Here." She opened her handbag and scribbled on the inside of a matchbook. "This is my address—it's just across the street from the park, ground floor of the house. You pick the night. Monday, Tuesday, or Wednesday?"

Phil knew he was going to give in, but his pride made him stare at the address with a skeptical face. "Will you put the gun in the yard or something?"

"Promise."

"Tuesday," he said, thinking it sounded conciliatory but not anxious.

"Good!" She had a genuinely happy look. "There aren't many men I have to chase after."

"If you point guns at them I'm sure you have no trouble at all."

"Hey. Let's have a truce. Forget it, OK?"

He nodded. He walked with her to the door. She snuggled against his chest and they kissed as if they were familiar lovers.

"See you," she said.

Pam's house was a surprise to him. He couldn't put his finger on why or what he had expected, but it lacked a sort of theme. Perhaps she had set him up to expect a web of intrigue. It was a stately old brick house on the outside but pastel and bare inside. Though the furniture was scarce, what did exist was old-fashioned, too sentimentally family-like to be standing alone in a pale room with echoing walls and semi-bare floors. A little solarium behind the kitchen was filled with flowering and budding plants, and at every window in the house was a pot of greenery. They were all florist-fresh and healthy, growing madly for her.

"I have a green thumb," she said, holding her thumb up to him. It wasn't green at all, but slender and pale like the rest of her. That was another thing—why didn't she have a tan? She had struck him as the kind of woman who would have a tan, a Scandinavian living room, and a pot of brown geraniums. But she wasn't.

"Have you lived here long?" he asked, flipping through a stack of magazines on the floor. She had three fashion, one news, two theater arts, and one six-month-old fishing magazine. He suspected it might have been left by a visiting male.

"All my life," she said with a sigh, returning from the kitchen with glasses of iced something.

"Thank you." It tasted like alcoholic lemonade with a bit of strawberry. It was all right. He settled into a hard wing chair. It made a creaking noise. "All your life," he said. "You haven't really lived here all your life, have you?"

She settled in the center of the sofa and seemed far away to him. "You know, *everyone* says that."

"Oh." Phil felt reduced to the most common and least interesting of all the people she knew. He ventured another risk at being a bore. "You have to admit that people don't often live somewhere longer than about five years these days."

"No, they don't. I haven't lived here all my life anyway," she said, sounding tired.

"Then why did you say you had?"

"Just to hear the same old thing again. I keep hoping that someone will come up with a new interpretation of that line that I can use some day." She crossed her legs and smiled and the distance between them became even greater.

He shook his head, wondering if she knew that she was opening herself up to be fair game for any comment. He felt like saying something really awful to her—what, he couldn't imagine—but didn't.

"Do you fish?" he asked.

"No. Do you?"

"No."

"What do you do?"

"I play the piano. Pick up women. Drive around the country. Tune pianos."

The smile that appeared was slow, as if she wanted to let him know that he was only amusing her.

He was sick to death of her and thought of the whole evening looming ahead. It made him irritable. "Either you were the most popular or most unpopular girl in high school, am I right?"

This time her expression was a little less practiced. He'd hit her somehow. She lowered her head. "I spent most of that time in reform school."

"*Reform* school!"

She laughed.

"And you've lived here all your life," he said knowingly.

"I've lived here a little over three years."

He was half through with his drink and wishing either

for another or for permission to go home. Why hadn't he followed his instincts?

"The first time I was arrested it was for drugs— marijuana—and then again for drugs and assaulting a police officer. And the third time they put me away for burglary."

"Burglary," he echoed.

"Yeah. Friend and I broke into a rich neighbor's house and stole his silver candlesticks. He beat his dog, so we thought we had a right. That damned dog tipped the guy off, though. I was young." She rolled her eyes in derision of a former self.

Phil sighed. How much would he swallow?

"I won't tell you any more about myself." She rose and went into the kitchen.

"Well, I wouldn't mind knowing if I thought any of it was true."

"Come out here and talk to me," she called. "I'm going to start cooking."

He went to her kitchen. Wet lettuce, cucumbers, tomatoes and carrots filled her drainboard. Deftly, like one who makes salad often, she plucked the lettuce leaves off the head and snapped their spines out. "I'm not really a liar," she said. "There's usually some truth in everything I say."

"Well." Phil leaned against the cupboard. "Well."

"You don't know what to think, do you?" She grinned at him. With an unnecessarily large kitchen knife she began to chop the carrots into medals. "I've never dated a musician before. Most of the ones I've met were in rock groups and either stoned all the time or stupid or both. Some are nice, I guess, but I've never been interested before."

"Well," he said again, determined to follow it with a real

sentence, "where I come from, people tend to be a little more straightforward. I don't know what I think of actresses."

"Oh, actresses," she said, dismissing the category.

"Give me one straight answer."

"OK. Anything." She glanced at him between carrots.

"Did you really steal silver candlesticks?"

She giggled. "Actually, it was a television set."

She showed him her scrapbook and photo albums. There was her family, the family dog, and a warrant for her arrest. He didn't know that they let people keep those kinds of things. She explained that because she had been a juvenile they hadn't had to take the paperwork seriously. It all gets thrown away when a person reaches twenty-one anyway, she told him.

She had been a pretty child, a pretty adolescent—even in the scrawny awkwardness of that age—and a stunning twenty-year-old. She had been a model then. "I got into trouble all the time because I was sloppy." Phil didn't detect a trace of sloppiness in the professional photos of her in bathing gear, holding sports equipment, eating a chocolate bar, nor in the studio portraits.

"I'm getting old," she said wistfully, caressing her own cheek with her palm.

He was touched by that. It made him feel close to her. So the show-off edges hid a real woman, worried about the things that ordinary women worry about. He said nothing, just tickled the back of her neck lightly with his fingers.

He stayed the night with her.

20

A s Phil came up the stairs, he saw Pam sitting in front of his apartment door, knees drawn up, chin resting on her crossed arms. She had a pathetic, abandoned expression that didn't change as he approached.

"What's up?"

She drew in a deep breath through her nose. "Where have you been?"

"Tuning a piano."

"What?"

"Come on in." He stepped beside her and unlocked the door. "Would you like coffee, Coke, beer?"

She unfolded herself and followed him in. "What kind of beer do you have?"

"Budweiser."

"Another St. Louis patriot," she said drily. "I'll have a Bud." She put her hands on the counter and swung one leg, then the other, as if warming up for dance class. "So what's this about tuning pianos?"

"You don't think I can live on what Glass pays me at the theater, do you?" He had never talked money to her, but he had always wondered how she lived on what seemed more like a fee than pay from acting. "I have to work pretty hard just to keep my old car in repair. The old wreck's about to turn the clock over again and it eats U-joints and mufflers and clutches."

"Oh." She turned her head back and forth to watch her legs. She could raise her toes above her face. "I'm rich."

"Rich? Must be nice." He sat at the table and watched her with admiration.

"My parents had a trust fund for me. When I was twenty-one I invested three-quarters of it. I'm one of Reagan's America, you know. Young, rich, successful."

"Mm."

"I own my house. I'm the landlady to the woman who lives upstairs." She stopped her workout suddenly and sat across the table from him. "You could be rich, too, if you wanted. Anyone can be if they want to."

"I don't agree. My father had enough money for mortgage payments and a secondhand Ford. Never had a trust fund to invest."

"Money's important," she said with a direct, almost accusing look. "Do you own any property? Do you have a pension plan other than Social Security? Do you have any assets?"

"No. But I don't think money's important."

She rolled her eyes. "God, you're trusting. The welfare state is on the way out, Phil. You'll be cold when you retire. Cold and hungry."

"I don't care. My life is interesting."

"Is it?" She sounded doubtful.

"I've had a terrific life so far. I've seen and done a hell of a lot. Known a lot of people in different places. Had some good times, had some bad times."

"Like what?"

"Well . . ." He couldn't imagine how to begin. "Well, come here. Come on, over here." He picked up his beer and sat on the floor beside the bed and pulled out the battered metal trunk without a lid. He looked over his shoulder at Pam, still sitting at the table. "Come on. This is my life here and I'm about to show you. Like you showed me yours one night."

She followed and squatted near.

He pulled out paper school folders that amounted to a pile of about eighteen inches. He opened the top one. "This is a theme song I wrote and sold to a Canadian television show that was never produced. When I lived in Madison." Underneath were several things he knew wouldn't be impressive, so he searched for the orange folder. "These three are television commercials that I wrote when I lived in Seattle."

"Seattle?"

"Yeah. Still get a royalty check from this one every now and then." He poked through them. It was the first time since he had been with Holly that he had inspected the stack. How much more there was now!

"What's this?" Pam reached into the trunk and pulled the corner of slick, brightly colored paper. Standing to unfold it, she peered at it. "What is that thing?"

"Just your standard movie monster. See there." Phil

pointed to the elongated letter gothic credits over the monster's hairy gray foot. "Music by Philip Benson."

"Very impressive," she said, folding the poster again. Her tone was neutral.

"My concerto, my sonatas," he said, still leafing through the folders. He supposed that she was bored with looking at musical scores, so he stacked them back in the trunk and took out the shoe box. "Photographs. Maybe this will entertain you."

She finally settled on the floor cross-legged and leaned against his shoulder. "Who's that?"

"Me. My first recital."

"Aww." She smiled at the little boy in the suit with one hand touching the keyboard. "You should wear that suit more often, Phil."

"This is Mr. Tackett, my piano teacher, his wife, and Katie, another of his students."

Pam took the photo and glanced at it. "Funny-looking old geezer. Parted his hair in the middle."

"Oh, I'm sure he was dashing in the late twenties. But that was the way men looked when I was growing up. Some of them still had those little Clark Gable moustaches, too."

"How old *are* you?"

"Forty-three. Here are my parents, standing by the secondhand Ford."

"Look like my grandparents. Nanna used to have a coat like that."

Phil started to have a queasy feeling. "There's Katie. My high school graduation photo." He started handing her the pictures faster. He slipped Katie's graduation portrait back into the box.

"Wait a minute. You have to show me everything." She plucked it out and studied it. "Another of Katie?"

"Yeah. Here I am in California. That guy with me was a big disc jockey in Los Angeles in the early sixties. He died of a drug overdose about 1971, I heard. This is the bungalow I lived in—life was cheap on the beach then. This is me with that monster when I visited the movie set. Katie again with her husband and two kids. My mother."

"Is that a cane?"

"Yeah. Katie lost her toes in an accident." Phil sighed involuntarily. "Here I am in Madison, on a peace march. This is the state capitol in Jackson, Mississippi. This is Elmer, half Indian, half black, a friend I had in Seattle—he could sing, Christ, he could sing. That's Holly, in Madison, and me—a sit-in for something or other."

"Look at your hair! You look like you'd been wandering in the desert for two years." Pam giggled.

"Madison is hardly a desert. Nice place. This is Eugene McCarthy—you're probably too young to remember. He ran for presidential nomination in '68. I worked at his campaign headquarters in Wisconsin. Here we are in Colorado again at Rocky Flats, protesting about nuclear weapons on the same trip that Holly met my parents."

"Katie again, too. Who's that kid?"

"Gordon. Katie's."

Pam looked at Phil slyly.

"Yes, he is," Phil said.

"Hit and run, huh, Phil?"

"It's not quite that simple. This is me, in Washington in '72, protesting . . ."

"I thought you were a musician."

"I am."

Pam put the photos back in the shoe box. "I have to go soon. Very interesting, your life. You don't still do sit-ins and stuff, do you? What is it this year? Starving in Africa? Solar power?"

Phil put his life back into the trunk, slowly, feeling a little dazed. "I suppose not."

"What's the matter?" She toyed with the hair on his temple, brushing it back with her fingertips. "You're not depressed, are you, when you look back at your terrific life?"

He shoved the trunk back under the bed. "You haven't finished your beer."

"Perhaps it's a protest against Anheuser-Busch, the capitalist pigs." She stood and slung her handbag over her shoulder and laughed. "I'll see you later."

Phil stared at the door for a few minutes after she had shut it, wondering what he did believe in anymore.

21

T H E day Phil got a small black-and-white television, he
watched President Reagan putting flowers on the graves of
Nazi soldiers in Bitburg, Germany. He listened carefully but
with detachment to the statement from Elie Weisel. To con-
sole himself for not feeling any passion about the day's
events, he drank a few beers and worked out on paper how
many piano-tuning jobs (if the car didn't break down) he
would have to do before he could afford an electronic
keyboard—the only thing resembling a piano he could get
up the stairs.

Money. Perhaps that should be his new creed. Pam and
so many others seemed happy enough with that kind of thing.
But Phil had decided that he didn't really like Pam after all.
She had put him off for a week, so he had given up asking
her out for lunch or a film. What was he doing fooling around
with that kid anyway? Whenever she wore her hair in spikes

he felt like her father. When she looked more normal, he felt shabby and worn. When she was naked, trim and bouncy, he wondered if he looked sagging and sallow to her.

He had spent a week wandering around in the loose boundaries of his current life debating both sides of the issue of What to Do About Pam. Whenever he saw her at the theater he was reminded of what he liked about her—how she laughed, the way her skin felt and looked, what she could do to him in bed . . . but he didn't want to be reminded. He sometimes resolved that she was not to be taken seriously, that he would have a good time if he happened to be with her until something better came along.

That didn't make it easier. She had managed to come and go as she pleased, taking his days or nights with her proprietary grace. Yet he had to approach her with caution. If he asked for her company she was busy. If he put his arm around her she suddenly had something to do elsewhere. But if she wanted *him* she didn't rest until he gave in.

The fact was, when they had a good time together, she was the prettiest, sexiest, the most entertaining, mysterious and powerful lover he had ever known. He would temporarily believe anything for the sake of those moments. Only when they were apart did he really dislike, distrust and castigate her in his private thoughts. Then, he could be objective and feel that he was using her as much as she was using him. Just hop into bed and sit in cafés with her, he told himself, and don't look past tomorrow.

She didn't even seem to notice the moments when he turned against her. He worked over and over in his mind the speech he would give when the time came to stop her, carefully choosing the words that would be the most effective, final and true, that would be his safety against her. As long as he knew she was dangerous, he was safe.

Mondays were his only completely free days—no rehearsals, no performances. Usually, he tried to schedule his odd tuning jobs on Mondays, but this one was empty. He felt joyously free after having spent a week without Pam, knowing his obsession with her was waning.

He packed a peanut-butter-and-banana sandwich and two peaches, dreaming of an excursion out of the city. It was a hazy, summery day, which indicated that across the river, in Illinois, the flat prairie would melt into a dull white sky. But he envisaged the openness of the drive to Cahokia and standing on the huge Indian mound. From there, if things hadn't changed in the years since he had been there, he could see forever.

Most important, however, was the idea of freewheeling down the highway, all his windows open, Beethoven's Eighth blasting out of his cassette player, smelling the fields and wildflowers. He hadn't been on the road for months, not even for an afternoon's drive, and he missed it. Suddenly, today, everything below his window was grimy and smelled of exhaust; all surfaces were tin, glass, asphalt, brick or painted wood. He felt he would choke. The need to breathe fresh air, to sail beyond the St. Louis Arch into the "wilds" of flat farmland, pressed on him.

He hurried to the car. When he reached it, he saw that the lights were still on. What a fool! When he tried the ignition, it made the sound he had dreaded—like someone being surprised with a light kick in the back—"uh."

"Shit." He scraped the posts of the battery but still—nothing.

Breathless from bounding up the stairs two at a time, he paused before his telephone. There was only one person he knew well enough to ask for a jump. He dialed her number.

She sounded sleepy. "What's wrong with you?"

"Not me. My car. I was wondering if you could come over and give me a jump. Battery's dead. I have cables."

She yawned. "I'm not Triple A. Really can't, Phil."

Phil thought of things to say that he knew he wouldn't say. His apartment suddenly became a box, his two windows tiny pinpricks of light. "I have something important to do today."

"Call a tow truck," she suggested.

He heard a noise like a cough in the background. She had someone with her. Not only had he stopped being her lover, but they weren't even friends—he was only someone she knew. "Sorry to bother you," he said and hung up.

He looked in the phone book for a towing service. There was no answer at the nearest one. The second number he tried told him it would be an hour before they could send anyone over, even just to jump his battery. Irritably, he slammed the phone down.

He made himself another cup of coffee and sat by the window, considering that he might have to satisfy himself with another walk in the park.

When the phone rang he hoped it was Pam, apologetically offering to come and help him after all. Instead, he heard a cool woman's voice, "Mr. Benson?" He knew it was a piano-tuning job.

"Yes, ma'am, what can I do for you?"

"I have heard that you can adjust pianos as well as tune them."

"Yes."

"Do you have references?"

Oh-ho, Phil thought. She sounded like a big fish, Harvardish accent and all. "Yes, ma'am. I can bring them with me."

"I would prefer that you send them to me first. You see, I have a valuable instrument and I must be *very* cautious. There is no point to taking references if one doesn't check them, is there?"

"No, ma'am. If you could just give me your name and address, I'll send them right away."

"Oh, thank you."

Phil had never had to use his references. Well, once or twice customers had asked to look at them, but he had felt that it was only curiosity. They consisted mainly of letters from piano teachers and music shop owners with whom Phil had become friendly enough to ask for endorsement, and also his certificate from a course in a small college in Dennison, Texas, which had cost him money, time and a hellishly hot autumn.

As he wrote down her address he decided to charge an extra dollar for the postage, envelope and photocopying— if he "checked out."

22

MRS. Lane not only gave piano lessons on a Bösendorfer to students with greasy fingers, but she also had a giraffe piano in her music room.

Phil had entered her house with the timidity of one who had grown up in the working classes. Even a university education (or part of one, in his case) didn't teach one how not to sweat in the presence of real money—that was an inherited trait. He had been so entrenched in his economic class that when he first began to tune pianos he thought those middle-class households were rich. In California, he saw crazy rich—a lot of money, but not ingrained. Just how far beyond the middle-class *rich* went was still something new to him. Standing in Mrs. Lane's foyer was intimidating enough.

"My regular tuner has gone away to France for *ten* months," she complained. She had already told him this the second time they spoke on the phone. Phil had imagined a younger woman from her voice, but now he saw that she was a woman of a certain age who didn't look that age, well-kept with regular visits to the salon for her hair, face and hands. Her hands were lovely but betrayed her age more than anything. Her skin was like oiled rice paper, fragile and thin.

Three eight-foot citrus trees in the front room were in the same proportion to the house as Pam's little fig tree by her front door was to hers. Above the fireplace was an enormous painting of an orange grove with a ladder and a gloomy sky. Mrs. Lane led him across the oriental carpet, past the vases and glass and soft leather furniture. Like a tourist, Phil craned his neck and saw a skylight at the top of the house and two balconies that overlooked the front room.

He realized that she must be a former academic who tutored to keep her hand in with the university. He had encountered many such teachers through the years. Her students paid well for their private sessions, no doubt, but it wasn't the money from lessons that paid for her groceries. No grimy children and recitals for parents in this house but probably earnest students such as he had been while working on his degree so long ago.

Neither did her music room have the overstuffed chair with tobacco crumbs and broken pencils under the cushion that Phil regarded as standard. Ancient stacks of music books, biographies, and student folders crammed into a narrow space were for the other sort of piano teachers. What would Mr. Tackett think of all this? Phil wondered, sizing the room; it was roughly as large as the Tacketts' front room and his music room combined. It had a walnut rolltop desk, a filing cabinet, bookshelves, two upholstered chairs facing each other by a bay window—acoustics, comfort, space, light. But most important of all, a Bösendorfer grand piano.

He had not known many Bösendorfers—two that he could clearly remember tuning and coddling. In his memory they were prima donnas with delicate clear voices, never booming like the Steinways. But when Mrs. Lane sat down and stroked the keys, a surprisingly masculine tone floated out. The keys were like a man's fingers touching her hands. As she played a simple Telemann, Phil found the relationship she had with her piano appealing. The expense was not wasted on her.

His mind began to wander with the music. Something subtle, not particularly physical, but rhythmical, reminded him of Katie—or rather what Katie might have been had she been less neurotic in her early years and later hadn't become so enmeshed in ordinary family life. Mrs. Lane was like a middle-aged version of the girl Phil had dreamed long ago would be his sophisticated wife, witty at the dinner parties they would have thrown for the concert crowd, slim and attractive even after so many years.

Several years ago on a visit home with Holly, they had gone out for dinner and a film with Katie and Louis. They had all had enough drinks to be warm and just a bit daring. Phil taunted Katie until she giggled and blushed and brought out her violin, which she had confessed she still practiced at least twice a week just for her own pleasure when everyone was out of the house.

He had accompanied her on the family piano with a song by Handel, something dangerously close to being "their" song, as with other young couples it might have been Elvis or the Beatles or Stevie Wonder. Although she was rounded by age and childbearing, awkward in posture and gait because of her foot, that evening she stood with dignity in a bright blue dress.

It was the first and only time since their theoretical bomb had dropped that they were not at odds with each other. Most of the time one or the other or both of them hurt with the bad memories. Katie had been awful to him at first after the shelter. He was haunted by the horrible scene in the hospital when he had tried to visit her—a pale, ill girl with dark-shadowed eyes and sores on her face shouting at him that he had tried to kill her and eat her, that he was a selfish rat who gnawed on anything or anyone when he was hungry. "Mrs. T was right—you only have room in your life for yourself!" she had said. "Even if there is only one other person in the world!"

Phil had recoiled in horror from her, never having seen anyone so ugly with hatred, feeling that she would never understand that she had been the most precious part of his life and dreams until then. He had stayed with his parents for a few weeks and then had run away from it all, taking a job in a music store in Kansas City. The bitter months of regret over every selfish act he had committed, every curt word he had ever said, every thoughtless or careless gesture made him hate himself as much has Katie apparently had.

What *is* a good man? he had wondered endlessly at that time.

When Gordon was born, he returned home. Katie had smiled when she opened the door to him at her parents' house; she showed him their baby, a bundle of smells and squirms, an unbelievably adult possession in his girl's arms. She seemed docile, not unhappy or happy, and sleepy-minded. Phil took Mrs. Doheny aside and asked her, "Does she still hate me?" When Mrs. Doheny said "No," it seemed tentative, as if she could have added, "Not today anyway." And when Phil drew up his courage to ask Katie if they could please get married when her divorce was final, he was given a mild rejection, as if he had merely offered her coffee.

Katie wrote him months later begging him to keep in touch with her and be her friend always. It was the only way in which he was allowed to be good to her.

The music that evening with Louis and Holly had led them to remember a time of a future so big and hopeful that it *had* to come into being.

Somehow the future had twisted and writhed out of their hands. How had that started? Was it latent in Katie because of her fear? Did it begin with Mrs. Tackett or Perry or the noon siren that sent Katie into hysterics? Or was it in Phil because of his lack of faith in himself? Somehow Katie had always been stronger because she *believed* in something, however misguided it was.

What Phil saw that evening was that—although two perfectly nice and loving people, an accountant and a high school science teacher, sat on the sofa watching them—somehow things had gone awry but that what they had imagined as children *could have been*. If . . . if . . . if . . .

After they had finished playing, Katie and Phil had both been so raw that they could barely look at each other or speak. He had made his excuses and taken Holly back with him to his parents' house. He recalled that Holly had been subdued the following day, no doubt jealous of Katie, although it wasn't Katie herself that Phil hungered for. That Katie had never existed, though the possibility had at one time.

———

"Here," Mrs. Lane said after playing the piece. She moved aside and put her hand on the bench.

Phil sat beside her and played a cavatina as if acting his role in transmitting the piano's love. It sang on its own for her. "This is a fine piano."

"Yes, but the lower registers have started humming." She worked out a scale low on the keyboard and tilted her head toward him. "Do you hear it?"

"My God." For the first time, Phil noticed (how could he have missed *that* when he walked into the room?) the giraffe piano by the bay window.

She smiled at him, knowing what he saw without turning her head. "Isn't it lovely? Not much for performance, but I couldn't resist having it."

Together they crossed the room to the antique. It was at least six-and-a-half feet tall, like a harp with a heavy mahogany frame and a keyboard stuck halfway down. Because the French provincial wallpaper showed through the strings, it had an unfinished look, though it was a carefully crafted piece. Must have cost her as much as a small house, he thought. It was made in the days when piano manufacturers still weren't sure what the piano was. This could have been the shape of things to come; instead it was an odd museum piece.

He pressed middle G. The thing vibrated although the note was barely musical. He watched the string wobble within the framework then peered down inside.

"It's just furniture," Mrs. Lane said, "not really in a state to be played."

"Yes, I can see." Phil put a finger here and there tentatively. He had only seen one in a museum once. Now there were no guards to make sure he didn't touch it. "I wonder

if it could be rehabilitated. Has an interesting voice, doesn't
it?"

"I know what you mean, but it's so out of tune that I
can't bear to hear it. Just a bit of extravagance. My husband
bought it for me."

"You shouldn't apologize for buying it." He straightened
up. She had been standing close behind him so that suddenly
they were standing face to face. She didn't move and he
couldn't. "I would buy one if . . ." He decided not to go on
and commit the social error of telling her how filthy rich she
looked to him.

"You would?" She sounded surprised and pleased. "Oh,
then, you're right, I shouldn't apologize. Tony, my regular
piano tuner, is horrified by it. He thinks it's just an expensive
monster. I think he learned to hate it because he couldn't
tune it for me."

"Oh." Phil smiled. He wanted to rise to the challenge
but decided he had better wait until she made an offer.

She finally stepped back and released him from proximity.
He returned to the Bösendorfer. "Would you like some coffee?" she asked.

"Sure would," he said. "That would just hit the spot."
He opened his kit and began to dismantle the piano.

After two hours of smoothing the hammer line, adjusting
screws, cautiously (Jesus, what if I slip?) filing the hammers
with his finest emery, checking the pressure on the keys, and
checking each string in its length along the lyre, he was
nearly ready to start tuning. Obviously the piano had been
cared for over the years but hadn't been adjusted in detail
for some time. Phil felt enormous pleasure in doing the job.

Mrs. Lane wheeled in a kitchen cart with a small pot of

coffee, sandwiches, a bowl of fruit and two large squares of carrot cake. "How are we doing?" she asked, picking up the coffee cup he had emptied earlier.

"I'm afraid I haven't started tuning yet. I'm enjoying this so much I'm being slow."

"Yes? Well, it does take time to do a good job, doesn't it?" she said mildly. So mildly that Phil thought she might be reproaching him in an underhanded way. "Why don't you take a break?"

He sat down in one of the two tightly upholstered Queen Anne chairs. As Mrs. Lane poured the coffee, he took one of the sandwiches and began eating self-consciously, feeling like a grimy workman in an elegant lady's house. She sat down and began to eat her sandwich just as ordinary people do. He squinted across the room at the musical score spread out in a long picture frame on the wall above her.

"That's a Bartok," she said.

"Oh!" Christ, what a bundle of money just in this room, he thought. This woman has so many *things.* His desire to jump up and study the score closely was dampened by the fact that he would have to lean over her. Later, he thought.

"Do you like boats, Mr. Benson?"

"Boats?" Phil couldn't imagine what might lie behind her question.

"Yes, do you like sailing?"

"Well, to tell you the truth, I've spent most of my life on land. Most of my sailing experience is on dollar-an-hour paddle boats on city park lakes except for a few times out when I lived in California." He didn't know whether to go on or not, so he waited to find out what she was up to. Trying to sell an extra boat?

She smiled enigmatically.

He did have an inkling as to what she was thinking. Some women are obvious when planning things for a man. He popped the rest of the crustless sandwich into his mouth and washed it down with coffee. He avoided her gaze by checking the room for other musical treasures he might have over-looked. The Bartok score and the giraffe piano were tops so far. Other picture frames contained prints of people and pi-anos through the ages. At least, he suspected they were prints, since he recognized most of them. In the back of his mind was a suspicion—was he imagining the whole thing or was she putting out signals to him?

"I think it might take a couple more hours to finish this job. I'm not intruding on your time, am I?"

"No, not really. But if you have other appointments you might want to come back another day this week. I'm always here in the mornings. My husband leaves the house about eight and I don't take students until one, and only on Monday, Wednesday and Friday. My husband returns about half past six or seven."

Phil nodded, mentally jotting it down. Married women were always so complicated. "I see. Well, perhaps I should come back another time. Oh—what about your students?"

She shrugged. "We can use the little piano."

Phil nodded, afraid to ask. "What about tomorrow, Mrs. Lane?"

"Yes, that would be fine," she said evenly. "My name's Joanne."

"Mine's Phil."

They smiled as if just meeting for the second time at a large party. "Please," she said, holding a hand out toward the cart, "have some fruit."

"Yes, thank you very much. It was kind of you to make lunch for me." He took a peach.

She rose slightly in her chair to take a banana, which she peeled *lentissimo*. "I happened to hear you play one night. I didn't realize when I phoned you about tuning the piano that you were the pianist at Glass's little theater." The way she said "little" made it sound as if she thought the theater was a hobby for Glass.

Phil was astounded to be connected from one career to the other and couldn't imagine how she could be so certain. Except that he had probably unconsciously played some of the music from the current play as he was fiddling with the piano. "Amazing," he said.

"What's amazing?"

"That you've actually been to the performances."

"Not really," she said casually. "Artists tend to run in packs. It's inevitable that musicians with the same interests would see each other and eventually come into contact. Somehow."

Phil thought she ate that banana with more class than a swan on a brook, but he was worried about the sound of fate working in her words.

"Would you *like* to go sailing, Phil?"

After Friday's performance, he sat down at the piano, idly remembering lace and crystal roses and coffee with real cream. A hand rested on his shoulder.

"Hi. You speaking to me?" Pam asked.

"What? Oh, of course, sure." Guiltily, he tried to summon up a smile for her, but his mind was filled with someone else's face, belly and thighs. Joanne didn't excite him the way Pam could (though she must have been something when she was young, he had thought when he first saw her naked) but she was tender and . . . almost professional. He couldn't deny that he had enjoyed the morning. The only problem had been the phone call from her husband immediately after sex, which had interrupted the afterglow. Joanne handled it so coolly that Phil understood it was routine for her—perhaps she had only been missing her regular piano tuner.

He suddenly realized his changed attitude toward Pam during the week. All the edge had been taken off—she would have to work hard to make him feel one way or the other about her.

"Buy you a cup of coffee?" she asked.

"Sure." They collected their coats backstage, and as they headed through the door, Phil slipped his arm around her waist, trying to reestablish himself with her. Getting back in the mood with her would make it easier to divert her if she quizzed him about what he was up to; he always felt so distracted by the last person he had slept with and transparent about having done so besides. But then Pam might not notice a thing—she didn't seem to be the most sensitive person in the world.

The play they were currently doing had Pam dressed in a business suit, as an aggressive executive. She still had her hair done up. A row of hairpins like staples looked familiar from another time and place.

Katie. Yes, Katie had worn her hair like that once or twice. When was that? Phil shook his head, trying to remember. Not in high school, but before . . .

He escorted Pam to his car and shut the door gently, staring through the window at her French roll as she bowed her head, buckling her seat belt. The hairstyle disturbed him.

He settled behind the wheel and smiled at her. Slowly,

not wanting to startle her into defense, he reached around and plucked the pins from her hair. It was simple but her hair was so lacquered that it held in a tight coil as it fell.

"Phil, what the hell are you doing?"

He mussed her hair with both hands and arranged it over her shoulders. "There."

"Well, well," she murmured with a sleepy, bedroom look on her face.

Palm up, he offered her the hairpins. She took them. When the car started he said, "New battery." A week ago, he wouldn't have been so glib. Neither had mentioned their last telephone conversation. Now it seemed remote and something to dig at her with. "It's a five-year-old Die Hard."

"Must have cost you a pretty penny." She tossed her hair a little more with her fingertips.

"I've been working pretty hard lately."

"Oh?"

"Tuning."

"Oh, Phil, really. Must you?"

He glanced at her, surprised by her tone of disapproval. "What's the matter with that?"

"Well, it's like being a plumber instead of an architect, isn't it?"

Phil took a corner a little too quickly and downshifted too jerkily. If he didn't have money that wasn't good. If he did have money it had to be gained in the right way. What did she want? Besides, he liked tuning. Sometimes he liked it more than playing, but he would never tell her that now.

Pam seemed aware that he wasn't reacting well to what she said but couldn't stop herself. "You may as well put on overalls and go talk with dreary housewives all day."

"Some of them are not so dreary."

"Oh. I see."

They were silent.

Phil was angry with himself for making half a confession and for underestimating Pam's reaction. What right did she have to judge him on this anyway? What had been going on that day he had asked her for a little favor? He enjoyed the revenge for the length of a few city blocks then caught sight of distress in her face. Her expression was not of anger but of things going awry for her. It made him sorry. Perhaps she did care about him. She's tough and I'm soft, he thought. Does that mean I have to swallow whatever she dishes up when the fancy strikes her? Are her rare feelings more precious than my frequent ones?

"I'm not hungry," she said, putting her hand on his thigh. "Let's just go to my place. I'll fix you something there."

"I'm starving."

"I'll warm up some soup. Made some today. Chicken."

"Yes, mother."

"Come on, don't be cruel."

"You mean—don't be as cruel as you are."

She shrugged. "I don't think you understand me."

"Do you want me to?"

She didn't answer except to give him a puzzled look. It was the kind of expression that was so sincere it made him suspicious that she was acting again. But he went inside with her when they reached her house.

She put the soup on and sat on the sofa, he in the chair, as always. "Phil."

"Yes?"

"I have to tell you about something. Someone."

He felt sicker inside than he wanted to. If it was over, why couldn't she just have left it as it had been for the last week, a gradual cooling down? Why did she drag him over here to parade her affairs before him? It made him realize that he still wanted her to feel this as an impending axe coming down.

"I've just broken up with someone," she said. "We had been together for a long time. I . . ." She made a helpless, speechless gesture, fingers aflutter. "When you and I . . ."

Phil had seen her weep onstage before, on cue, convincingly, but what he saw now was a startling disintegration. He moved to the sofa and put his hand on her shoulder. "Hey, hey."

Eventually, he learned from her about her previous lover. She had never been faithful, but it had never mattered until Phil came along. Her irritability, vagueness and capriciousness came into perspective with the detail of someone else.

She said, "You're different."

He found himself excited by the fact that she cared so much about him. He held her and rocked her like a comforting father. He thought of his little fling with Joanne Lane, which had been indulgence in a fantasy—what my life might have been, what Katie might have been like if . . . if . . .

But with Pam clinging to him with her damp face and relief at his affection, he was suddenly determined. There will be no more "might have been." I have a future at last with someone, a future I can make. It starts right this minute.

23

P A M blinked at him, cat-like, her chin in her hands as she leaned on the piano. Above them on the stage, two young actresses were reading lines to each other. A ladder shook center stage as a lighting technician changed bulbs and fiddled with gelatin filters.

"I'm going to be in a luggage commercial," she said. "My agent just phoned this morning."

"A luggage commercial!" He looked up from the keyboard but continued to play. Once, when she was talking to him like this, he had stopped and she said it spoiled the "old film effect." She saw him as Gene Kelly and herself as Debbie Reynolds, chatting in the lead-up to a burst of song and dance. Phil smiled and tried to imagine what Gene Kelly would say to such a line. He couldn't summon up anything witty so he just continued to grin and play.

"Yeah. Relatively big bucks. It's a semi-national," she

said. "They're doing four regions, mainly because of accents—southern, eastern, west coast and midwest. This company here in town is doing one of them and I am, of course, Miss Perfect Midwest Elocution." Pam laughed.

"You do indeed have a beautiful voice, Miss Elocution," Phil said quite sincerely.

"They also made me twirl when I auditioned and I am a perfect twirler, too."

"*I* knew that."

"I've got you twirled, haven't I?"

"Yep." He looked back down at the keys. "And luggage is OK to advertise. Politically."

"OK politically?" She laughed loudly, standing up straight. "I'd advertise cigarettes or nuclear bombs if they named the right price. A job's a job. This will be shown from Chicago to Mississippi, Utah to Pennsylvania."

Phil shrugged.

She put her hands over his and moved her face close, staring deeply into his eyes. "You have a price, too. You would write a jingle for infanticide if they paid you a million."

"Wouldn't." He kissed her.

"Yes, you would."

"Wouldn't."

"Well," she said, "I will use my connections to find out if they want a tune for luggage. Not for a million, though. Whadya say?"

"OK."

"Oh, Phil, while I'm cooking, would you go down in the cellar and look at my hot water heater? This water's just tepid."

Rather than show his aversion to the idea, he laughed.

"I don't go into cellars for any woman. I'm a bedroom man myself."

"Oh, come on."

"I don't know anything about hot water heaters anyway."

"Just take a look."

"No." He tried desperately to think of a way to distract her from the idea. Rising from the kitchen table where he had been reading the newspaper, he crossed over to her and put his arms around her. "You're so beautiful when you cook."

"Goddammit," she said, scraping at the potatoes in the frying pan. "Would you *please*."

Phil backed away from her. "No," he said simply.

"What's the matter with you anyway? Afraid of the dark?"

"Something like that."

She turned suddenly and pulled open the cellar door then tugged Phil's arm. He pulled back, mule-like, resisting her. Pam laughed. "Scaredy cat, scaredy cat," she taunted.

Phil could see the darkness beyond the door and smell damp concrete walls. He fought her more viciously than he intended to, swinging his arms up and away then almost at her once freed from her grip. "I said NO, I mean NO!" he said, furious at having to play children's dare with her.

She stopped suddenly and looked at him. In her eyes, she had the bright, victorious look of a someone who has discovered a useful secret.

Phil felt as claustrophobic from the confines of Pam's personality as he did from her cellar and retreated to sit on the steps of the front porch until dinnertime. All seemed forgotten—or stowed away—by the time she called him back in again.

———

Katie hated it when Louis cut out articles while reading the newspaper. It wasn't the clipping that bothered her but his secrecy about it. A silly thing, really, but she had noticed that he was quiet about the things he saved, pocketing them immediately as if ashamed of what he had chosen or as if he didn't trust her with the knowledge that the cutting contained. Years ago they had argued about it—one of their few unresolved disagreements. The result was that Katie felt the same way about it as she might if those cuttings were letters to her husband from another woman. Twice, she had discovered what he had saved. Once she found an article in his pocket while searching for his keys; another time she memorized the empty space and compared it to a paper she then bought herself. She understood that he was trying to protect her by removing stories about neutron bombs, nuclear power plant accidents and weapons testing. But it wasn't so much what he did as how clumsily he did it that annoyed her. Almost as if he were signaling to her that there were things she shouldn't be told.

"It's hot already," she said across the breakfast things on the table. "I think I'll bring the fan upstairs."

"Yeah."

What Katie saw of him at that moment was the shiny top of his head, where some wispy hairs still grew, as he held the newspaper on his lap and carved out his secrets. Louis looked as he always did before work, suit and tie, hair carefully blown dry to look just a bit fuller on the sides. He had lost all the hair where once he had worn a Beatlish fringe.

"I'm going to sew my underwear to the trees today," she said.

Louis glanced up. "What?"

"Oh. You were listening."

He sighed impatiently. "Of course I was."

The phone rang. They looked at each other and Louis's reluctant expression won out; Katie crossed the room to the phone.

"Mom," Gordon said, "let me talk to Dad."

Katie was taken aback by his abruptness. "All right and good morning to you, too."

"Mom . . ."

Katie held the phone out to Louis. "For you."

Louis put the newspaper and scissors down on the chair with a puzzled look on his face. "Hello?"

Katie watched him at the phone, wondering what Gordon had to say to Louis that he couldn't tell her. She calculated for a moment—her birthday was still months away—no one's birthday was near. If it was about Gordon and Eva themselves, surely he would have been able to tell her. Then she saw Louis glance at her and say quietly, "Yeah, OK." And then, "Yeah." He put the phone down.

Katie studied him as he came across to her, knowing bad news in his walk, the heaviness of his hands on her shoulders, the softness of his voice as he leaned over her and said, "Katie, your daddy died this morning."

It was strange to have the Doheney family together without the usual noisy and happy chaos. Still, the grown children and Margie's grandchildren made enough noise. Katie sat with her back to Granny Byrne's mirror, which was draped with a velvet scarf that someone had found in the linen cupboard. There had never been a death in this house; the covered mirrors, curtained windows at midday, and her solemn sisters, brothers-in-law, son, daughter-in-law, nieces and nephews, and her husband made Katie feel strongly that her father had indeed gone out of the world. He would have hated the scene. He would have hated the darkness, the gloomy faces.

My father is gone. My father, the funny little man who had freckles on his hands until they turned to liver spots. My father, who opened the door to the earth and let us out.

Katie stared across the room at Phil—no, Gordon—who was leaning on his cheery wife, Eva. How strangely he resembled Phil today. With a change in hairstyle from long back to short, Gordon had acquired Phil's sort of jaunty sandiness. A friend had once said to her, in one of the most intimate conversations she had ever had with another woman, that it seemed whenever a woman carried a child she shouldn't, the child ferociously clung to its father's face and character, as if knowing the physical similarity would be the only birthright it would ever have.

You and I, Gordon, were freed from hell by the man lying in that room upstairs. We would have died. And afterward . . . he prodded me back to life, teased me, cuddled me. He told me that Phil hadn't eaten my foot, even though I thought he had. He sat on my bed and drew a funny picture on the sheet because he saw the doctors writing on sheets all the time. He stroked my face and said, "Katie, you know he wouldn't have done a thing like that. You're as precious to him as his own mother and father." But when Phil came to visit we could hardly stand to look at each other. His face was horrible to me.

"Katie, just forget about it," Daddy had said. "Every minute of it is time off your purgatory and, sweet darlin', you'll go straight to heaven if you forgive and forget."

But I told him everything about the cans of new potatoes and the smell of adhesive tape in the first aid box and the oil stain on the floor that I stared at while counting to 2,470 while trying to count to 130,000 for each person who died in Hiroshima. But Saint Hiroshima wouldn't let me finish— she put her face in the oil stain, her eyes unseeing and speckled with gravel. I tried to count the gravel in her eyes but he said, "Come on, Doheney, hold this for me." It was too heavy, my arms trembled, I couldn't even hold a silly little hatchet and dropped it on my foot and he didn't even notice until I showed it to him and he just said, "Oh, something to eat," and put his finger on the blood.

"Mom?"

"Katie?"

Katie put her hand to her throat, which was sore and constricted. Louis pressed her hand solicitously. "Could we open a window, please?" she asked.

Someone moved and the sun poured into the room, revealing all the pasty expressions of mourning, red eyes and noses, and frown marks creasing brows and mouths. Margie's hair was oily and ill behaved; Mary-Rose's jowls were sagging. Louis's eyes and mouth were lined with years of expressions; Margie's husband squinted in the brightness as if the daylight hurt him. All of those who were young in Katie's memory were getting flabby, gray-haired, and secretly bad-tempered from disappointment. The carpet was covered with crumbs; the furniture was dusty.

Except for the piano. There were streaks made in the dust at the edges where it had been opened. Someone had been playing it recently.

Katie stood. "Anyone like some more coffee?" she asked.

———

She sat with her mother after convincing her that it wouldn't hurt Daddy to have a bit of light in the room. "I feel like I'm suffocating today."

"I knew you would take it hard, Katie." Her mother sounded much as she always had when her children told her things about themselves that she had already suspected. But her gaze didn't linger on Katie; instead she resumed a steady focus on the waxen figure lying in the bed.

He had suffered a massive heart attack while on the toilet. According to the doctor, a lot of people went that way— Elvis Presley, Catherine the Great . . . Katie had heard a different version of Catherine the Great's death but she didn't want to bring that up in front of her mother. In spite of her shock, Katie considered it a good way to die—no drawn-out illness, no long stretches of senility in a nursing home. But why now? Why not in ten years when he was an old man? Of course, she could remember his thirty-fifth birthday, when she had thought he was so terribly ancient. But now she had passed her own, and her fortieth, and a man dying in his sixties seemed far too young.

The neighbors had brought hams and roasts, chocolate cakes and strawberry-rhubarb pies, muffins, cheeses, green-bean casseroles, and even a bottle of Irish whiskey. Katie and her sisters took condolences from people who hadn't actually spoken to the family for years. When they answered the phone they found on the line insurance men, undertakers, and long-lost relations who had heard from Cousin So-and-So about poor Cousin Tom.

"Are you going to have a good ol' wake for 'im?" asked a man on the phone whom Katie had never met.

Katie had a feeling that if she had responded in just the right tone of voice the man would have gone to the bus station immediately with the prospect of sleeping on her mother's sofa for a week or so. "No, it's fairly quiet here. Just the immediate family."

"Ah, well, too bad. The Tom I knew deserved a good wake."

"Thank you," Katie said politely. "Well, I'll let you go now. Long-distance calls can be so expensive." She smiled and rolled her eyes at Margie, who had described a similar conversation earlier.

"Come on, Katie, Mary-Rose has laid the table."

Katie joined the family for sandwiches and cake. Some bit of conversation at one end of the table with her mother, Gordon, Eva and Mary-Rose's boy, Mike, seemed to stop abruptly when Katie hobbled in and sat down. Katie smiled across at Eva while she helped herself to slices of beef. "You kids look thick as thieves."

Gordon gave her a shrug.

Katie's mother poked at her food absently.

"Eat, Mama," Mary-Rose said.

"I'm not hungry."

Louis cleared his throat and spoke across the table to Katie. "While you were on the phone, Frances was saying she might move into an apartment."

"Is that true?" Katie looked at her mother with surprise. It had never occurred to her that this house could be anything other than her parents' house.

"Well, I think it's a little big for me, don't you?"

"Maybe you should wait a while until you make a decision like that."

"Well, I was thinking," her mother said, pushing her plate

back, "that if Mike and Gordon and Eva could all get along maybe they could live here and I could take Gordon's apartment. It's a nice little place—just big enough for me and too small for them."

Katie felt a sudden swell of hope, almost as if she herself were being given the house, too. She had fretted over her son's life silently. It was always hard to get a start. Eva did sewing and tailoring at home, and their apartment was forever strewn with fabric, patterns, pincushions, and scissors —and Gordon's books were crammed into one bookshelf and in stacks on the floor, which always made her feel claustrophobic when visiting. Eva could use Katie's old bedroom for a sewing room; Mike could take her parents' old bedroom downstairs and if grandchildren came along . . . She wanted to jump up and clap her hands together but held back. It was hard being both a grown daughter and a mother-in-law in the same conversation, so she just grinned at Gordon.

"And you would keep the piano here?" she asked.

"The piano?" Gordon asked, his face reddening.

The room went silent as all the sisters and husbands and children and the newly widowed mother glanced between Katie and Gordon.

"I mean," Katie said, "I just wondered what would happen to the piano."

Katie's mother made a prim face, which made her look a bit like the middle-period Lillian Gish—a hard-working, good woman. Katie knew that face well and knew what it meant. Secrets. "I don't see any reason to move the piano. It wouldn't be in your way, would it, children?"

"No, not at all," Eva said.

Katie glanced at her son, who was murmuring to Eva, asking her if she wanted another cup of coffee. Secrets are always intended to protect the people you love, not hurt them, Katie thought. I just hope he doesn't have piano-playing genes in him, that it's just a pastime and not a passion. But she couldn't help feeling hurt that he had hidden it from her all these years, even though she had actually known for a long time. It was like being a citizen of a supposed democracy and not being trusted with information or consulted for opinions. Her family had a government that lived elsewhere other than her house. Secrets were also secret weapons.

Louis said, "Am I missing something?"

"Mother," Katie said, "you should at least have some chocolate cake. Mrs. Townsend brought it over. If you don't eat *anything* you'll be dizzy."

The family geared back into action over the chocolate cake. As Mike started to elaborate on a memory of the creamery can that had been rusting by the back door since he was a tyke, Katie caught Louis's eye and mouthed, "I love you" across the table at him.

She suddenly felt so fond of him, a feeling that usually stretched out for days at a time into an everyday thread of affection. But today it was so thick and tangible and tangled. She knew Gordon hadn't owned up to his piano playing because he wanted to be Louis's son first and foremost— which he was, never mind his face. Katie also knew there were other family secrets. Well, perhaps not secrets but silences and taboo subjects. When had anyone discussed the Bomb around her last? No one even knew how she felt anymore.

The truth was, she no longer felt anything. It hadn't happened when she was most prepared and expecting it. Perhaps the Bomb never would fall out of the belly of a plane onto her house. No one *really* took it seriously anymore. Threats and promises that are not carried out become nothing but words.

As they all sat here, grieving the loss of their patriarch, in a year's time it would be an occasional grief. Mary-Rose might say, "I was thinking of Daddy today. Do you remember when we went camping near Marble?" And the grandchildren in ten years' time would vaguely remember a funny old man, rather untidy but good-natured, whose old house smelled a certain way.

Katie had her bad memories, but they were some "damn fool thing" that involved three people, not the world. The effect had been to make her treasure sunshine and the wind and the sight of trees and grass, just as losing Daddy made her love Louis even more.

The world would have to find a brand-new way to scare her now.

24

Dear Katie,

I don't know how to tell you how awful I felt when your letter came this morning. You must remember how much I used to like your father in the old days and how much more he meant to me for saving our lives. Well, I may not have seen him much in the past years, but it hit pretty hard to hear that he's gone. Please give my love to your mom and tell her how sorry I am, too, will you?

Things are okay for me. Maybe more than okay—I've got a beautiful girlfriend who is an actress at the theater where I play. She makes life interesting and keeps an old man like me running. The job is one of the better ones I've had. Maybe I'll get around to writing some music again one of these days.

Good news about Gordon and his wife getting your old house. Sounds a little Old Worldy to have the grandkids take over the ancestral house, but I'm glad to hear it's going to stay in the family. That's a great old house. Tell Gordon hello for me and sorry that

I haven't sent him a wedding present yet. One of these days. I hope before he has a couple of kids!

Sorry this is short. Just about time to go to work. Take care of yourself and Louis and the kids.

Yours always,
Phil

Just as he locked his door on the way out, he remembered that he had been commanded by Pam to wear the new jeans she had made him buy ("I'm sick of seeing you in flares," she had said. When he protested that they were boot cut so he could get his feet through the bottoms, she had silently pointed to the zips in the ankles of her jeans. "This is 1985, darling.") So he shrugged and went back in to change his clothes.

He was forcing his feet through the narrow denim tunnels when the phone rang. "Yeah, yeah." He reckoned it to be Pam, urging him to hurry over to her party. Urging was actually unnecessary—he had discovered that he hated every minute apart from her. This last week he had suddenly realized that he was crashing down into love with the recklessness of a kid.

It was Joanne Lane. "You haven't phoned me," she said.

"Well, I know, but . . ." Lamely, he let it hang. He couldn't even think of a decent excuse other than that there was definitely someone else—someone with less money but more time and bouncier breasts and no husband.

"Will you meet me at the cathedral down by the arch on Tuesday morning?"

Phil hesitated. His main worry was that Pam was going to phone and his line would be busy; then he would have to come up with a story. Perhaps he should have been a little more considerate to Joanne, anyway. He could see her and explain that he was deeply involved with someone else. Apparently even more involved than she was with her husband. "All right," he said.

"Ten a.m.?"

"Fine, yeah, that would be terrific. Look, I'm sorry to rush it but I'm late for a party."

"Good, very good," Joanne said with her oddly approving voice. "Have a good time and I'll see you on Tuesday."

"Yeah. Bye, Joanne."

He hurried out before the nagging phone could start again. When he reached Pam's, it was difficult to find a parking space. How many people had she invited over, anyway? As he went up the steps, he found her on the front porch, wineglass in hand, her hair standing straight out on top with a scarlet streak sprayed in. In the light of the street lamps, he could see that her eyelids glittered. She was like an exotic bird. A young man in shirtsleeves stood with her.

"There you are," she said, coming forward and kissing him. "Now, you just wait a minute." And she disappeared inside the house.

The young man appeared at loose ends. "Hi."

"Hi," Phil said.

"Everyone's in there bitching about the hijacking. I was getting pretty tired of it."

"Oh. Yeah." Phil could not imagine why the kid was explaining his presence on the porch unless he was nervous about being caught alone with Pam. It didn't worry Phil, but suddenly he couldn't think of anything to say except to talk about the hijacked plane, which, last he heard, was now in Algiers with American tourists still aboard. "It's like the weather, isn't it?"

"Weather?"

Phil tried not to sigh with impatience. What the hell was Pam up to anyway? He tried to peer through the window at the people inside but could only see the tops of two heads. "Lot of people?"

"Yeah. She always throws a good one. It's her barbecued meatballs and wine that bring all the important people around."

"Oh. Well, looks like I came for the night air."

Pam returned with a pillowcase. "Come on, Phil."

"What are you doing?" He backed off when she opened the pillowcase and moved it toward him.

"I have a surprise for you." She laughed and stepped closer. "C'mon, play fair."

"You don't expect me to walk into a party full of strangers with a bag over my head."

"Don't embarrass me," she said through her teeth, "or I'll put you in the cellar."

"Please, Pam, *please.*" He wanted to sound as stubborn as she did, but it came out a little more desperate than anything.

She studied him. "All right. But you have to walk in backwards."

Relieved, Phil allowed her to guide him as he went heels first into the house. Pam glanced from his face to others, waving them aside, looking mischievous. "OK. Turn around."

It was like a fantasy; it was as if he were in a film where Merle Oberon gives to Cary Grant the thing that he couldn't have because he paid for her operation or something.

A Steinway baby.

He was aware that the room full of drinking, chattering

people had gone quiet and they were all watching him. The piano was his. He was embarrassed by the size of the gift but overcome by its presence. It filled her front room like a locomotive in a two-car garage.

"Go on," she said. "Touch it."

He sat down and struck middle A. "It's out of tune."

The party burst into life again with laughter. Vaguely he heard Pam shouting, "I told you he'd say that, didn't I?" But he attacked it with "St. James Infirmary Blues." At the point of putting "a twenty-dollar gold piece in my pocket so they'll know I died standing pat," he realized he had made a terrible oversight.

"Pamela!"

She turned from the woman she had been talking to and smiled at him.

He crossed the room and squeezed her as if she were the most precious thing in the world. For, at that moment, she was.

She was still a little drunk as they rolled around in bed, where they had collapsed, not even sure that all the guests had gone home. Her fingernails dug into his buttocks as he moved.

"I love you," she said. "I believe in you."

He covered her ears and eyes with kisses. "I'm madly, insanely in love with you."

She blew at his face. "Tell me you like it."

"I love it."

"Tell me that it makes you feel ambitious. You have to earn it, mister. You have to go out and conquer the world."

"I'll conquer the world."

"Tell me how wonderful I am."

"You're fucking fantastic, lady."

"Tell me . . . tell me you're going to . . . oh, Phil . . . tell me."

"Whatever you want. It's all true, it's all wonderful, it's all I can do to keep from exploding."

Her fingernails dug deeper.

He had been dreading the time with Joanne, but from the moment she picked him up in her luxurious car he felt happy and peaceful. They boarded a riverboat and chugged on the quiet, broad Mississippi. With a click of her fingers, mint juleps arrived. It wasn't the usual tourist fare, though there were other people on the boat. Just as he had decided not to ask her if it was *her* riverboat, she asked him again if he would like to go sailing with her on her own craft.

Phil had his feet up on the rail, enjoying the humid breeze blowing off the water. He admired the scenery—the shoreline of trees, anchored boats, the houses and buildings peculiar to life near big water—low and flat behind wooden piers strung with Christmas lights even in June. He saw yellow ribbons tied on some of the trees, probably for the American hostages still being held in Beirut by Shiites.

"I think I'd better be straight with you."

She lowered her sunglasses to the tip of her nose and peered at him with a faint smile. "You have a girlfriend, don't you?"

"Yeah. I don't want to wreck it. It's a good thing right now."

"Ah," she said, stretching out. "Sometimes you sound so young, Philip. You still have faith in things."

He grinned. "I know. I feel young right now."

"That's all right. I understand. After all, I have Arthur. I

just like to have a little company every now and then. Someone who knows Locatelli from Vivaldi."

Joanne was always so cool. He felt that it wasn't a deep
friendship but that somehow she might always be there, as
free and flowing as the river. He leaned over the rail, looking
for the white flash of a bass or the greedy mouth of a sunfish.

"Bet there are some gigantic catfish at the bottom."

"My granddaddy wrestled out a six-footer bare-handed
once."

It amused Phil to think of Joanne having a "granddaddy"
of that kind. He smiled over his shoulder at her, encouraging
her. "Was he from St. Louis?"

"No, I grew up in Cape Girardeau." She pointed down
the river as if they might catch a glimpse of it a hundred
miles away. "One of my earliest memories, when I was about
five, was Pearl Harbor Day. Granddaddy and I were at the
river fishing, and my father drove over in the old Chevy to
tell us."

Phil calculated quickly. Christ Almighty. He felt as if he
had been struck with a hot wind. Here he had been, thinking
of himself as the "younger man," and she was only about
six years older than himself. Six years. That amount of time
meant nothing anymore. Six years ago was an eyeblink ago
in my life. That was even after Holly, it was so recent. He
sat down beside her again in the deck chair and, without
actually looking, imagined all her wrinkles and sags and other
nuances that indicated she was a woman well past her prime.
Other people might even see them as contemporaries. Am I
this close to being an "older" man?

He wondered suddenly how Pam saw him.

Wanting to cover up his sudden insights, he groped for
something to say. "Funny how we date our lives with events

like that. For instance, I was just thinking about the Kennedy assassination when we first got on this boat. I was living in California then and went sailing that day with a friend. We heard the news on the radio that he had been shot."

Joanne said in her calm voice, "Yes, I remember that day. I was at home, scrubbing the floor. As soon as Arthur phoned with the news that Kennedy was dead, I invited some of our friends over to celebrate the death of the papist."

Phil turned his head away lazily, feeling light and numb, as if slightly drunk, from the shock of her words. The chair he sat in seemed to have no substance. Important things that he had *known* somehow turned out to be assumptions. It had been so easy to find Katie-ness in Joanne, but it wasn't really there. But God knows, he thought, perhaps Katie herself would say such a thing these days.

"Lunch?" she asked. Her lovely narrow fingers were arranged like furling petals around the mint julep glass.

"Yes," he said, wanting something to do as a distraction rather than actually wanting to eat.

Phil watched the Mississippi rolling and sloshing at his feet. He thought of blues songs about this river. He remembered a café in Jackson where he had eaten the world's best cornbread and ribs and had heard truly great piano playing. That old man (what *was* his name—Phil had thought he'd never forget it) might still be sitting there, flirting with the old ladies and rattling out cakewalks and rags and weeping over the blues.

Them's what can don't always do, he thought, seeing a McDonald's waxed paper cup float by. I might not be able to do what I used to dream of, but I *can* do. I can try.

"Joanne," he said, turning around to her. "What exactly

does your husband do? Is it something that would be useful to me?"

"Are you looking for connections, Phil?" she asked, smiling. "You're looking *at* a connection."

"You." Phil leaned over and kissed her on the lips. "I should have thought so. Hollywood or Broadway?"

She laughed. "Why don't we start with St. Louis and see how it goes?"

"I'm in your hands, ma'am."

She nodded, smiling her mild smile at him as if he had made the reply she expected and approved. "I'll see what I can do."

25

    P H I L escaped from a boring man, who wanted to talk about the gold and silver market, by wandering into the kitchen for another drink. He didn't know many people at this party but intended to have a good time somehow. They had passed the hat to give money to the Mexican earthquake relief fund, so he felt that at least it was ideologically OK, even if the people all seemed more the type to have their consciences assuaged than to want to really help people outside their borders. Pam had been invited through an acquaintance from her investment contacts. Phil took the tack that he might find someone who needed a piano tuned or repaired.

    Phil could hear bits from a conversation in the utility room, where nonsmokers had congregated to sit on the hostess's washer and dryer. "What about this guy you're with now?"

    "Oh, he's all right."

Phil was gripped by the casualness of the reply. It was definitely Pam's voice. All right, am I? he thought. She opens her legs and says it's never been so good (which he knew was a lie, but he thought if she kept lying, she might start to believe it) and then says I'm "all right"?

"What does he do?"

"He's a pianist. At Glass's theater. Not exactly Mr. Success, but Phil's a nice guy. He's a little older than most of the men I've gone out with, but he's putty. It's remarkable. He's really devoted to me, watches me move around the house with big puppy dog eyes and whenever I say jump, he jumps. I gave him a piano and he didn't even flinch. I thought it would make him squirm . . ."

Phil poured himself a double bourbon and rejoined the boring man, who was still standing by the front curtains staring mistily at the other guests, to ask him about commodities.

"Is it really true or is it just a cliché about pork bellies being a passionate issue in the market?"

While Pam was in the bathroom, Phil stroked himself under the sheet, trying to work up something, knowing that she was interested in sex tonight. But, when she came back and crawled into bed with him, it was hopeless.

They lay quietly, each staring diagonally over the other as if the will to try had left both of them. Phil pulled her closer to his chest; she was tame and compliant. He felt ancient and useless. Pam was the source of their power together, but now she was still.

"Too much to drink?" she asked, kissing his shoulder.

He petted her hair, those long coarse strands he had been

so intimidated by when he first caught sight of her. He laughed. "Radiation poisoning."

In the cinema, his knees ached from being tightly wedged against the seat in the next row. It was a tighter fit than Glass's theater. Picking popcorn hulls from between his teeth with his thumbnail, he started to think more and more about his bladder filling up with the extra-large orange drink he had bought to cover the popcorn thirst.

Pam was completely wrapped up in the film. He should have known that she would be a Peckinpah fan, what with all those guns going off, throats being cut, and blood spurting everywhere. He hadn't liked these films when they were new, and the intervening years hadn't jaded him. But with difficulty, he watched the action rather than turning his head away at the worst violence. Pam made the same soft "hhh" sound that she did during sex sometimes, which disturbed Phil not just a little bit.

He finally closed his eyes when they brought out the Gatling guns again.

He wanted a day back from his childhood. Any day in which he was merely a boy wandering in an empty field or playing his grandmother's piano or sitting in the back seat of the old Ford while his parents sang along with Rosemary Clooney and the car radio.

A time before Pam and her playful fascination with cruelty. A time before Holly and her need to "find herself, as a woman and human being." A time before Katie and the shelter.

He feared the power of love to pull him in once again. Just as Katie had taken him into the shelter in her worship of Saint Hiroshima. Just as Holly had sent him away with a clumsy understanding of his own inalterably male attitudes, which stunted her personhood. If he opened his eyes to this film, to carrying guns to frighten people for amusement, to manipulations like gifts of baby grand pianos to make people squirm, what would happen to him this time? Every time he fell in love, he had to worship another god, good or evil. What was it this time?

He glanced over at her. She was beautiful, shining out and turning heads with her grace and manners and dress. She was intelligent, talented and ambitious.

She's going to destroy me, he thought. He smiled.

The house lights brightened. A sober and sick crowd stood, murmuring, collecting coats and handbags from the snapping jaws of the seats. Pam's familiar hair and shoulders ahead in the crowd led him on. She didn't wait for him until they were outside in the cold January night.

Pam turned her head. "What a movie, huh?" she whispered.

Phil put his hand tenderly on her face. "I love you."

He listened to the phone ring a few times, then reluctantly left the piano to answer it. Answering the phone at Pam's was a strange experience sometimes; even though he had lived there for six months, he still picked up the phone to men with bedroom voices wondering if Pam was "around," apparently unconcerned that another man had her phone in hand. He dutifully took messages from men named Pete or Kevin or Jay and handed them over to Pam, whose reply was usually, "Oh!" and nothing else. He never asked. He didn't want to know.

"Phil," Pam said, "have you heard?"

He paused. "I guess not. Heard what?"

"The shuttle blew up this morning. I just found out at the hairdresser's."

"The shuttle?" he said. "You mean the space shuttle?"

"No, the weaver's shuttle. What do you think? Isn't it a shock?"

"Well . . ." He felt confused and looked across the room at the dead television screen, wishing his arm were long enough to reach across the room and turn on the cable news. "What happened to the astronauts?"

"It blew up," she said simply, then laughed. "What a way to go, huh? One second, headed into space and the next, *blooey!*"

"Christ."

"Hey, I gotta go. Listen, when I get home this afternoon, would you remind me that I have a surprise for you?"

"A surprise?"

"I'll tell you later, dear. Bye."

Phil settled down in front of the television where, at first, people were being interviewed about what they thought might have happened. Then came the film of the spectators watching the shuttle, their faces changing from excitement to horror, and then the shuttle itself catching fire and disintegrating into smoky white streamers in the sky.

The fourth time he saw the film clip, he started feeling sick and turned the television off.

It was the same feeling he had experienced as a boy after learning that the dog the Russians had put into orbit would just go around and around the earth, dying of asphyxiation or starvation. Or watching the Zapruder film of President Kennedy's head blowing up. Or news coverage of Viet Nam and massacres in the Middle East.

But I always recover and forget, he thought. None of

these things has ever happened to *me* except for a phony nuclear attack. I've survived all the horrible things that have happened in the world with varying degrees of tiny scars.

There's always something to make up for it. For instance, Pam bringing me a surprise tonight. I'll forget about dead schoolteachers and astronauts, won't I?

What could it be? A surprise . . .

He imagined something gift wrapped on the kitchen table—a book, a record? No, she wouldn't have mentioned that over the phone, just plunked it into my hands as we do with little gifts. An event—we're going on a trip or to see something, or the governor has invited us to a party.

Hungry now, he searched in the cupboard for something to eat. All he could find was a nearly empty box of graham crackers. He rummaged through and found a large corner and good crumbs. The cork-colored dust stuck to his fingertips, which he licked absently.

She's taken a job in New York? Someone asked about me and I will be getting a phone call from a music publisher?

Tapping his fingers, he started to string together a bit of a melody. Not quite consciously, he worked it out in a quizzical hum.

Maybe she wants to take me home to meet her mother. Maybe her mother is coming here to stay. Maybe she's pregnant and wants to get married and keep the baby. Maybe she's been told she only has three months to live. Perhaps the stock market has crashed and she's lost all her money and has to become a cocktail waitress.

He shook his head. The melody was stronger. Suddenly alert to it, he moved to the piano and rifled through the papers for something to write on. A splattering of fresh green notes came from the felt-tip pen. He paused, distracted by the sound of his mind, and played the piano for a long while. It came easily and surprised him with tempo and key changes, rather gypsyish but still cheerfully quizzical. A run here? Sounds too childlike, but aren't surprises for the childlike? Always have liked these notes in this key but have never done it. Yes, this works. No, that's shit. Garbage. That's better. Yes . . . that needs refining.

After a couple of hours of playing, noting down what he'd done and then playing it through several more times for the sheer pleasure of hearing it, he put the pages of the composition together with a paper clip.

Under Pam's bed was the trunk that he had carried with him for years. He pulled it out. Crinkled, bent at the corners, and still smelling faintly of the cat urine from Holly's cat, his most recent composition until today sat on top of the heap. It reminded him of how long it had been since he had written anything down. Seldom had anything come to him so completely as today. Bits and pieces of undeveloped melodies still whispered within, but he could never quite get a grip on them or find their complementary phrases.

He put the new work, labeled in a confident hand, "What Is It?" on top of the others, making a note to look at it again in a few days after the first thrill of having done it was quieter.

She's got a part in a film, he guessed, and we're going to London, Venice or Paris.

When she came home, he glanced at her bag and the shape of her pockets, wondering if she actually carried something for him. She was wearing one of her most intimidating outfits—a billowing tigerskin print shirt over black leggings, her hair sprayed with a pink streak and standing outward just on one side and her neck, ears and wrists laden with costume jewelry. If his mother, in 1942, could have foreseen this woman as an object of little Phil's passion, she would have killed him in his crib.

Pam collapsed on to the sofa with an ordinary sigh. No guess-what-wait-till-you-hear-this. "What a day. Everyone's talking about the shuttle." She rose suddenly and switched the television on, then settled back. "I haven't actually seen the film yet, have you?"

"Yes. It's terrible." He stood by the sofa, wondering whether to say anything about the surprise. She had said "remind me" on the phone, hadn't she? But he hated to be uncool, so he just stood and watched a variation of what had been on earlier—people talking endlessly about what appeared to have happened, about what might have really happened, what they didn't know and why.

"What are you pacing around for?" she asked irritably.

"I'm not pacing."

"Well, you seem nervous or something."

"Well . . ." He was embarrassed.

"What?"

"What's the surprise?"

"What? Oh! God! Thanks for reminding me. I have to write a check." She opened her handbag and wrote out a check and put it on the coffee table.

Phil stared dumbly over her shoulder at it. It was made out to Chester.

Pam tossed her handbag aside. "Would you be sweet and get me a glass of wine? I'm bushed."

"But . . . what's the surprise?"

She laughed. "You're just like a kid." She batted at him playfully with a sofa pillow. "I knew it would work. I told you that as a reminder, like tying a string around my finger. I promised to pay Chester for that picture frame. If I had told you to remind me about something like *that* you would have forgotten, too."

Phil couldn't quite make the connection between his surprise and the picture frame. "So . . ."

"There's no surprise. Don't be such a kid." She picked up the television listings. "I suppose we'll have to watch these great American heroes burst into flames all evening, won't we?"

Phil went into the kitchen and stood with the refrigerator door open, not seeing the wine that he was supposed to be looking for. He hated her. He hated her. What a fool, what an idiot I am. What am I doing here? Is it just the sex? But he liked hating her. As long as he hated her, he was safe. He could keep himself from believing in her and in the future.

I'll show the bitch. I'll show her. Somehow.

26

"I t ' s the Libyans again," Chester said to a new actor in the group.

Libyans? Phil thought. Chester frightens me. He experimented with an appoggiatura like a kitten batting at a ball of yarn, trying not to listen to Chester.

Glass tapped him on the shoulder firmly. "I want to talk to you."

When Phil turned, Glass was already up the aisle, headed for his office. Phil followed, remembering a time when he had been caught by the principal as he threw spitwads at the teacher's back. Was this because he had dashed in late for the dress rehearsal? But it was only a minute and no one seemed to being doing anything yet. He didn't think Glass had even noticed.

Glass was already sitting behind his desk. Phil stood, there being no chair for visitors. Glass moved his telephone off a stack of papers, glanced through them, then up to Phil.

"I hear we have a mutual friend."

"Oh?" Phil was thrown. He hadn't expected such an opening line.

"Yes. Joanne Lane. She's a dear friend of mine."

Phil took this extremely warm statement to mean that Glass had slept with her. Why not? Phil had known that the only weakness in Joanne's strong tendency towards men in the arts was her husband, who was "in business." He could easily imagine it, especially after having seen Mrs. Glass, who had a lovely dark face but suffered from a surfeit of bagels and cream cheese. Occasionally, she brought around a box of them to express the management's goodwill toward the actors and staff and usually ate two or three herself.

"Yes, Joanne spoke highly of you," Phil said.

Glass's face became puzzled for just a second or two. "Well, she tells me that she's heard some of your original compositions and she thinks I should let you score the next play."

Phil was surprised that his request for "connections" would hit so close to home. For a moment, he was sweating with embarrassment. He feared that he would be seen as he had seen others—as someone with more friends than talent. Or wasn't this the way of the world? It had bothered him but had remained a moot point since Joanne hadn't pulled any strings until now. The last time he saw her had been at a large party; she had stressed that he should bring "his friend" but never said more than a greeting and goodbye as she flitted around in the great press of well-dressed people who all seemed to know each other.

Why couldn't he have asked Glass himself? Why had he been shuffling around all these months like a quiet child?

Why did he have to wait for others to do things for him?
Well, it was a plum and he was going to take it.

"Would you like to hear . . . ?"

Glass waved his hand impatiently. "I like music, but I
don't know anything. I trust Joanne's judgment. Here's the
script. You do it, get her to have a listen and tell me."

"I . . . well, thank you. I really do appreciate . . ." Phil
couldn't think of anything more awkward than trying to gush
at Mr. Glass.

"Flat fee or percentage of door?"

"Uhm," Phil said. "Percentage."

"Good boy," Glass said even though ten years at most
separated them. "I'll ask my attorney what percent music is
worth and get back to you."

"Thank you."

Glass nodded and stared at his desk in sudden intro-
spective busyness. Phil started to duck out, recognizing his
boss's moods. "Wait a minute," Glass said.

"Sir."

"All the rules still apply. I expect you here and I expect
you to work while you're here."

Phil wondered if that meant a warning for past behavior.
"Right. Of course. Thank you."

I'll do it, he thought. And I'll do such a hell of a job that
everyone will notice.

Joanne stripped and lay on a giant white beach towel
under a sunlamp. He played to her bare back and bottom.
After going through half the score, explaining the action and
playing the bits, he stopped, thinking she had simply fallen
asleep.

She raised her head. "It's too classical. Jazz it up."

Pam came out of the bedroom wearing her bathrobe. "Phil, I think it's really too late to be banging away on the piano. I have to be up early tomorrow."

"Oh, sorry, sweet," he said absently, marking a change in a riff on his score. He glanced at the script. "I assume you'll be playing Amelia in this one, right?" he asked. He had never read a script before and was imagining who would be what. Pam hadn't talked about it at all.

"No," she said.

Something in the "no" sounded meaningful. He studied her face. "No?"

"No. I'm not in this one."

"You're not?" Phil couldn't imagine that Glass had passed her for an audition. Besides, she would have stormed and fumed about it so all St. Louis would have known.

"No. I'm going to be starting rehearsals for the American in a few days."

"Oh."

"I thought I had mentioned it."

"You know you didn't."

"I thought I had."

"Then why the guilty look?"

She changed her face to a smooth, cool expression. "I thought I had mentioned it," she repeated. "I don't *belong* to Glass, do I? Besides, you should be happy for me. The American is a better theater."

"Congratulations." He put the script down, suddenly recalling a conversation with Dennis, who was playing the lead in this new play. Phil had mentioned Pam in his misguided notion that she would be playing opposite him and Dennis had become very distracted. Now Phil understood that he was one of the last to know.

"You're angry with me. You should be happy for me."

"I said congratulations. American. Good. Thank you for letting me know the good news."

"Well, it's probably better that we don't spend day and night together anyway, isn't it? Be a break to have separate theaters for a while."

"Perhaps we should have separate lives. Then maybe I'll know what you're up to."

She frowned and walked back into the bedroom.

Phil made a few more notes on his score, crammed it into his folder, turned out the light, did his bedtime ablutions, and then stood in the bathroom, dreading the moment of going into the same room with her.

She wasn't asleep. As soon as he settled down, she clung to his back, sobbing. "Please don't ever leave me. I love you so much."

"Yes. Mr. Rich and Successful."

He felt something irregularly shaped and metallic against him, between the softness of her breasts.

"I'll shoot myself if you leave me."

Phil felt a heavy, heavy weariness course through him He could not bring himself to make the effort of telling her to get the gun out of the bed. Instead, he lay there, imagining the pistol that pressed against his back. It wouldn't matter which of them it hit if it were really loaded, if it went off. There would be a lot of blood. He closed his eyes, trying to breathe, knowing that the water was stinking and Katie's foot was rotting and the food had gone so long ago that they couldn't even think about eating anymore. In the corner of the shelter, Mr. Tackett sat with his recital suit on and spoke to Charlie, who kept wiping his forehead with a bandanna as if it were still that hot summer's day in the piano factory.

"The kid's all right, but he doesn't have it," Charlie said confidentially to Mr. Tackett.

"He's great," Mr. Tackett said. "I mean *great*, a genius."

"He can't even open the door to this fucking hole and crawl out, he's so great." Charlie glanced over at Phil and suddenly grew quiet with embarrassment.

"I heard that," Phil said. "It has nothing to do with pianos."

"No." Mr. Tackett and Charlie spoke together, shaking their heads and trying to look friendly.

Phil's leg jerked in the bed and he realized that he no longer felt Pam against him—neither her breasts nor her gun.

Katie had thought that Louis was asleep, stretched out along the sofa, the right half of his face buried in a sofa pillow. She was just about to get up from the chair and switch the television off when her husband murmured, "That reminds me—we need to get some new luggage for our trip."

Katie settled back and resumed her crocheting then looked at the television. She lowered the hook and yarn into her lap again and stared in disbelief.

There she was—how long had it been since Katie had seen her?—in a flowing, flowered dress, twisting this way and that to look at the six or seven pieces of luggage at her feet. "I need something big," she said, pointing to the largest suitcase. A twirl, and the skirt rippled out around her slender legs. "I need something small and something flat." Twirling and pointing again. "I need it all!"

Katie went cold and sick. Something bad is going to happen on this trip, she thought. Something very bad. And I can't open my mouth because they all think I'm crazy anyway and Louis has been waiting all his life for this trip. Something *awful* is going to happen.

A man in a business suit appeared on the screen, picking up the bits of luggage, hanging one piece by the strap over his shoulder, tucking another under his arm, holding others awkwardly in his hands. He gave Katie a weary smile and followed Saint Hiroshima off-camera into the depths of an airport.

27

O P E N I N G night parties were always more fervent when the audience had reacted well. Phil drank too much, smoked too much, and talked to everyone who stood in his path. He kissed the lovely blonde when she praised his music; laughed with Harry, the soft-hearted critic who loved everything theater; and even chatted socially with the unsmiling Glass, who studied the frolic dismally like a parent responsible for everyone's virginity.

Glass related an anecdote about an actor he had known on Broadway who had suffered an epileptic fit in the middle of *Look Back in Anger* and had received a standing ovation. Glass smiled. "He was playing Cliff, too."

Phil could only laugh at the idea of it, assuming the character made a big difference, since he didn't know that play. It was on the list that Pam had compiled for him of "must reads," but he hadn't worked his way to it yet. Full of gin and tonic, Phil began to feel positively affectionate toward his boss.

"Why did you leave Broadway?" he asked Glass.

"I lived in New York for thirty-five years. That was about twenty too many. I prefer this side of the Mississippi." Glass was suddenly beckoned loudly by someone across the room. "Excuse me," and he was gone.

Joanne had come to the party. Phil first searched for Pam. She usually had admirers hanging around her during these parties, but she was only a visitor this time. He couldn't see her in the crush of people. Where do they all come from? he wondered, as he did every time they opened. All relatives and friends? Some of the faces changed from play to play, but there were still only a few expressions—the eager, shiny eyed ones or the bored or jealous ones. How many husbands and wives had he seen glowering? But the bored, cool ones were the worst. If you happened to catch their eye, they would look sideways in a second without turning their heads.

Seeing that Pam was not within sight, he headed for Joanne. "You look gorgeous tonight," he said, kissing her cheek.

The compliment was sincere, for she was in an elegant plum-colored dress with only a simple brooch. Standing among the younger folks in their modish dress, her appearance sang out with good taste followed by money. "Thank you, my darling. Look, I think your music was splendid," she said.

"You really do?"

"Yes. Splendid. Believe me, I felt I had something at stake here and I was pleased. I know that Glass wouldn't tell you this, but he thought it was marvelous, too."

"Oh, well, that does mean something," Phil said, feeling

high with the praise. He had suspected that Glass liked it.

"Give me another kiss, Phil. I have to go to another party tonight." She raised herself on tiptoe to receive the kiss. "I wanted to talk to you before I went. Look, if you should have some morning free, give me a call." She smiled.

"I'll keep it in mind."

Joanne glanced around, then wrinkled her nose at Phil. "I'm sure she's vintage Coca-Cola, darling, but you like brandy, don't you?"

Phil laughed and squeezed her hand and watched her go. He noticed the way the younger women turned to look over their shoulders at her as Joanne passed through to the door. She was one of those people who knew how to attract attention without doing a thing.

He retreated to the bar at the end of the room and saw a woman about his age pouring herself a drink. He recognized her as the playwright. Earlier he had noticed her edging away from people and standing near the window, glancing out as if waiting for a ride home. In spite of her grim face, Phil was too happily expansive to be put off by her appearance.

"Hello," he said.

"Hi." She smiled briefly, politely.

"Are you a native of St. Louis?" he asked.

"I've lived here sixteen, seventeen years." She drank nervously.

Phil wanted to put her at ease, to make her feel as good as he did. What was she looking so tight-assed about? It had been a good performance. "I like the play," he said.

"Oh, thanks. Aren't you the lighting man?" She squinted as if to get a better view of the memory of his face.

"No. I wrote the score."

"Oh." She looked down at her drink, then back again. "I don't know how I feel about music with it."

Pam appeared and slipped her arm around Phil. Phil patted her back. "I can understand your viewpoint. It's different."

"I think it's pretty damned distracting."

"Well, I've tried to score it sympathetically or. . . ." Struggling for the right word, he held back from saying that he knew the music end of things and wouldn't presume to tell her that he didn't like the dialogue in Act Two.

"I know the music is Glass's pet project, but I think it's a cinematic device, not a dramatic one. I think film is creeping into theater too much these days. Special effects, music, realism over abstraction." She stared over his shoulder into the other room.

"I suppose I like realism. I'm that kind of guy," Phil said. "Perhaps it's my lack of literary education but—for example—sometimes things get a little too abstract. I don't understand why Oliver wanted to get away in the first place." He was interested in an explanation of the behavior of these imaginary people whom he had watched day after day.

Her mouth twitched, almost smiling. "I don't talk down to my audience by making everything crystal clear. Do you know why you do everything you do?"

"No, but aren't you trying to communicate with the audience? I suppose I could record all the random sounds on a street and call it music, but it wouldn't be."

"Come on, Phil," Pam said, tugging at him.

The playwright glanced at Pam with that same twitch, as if she were watching from a distance. "Maybe that would be more interesting than what you *do* write," she said.

"Now, all I want to do is have a serious discussion about art," Phil said to Pam. He knew that he sounded just a bit too drunk but, dammit, he was sick of people just saying polite how-dos and tiptoeing or getting downright nasty rather than attempting any sort of discussion. Here, in this house full of people in various kinds of arts, couldn't one have a little intellectual stimulation? he speculated. Where is the spirit of Paris of the twenties or Greenwich Village of the fifties? Where are the rebels and thinkers of the new generation? Has everyone become a businessman or public relations officer at heart?

Pam pulled at his arm. "Don't make a fool of yourself."

"It's too late," the playwright said. She laughed in Pam's direction.

Pam laughed, too.

"How have I lived my whole life without you?" Phil said, feeling betrayed by and hating the woman he loved.

She found him in a nearby café. She knew his habits, his propensities well enough to look for him in a place serving pie and coffee in the middle of the night. Reluctantly accepting her presence across the table, he watched her practice her profession. Now she played the part of the contrite lover. He had seen the expression many times from below stage where he plunked out those god-awful tunes for god-awful plays. But she was a good actress; even now, he wondered if her air of apology and hopefulness might not be sincere.

The waitress brought Pam a menu and poured Phil another coffee. He stirred the heavy spoon, clink-clink, against the mug. "You know what I hate about the whole thing . . ." he began.

She lifted her head, frowning. "You act like something

really big happened to you. It was nothing. How many times do you have to whine about your hurt feelings?"

"Thanks. You're a pal among pals."

"I'm sorry. I'm just not much of a therapist, Honky-tonk. I think *I* need help," she said. Ivory face, ebony hair, mahogany eyes, magenta dress. She had never been so beautiful. "I want to destroy you." She widened her eyes and outstretched her clawed hands melodramatically. Then she withdrew and stared at him. "It's true, Philip. I would love to get my fingers into you and just sort of squeeze until you come oozing out, and then I would make you into something else."

"Why is that?" he asked, feeling only academic interest. He couldn't believe she actually had such a clear thought about him in her mind.

"Because you're the only lover I've ever had that's been *nice* to me. I mean, you actually try to be good to me, don't you? It drives me crazy. But you would leave me in a second, wouldn't you?"

"I haven't." He couldn't yet say that he had been sitting there for forty-five minutes deciding to do that very thing. It had only been a matter of planning the strategy—where would he stay until payday? What about his job, if she should get another part in Glass's theater and they had an ill-tempered breakup? That the piano would be left behind was the first and easiest decision—she could eat it, for all he cared.

"No, what it is . . ." Her tapered fingertips, which many times had traced lines all over his body, now zig-zagged across the paper place mat, connecting the dots of sister coffee shops in Missouri, Kansas and Illinois. "I hate this moral attitude you have. It really gets to me when you're a goody-goody, Mr. Idealism. You'd probably like to take a gun out and shoot that bitch right between the eyes as much as I would." She pointed her index finger at his brow and crooked her thumb, trigger-like. "But your *ethics* won't let you admit it."

"I never even think about killing people."

"I'll bet you do." She smiled, lowering her head.

"I don't. You're sick."

"You didn't like her because she treated you like a stage-hand. The great genius, Philip Benson, the fucking *artist*. You were not appreciated for your true value." She put her hand over her heart.

"Shut up. Go away." He turned sideways and fetched a cigarette from his jacket pocket.

"Don't take it out on me." She sighed. "You know, Mr. Genius, even with your important new position as musical composer and director, Glass would still give you the boot if you were even so much as five minutes late to work. That's how important you are."

"You're mistaking me for someone else, Miss. I learned long ago, when I had a moment to think, that I have a great workable mediocrity."

"You still have the faith; you can't fool me. You got the religion too early, didn't you? What's that in your special box? You think someone's going to come along and publish all those moldy compositions once you're dead or something?" She shook her head in contempt, smirking. "But you're not even ambitious. You've made this little baby step forward and you think you're on top of the heap now. Everything's taken care of." She spread her hands out as if feeling the sun on her palms. "Don't you ever think about something *big?*"

His skin prickled at her voice. It was her real voice, which wasn't the horn calling across the meadow or the soft mew of a kitten but the quartz voice, hard, crystalline and cold. He felt like hurting her. "What do I do—something like your gigantic leap to the American?"

"Well, I am just a few years younger than you, aren't I? But do you think I'm going to stop there? I'll be in films and you'll be doing little songs for those depressing little artsy productions of Glass's. In fact, one of the reasons he probably likes you so much is that you're just like him. Just as happy in a stupid little hole in the middle of nowhere."

"I don't think St. Louis is nowhere. It's a good place."

Pam rolled her eyes. "And somehow being a genius—"

"I never said I was a genius," he said calmly.

"—being a genius," she continued in a louder voice, "will get you somewhere just like God looks after his chillun, right? You think the world will find you because you're good. It's like being a Catholic. I still get shivers when I see a cathedral because, no matter what my mind says, I know God knows that I don't believe in him and he's waiting to prove me wrong. The saints weep for me when I'm wicked even if I don't believe in them." She took his hand. "You got your religion bad, don'tcha, boy? You're a bag of worms in there, knowing that you're really a genius but scared that you'll never blaze up to the forefront of American music. Scared to even try. You don't have an agent. You don't hang around with the right people. And if you did, you'd treat them with that purist attitude of yours that smells like failure."

"You don't need to go on like this, Pam."

"To all the world, you're a zero."

Phil leaned back further and regarded her. "You have all manner of guns, don't you, sweetheart? The trouble is that your ammunition doesn't hurt me. I don't care what you think about me anymore. You don't even really know me—you can't imagine how it feels to be me and you don't even try. All you want to see is something of a certain status hanging on your arm, right? You know what someone called you tonight? Vintage Coca-Cola. I think that's good."

She smiled too quickly at the epithet. "I don't care." She didn't drink her coffee and left him to pay for it.

28

S H E entered the kitchen, rustling with silky material, looking businesslike with a jacket over her dress, her hair tamed
straight and tucked behind her ears. Her scent came across
the table like a deliberate reminder of the smell of her in bed.
"I'm sorry," she said. "I had quite enough to drink myself
last night, you know."

He glanced up from his receipts, check stubs and tax
forms. It took him a moment to focus on her face across the
kitchen table. Need glasses, he thought as he always did while
reading or writing.

"You aren't even very affectionate anymore." She hung
her head as if to hide the tears she wanted to punish him
with.

He almost smiled. During his life he had heard that line
a few times. He had finally figured it out—at the end of a
love affair, a woman is sorry because a man doesn't want to
hold her anymore, but the man is *also* sorry that he doesn't

want to hold her anymore. However, a feeling of general grimness and confusion about what the next steps in his life would be buried the possibility of even a wry and wrenched smile; he put his pen down. "You don't even like me. Why should I kiss you?"

"I *love* you!" she said angrily. "I want to help you. You could be successful. You've got what it takes. Look, I'll find you an agent. Forget Glass and his two-bit job—"

"I like my job. It's the only job I've had in years that I've liked and I'm *doing* something with it."

Pam shook her head. "It's peanuts, Phil. Let's get you some new clothes, a haircut. A trip to New York. Dust off some of those old songs of yours. I think you could be something—why do you think I bought you a piano?"

Phil nodded. "I get it. I'm an investment with potential for expansion. No, thanks, lady. You were probably making more sense last night when you said I smell of failure." He tapped his pencil on the papers at his elbow. "Excuse me, I have to finish this mess."

"Let's go to California. Meet some of the right people in the business. It would be good for both of us."

"I don't want to go to California," he said. "I've been there. Raymond Chandler was right."

"New York, then."

"New York is full of tiny, grubby rooms. Can't breathe there."

"Miami then," she persisted, sitting down in the chair next to him, her elbows on her thighs, hunched forward.

"You must be joking."

"*What* do you want to do with the rest of your life?"

"I'm happy right here at the moment. Besides, you never

know what's going to happen. Making plans only leads to disappointment."

She flung her arms backward and arched her back, appealing to the ceiling. "Let fortune fall from the sky!" she sang.

"You're a sarcastic bitch."

She sat up straight and stared at him. "You know, what made me love you is that you're good at what you do. You're good on the piano and you're good at composing. I'm not going to say this straight to you ever again because I know you think I'm full of bullshit from being around the theater crowd. But I really *believed* in you, and not just for yourself but for me. You don't know how I've strained to see those judgmental little twitches of your mouth because I know if you don't like something, it's garbage. I've tried to impress you and, even though you never said so, I think I'm better at acting and singing than I was when we first started being together. But it's not just me I care about—every day I see you just wasting yourself because you don't even care. You don't care about anything personal. You have all these high-flown ideas about single-handedly stopping wars or racism or pollution, but you don't give a damn about *people*. Including yourself."

Phil had heard this speech before. Some from Katie; some from Holly. Now, listening to it for the third time, he wondered if it might be true after all. No, it was just a way of arguing, wasn't it? There's no defense against women saying "you don't care" because they just can't look inside.

"You tell me one, just one, useful thing you've accomplished in your life that has really made a difference to other people."

Phil glared at her silently. Finally he said, "Do you think I'm going to let *you* judge *me?*"

"You're an arrogant little shit. Who do you think you are?"

"I'm . . ." Angrily, he stopped. "I don't have to listen to this. I don't have to justify myself to you."

"Then who do you justify yourself to and what do you say when you do?"

"All you care about is outward success—money, things. I have a different value system. I don't care about getting rich."

She stood up suddenly and screamed, her hands curled with frustration. "You're a fucking *musician!* Not a philosopher!" Bending over him, she said, "Success doesn't just mean money, it means reaching people."

"Shut up, Pam. Just shut up." He started to gather up the papers scattered all over the table. "I don't know why I'm even listening to you. You don't love me."

Her arms fell limply to her sides. "I wish to God I didn't."

"I'm just someone you can lead around by the nose, aren't I? Putty. Following you around the house like a puppy dog."

Her face and neck went bright red. She sat down. "That bitch."

"Who?"

"Shelly. She told you I said that. I didn't know you even knew Shelly. You haven't been sleeping with her, have you? We'd all better go for blood tests if you have."

"I don't know who the hell Shelly is. I heard you say it yourself. Accidentally, I heard it. At a party."

"Yes, I know what you're talking about. I was giving her a line. I didn't want to make you sound too good or she'd be over every day with homemade apple pie, pinching your behind while I was out of the room. Little snake."

"So." Phil felt a bit foolish and embarrassed at having reported overhearing her private conversation. "So, you were giving her a line, you give Chester lines, and your agent lines. How do I know that you don't give me lines? You act like a selfish brat most of the time."

"Who took you out of that depressing apartment? Who gave you piano? Who has tried to make you dress like a mature man and not a leftover from two decades ago? Who's harrassed her agent regularly trying to get you work—however hopeless that was?"

Phil was stunned. It was all true. He stared down at the table, too ashamed of not having a good rebuttal to meet her eyes.

"Did you really believe that I felt that way about you—those things I said to Shelly?"

"Well, yes. How could I help it?"

She shook her head. "That's disgusting. That's really disgusting. And you put up with it, thinking that. You have no pride at all."

"Please, stop. Please. Let me think a moment."

"You know what? You've been talking about being a good person and hinting around that I am some sort of monster. Meanwhile, I've been *doing*. It's not enough to talk, sweetie." She pointed her finger at him.

Sighing heavily, Phil said, "Oh, Miss Philanthropist of the Decade, right? Nothing for yourself."

"Don't you even want to impress your one-footed friend back home?" Pam glanced away furtively as she said it.

"What are you talking about?"

"Katie. Isn't that her name?"

Phil detected jealousy in Pam's voice, the sickness over his old love, which had ended when Pam was barely in school. Something woke in Phil, the old feeling he used to have when kids at school laughed at Katie for being afraid or silly. He was fed up with Pam and her sneering. "You don't know shit about Katie. You don't know shit about anything."

"You're thinking of leaving me, aren't you?" she asked.

He gazed at her. "Yes."

"Well, honey, I'm going to do you one last good turn. I'm not going to ask your permission and you can tell me later that it's the best thing that ever happened to you."

Wary of her assured tone, he watched her as she seemed to plan something out.

"First," she said, "go get me a bag of split peas from the pantry."

"What?"

"You heard me. Go on." Clapping her hands together as if for a pet or small child, she nodded toward the pantry door. "Split peas in the plastic bag."

"What's your game, lady?"

"GET ME THE GODDAMNED PEAS!"

Phil rose reluctantly from his chair. Inwardly boiling and wishing that she would disappear off the face of the earth, he stood inside the pantry and pulled the string for the over-head light bulb. It smelled like spices and dust and vinegar. The top shelves were packed with jars of tomatoes and pickles given to Pam by an aunt of hers who lived across the river in Illinois. At eye level were more commercial things—soup, packets of instant sauces and flavored rice dishes, boxes of mashed potato buds, and bags of spaghetti and spinach pasta. On the bottom and widest shelf were rarely used pans, casserole dishes, and cutlery in boxes. Phil impatiently shuffled the pasta around. He could only find a bag of dried butter beans.

"I don't see—"

The door slammed shut.

A prickle of rage ran over his skin. "Not funny, Pam. Open this door."

"No."

He could hear her footsteps moving out of the kitchen and into the front room.

The light went out.

Her steps came back into the kitchen. "Gosh, Phil, I've blown a fuse somehow. I'll have to go to the hardware store." Her keys jangled.

"Let me out of here!" He pounded on the door, beginning to sweat in this tiny dark room. No window, no air. A thin grey mist of light came in under the door but dissolved a few inches into the room. He hammered the door with his hands. "Pamela, you bitch. You whore. You stinking, blood-sucking . . ."

The front door slammed.

He sat down on the floor in a lotus position and took six deep breaths, in slowly and out slowly, just as the psychiatrist had advised him to do whenever he was feeling shut in. Four . . . five . . . six.

His heart was still hammering, and he felt the glass jars of vinegar and watery tomato juice hovering over him, sliding silently toward the edge of the top shelves.

One . . . two . . . He started deep breathing again but became giddy. He felt his heart was going to burst with the pounding; his guts started to churn and cramp; the sweat rolling down from his scalp and armpits, and in the waistband of his jeans made him shiver with cold.

"Pam! Let me out! The joke's over! Let me talk to you!" He battered on the door, hoping that she hadn't really left, that she was standing by the front door, waiting for him to confess and beg. "Pam, I love you. I'm sorry. Let me out. Let me talk to you. Please. Please, Pamela, let me out of here." Please, please.

He sat down again, this time finding a box to perch on, and breathed slowly. I can take it, he thought, shutting his eyes. I'm just in the pantry. The kitchen's right there. It will be all right. Nothing's happened. No bombs. It's just the pantry.

But he had waves of a sensation of being deep under St. Louis, buried. The earth pressed from above and the sides, not from below.

Calm down, he thought. Calm down and wait. She'll be back.

He waited with his eyes closed, arms wrapped around his sides, huddled and hugging himself.

He regretted the way he had been with her. Never before had he been so rough and cold, never before had he felt so justified and yet so guilty. What has happened? Is she really as good as she makes herself out to be? Have I been seeing selfishness and malevolence in a decent human being only because I am so cynical? Are the things she said *true?* Sometimes he thought he might have an old-fashioned prejudice against actresses but, in fact, there *was* something basically dishonest about her. He could never sort out her acts from reality, partly because she couldn't either. What if he had been better to her, expecting the best rather than looking for the worst? What if he had been less easy-going and not let her order him around, thinking that she had every right to shape him?

It was too late now. It had been a fragile thing with many, many treasured moments, but it was broken now. He couldn't see how they could ever be happy together again. Or could they?

Isn't it *me* who is being unforgiving? And for what?

I have spent our whole time together waiting for the Bomb to drop instead of just loving her.

It may have been forty-five minutes or twice that long before Phil heard the front door open again. He had put himself into a trancelike state with deep breathing, his eyes closed, his imaginings alternating between taking a walk in the park and simply getting up and opening the door into the kitchen.

"Pam!" he shouted. "Let me out! Let's talk."

She didn't answer him. He put his ear to the pantry door and could hear her punching telephone buttons. "Hello, Sue. Glass around?"

"What are you doing?" Phil shouted.

"Hi, this is Pam. Look, I don't know how to tell you this. It's awful. Phil and I had a terrible argument and he's so drunk I can't let him drive tonight." Her voice had an edge of tearfulness in it. "I've tried gallons of coffee and cold showers. Look, you won't fire him, will you? It's my fault about the argument. Oh, no, look, please, Mr. Glass . . ."

Phil pummeled the door until he felt his fists were bruised. "You lying bitch, let me out of here! I'm going to pull your hair out lock by lock!"

"Yeah, I'm afraid so," Pam said. "Please, Mr. Glass, if you only knew how much this job means—"

"DON'T LISTEN TO HER! I AM NOT DRUNK! HELP!"

"I'm sorry." Pam put the phone down.

Phil, breathing as if he had run several miles, listened to Pam's footsteps on the linoleum of the kitchen floor. "What the fuck are you doing?"

"I have to go to the American now, dear," she said calmly. "I am going to leave you in there tonight because I want you to think. Think like a philosopher while you're there—wasn't it Descartes who sat in a closet for days?—and come out like a musician. You've lost your job, but when I get home, we can pack up the car and head for New York City. It's the best thing, Phil. For both of us."

"You . . ."

"I love you. You'll see."

"That job was the best I can do, Pam. You don't know. How can you know *anything* about it?"

"Come on," she said lightly, "think positive."

"Positive*ly*," he corrected. "Ignorant slut."

"If you get hungry, there are some of Aunt Lillian's prunes behind the tomatoes." Her footsteps left the kitchen, and the front door slammed again.

A siren. Like a nightmare Gershwin trumpet. Screaming siren. The bulb burnt out yesterday, didn't it? He groped in the darkness for Katie, the only comfort left in the world.

He sat upright suddenly, his ears hammering with pressure. For just a fraction of a second, he thought about being cold and sore; then everything was wiped away with rage.

His shoulder and hip were stiff from the attempts he had made to knock the door down. It was a solid old house and the door wouldn't budge. He couldn't even make the hinges creak.

I'm all right. I'm all right. I'm going to get out of here.

Holding his hands out, he touched the metal shelves and explored. Even the faint light that had come in under the door had left as he had dozed off. He groped and found an assortment of kitchen tools on the lower shelf. Nothing seemed immediately useful, but then he wasn't sure of what to do. He didn't know the first thing about picking locks.

Get my stuff into the car and find a motel. Lost my job, Christ, lost that job. He buried his face in his hands.

Suddenly, he remembered seeing matches and candles on one of these shelves one day while looking for rice. Patting his way across, he finally found them. He struck a match and lit the candle.

For a long while, he held the candle, staring at the long tapering shape that had always stood with a bright, clean wick in the center of Pam's table at dinner parties. It reminded him of a Buddhist monk whom he had met years ago. Has it been twenty years now? Where has all the time gone? How can the world be so much worse now when it was so bad then? Will it do this all through my life, just get worse and worse? Everything is ugly, polluted, superficial, murderous or dying. People are crazy, art is meaningless, the country-side is spoiled, cities fester like splinter wounds in the earth's flesh . . .

Monk: The goal is called Nirvana.

Phil: Nice name. Sounds like a pretty girl.

Monk: Yes, indeed. See this flame. See how real the fire

seems—warm, bright, burning, changing the wax. I blow it out—so. Gone. Where has it gone? Nirvana. Where did it come from?

Phil: Well, the matches come from Safeway. I don't know where the fire's gone. It actually doesn't sound like a very promising or interesting place to me.

I was such a smart one, Phil thought. I knew everything at one time or another in my life.

The monk hadn't crossed his mind for years. Even at the time he hadn't taken that particular conversation seriously. He had dismissed it all as something all right for a man like that, a man who seemed to have found his own way toward happiness. Just as his father had eventually found happiness with a new Oldsmobile, Katie with a harelipped accountant, America with Ronald Reagan.

I've never been happy; I never will be happy. It's only getting worse as I stumble around the country. Pam is right, absolutely right. I'm a bag of worms.

Perhaps she really wants the best for me. Perhaps she really admires me. I'll only disappoint her. I'm a failure in all ways.

Oh, Katie, Katie, if only you hadn't abandoned me! Phil felt a sudden revival of the old wound, brought back by the darkness and closeness of walls. He had loved no one more; he had wanted nothing more in life than to please Katie Doheney and make her proud. When she melted away from him, so had all his confidence. When she took him underground, she had only proved to him that he was nothing. Even she hadn't wanted him afterwards. She had cast him away from her and had taken his son with her.

"Katie, Katie," he whispered, weeping, remembering driving around with her, remembering sitting on her piano bench in the Doheney house, remembering loving her from across the high school grounds as she walked with friends, remembering how they had planned their lives—he, the pianist at the symphony; she, violinist. Giving lessons during the day. A music room full of love and life and hope and achievement.

Oh, Saint Hiroshima, why did you hate us so?

Phil moaned in anguish, stretching out his fists as if trying to shake off the bondage of his first imprisonment before he could even begin to think of his second.

Wax dripped down the candle and rolled onto his hand, making a tiny warm dot of white on his skin. If he were to disappear, who would notice? There would simply be a nothingness where Philip Benson used to be.

Sighing, he looked around the pantry, now able to see. The candlelight cast darting shadows as he breathed and moved. For the first time since living with her, he discovered where Pam kept her gun. It was in a plastic bag hanging from the hook on the inside of the pantry door. He had never looked at that side of the door.

He stared at it, remembering that first night when she had frightened him so badly. He had made such a fuss about the gun and hadn't seen much of it since then.

His old lover Holly had a friend, Jane, who was slightly deaf and had a misshapen jaw that Phil had always assumed to be misfortune from birth. Then one evening at dinner in a restaurant with Jane and Rick, he noticed that her hair was askew somehow. There seemed to be less on her right side than her left. He couldn't remember ever seeing Jane's ears or earrings or anything but the fuzziest of permanent waves on her head. He later asked Holly what was wrong with Jane.

"She tried to shoot herself. She didn't miss but she didn't do the job. She has a big hole in the side of her neck."

It isn't good to miss if you try to shoot yourself in the head. How would *I* "do the job"? I would like to go with some dignity, perhaps. A little bit of style. A knife. The Buddhist monk would prefer that to a gun, too. Holding the candle toward the bottom shelf near his knee, he found the box of stored cutlery and utensils. He pulled out the biggest, sharpest kitchen knife. Like this one, he thought.

He sneered at the gun. That was Pam's way, the All-American way. No matter. If I do anything, I won't use her plaything. *She* would never have the courage for something like this. He admired the knife's sharp edge, remembering sharpening it himself, recalling the roasts and hams he had cut with it.

Japanese, Romans, they know the noblest way to nothingness, he thought. Calm, accepting faces. Like in the films. No dread, no pain. Must be simple. Must be the best way.

He blew out the candle and put it down, then grasped the knife with both hands, holding it with the tip pointed at his stomach. With one hand, he pulled his shirt up to feel the steel against his skin.

Nothingness. Nirvana. Simple.

He thrust the knife forward.

"Shit!" His breath left him in a gust of surprise. He pulled the knife back out and stared at it with shock. It wasn't supposed to hurt. As his fingers began to tingle, the knife slipped away. He held his hands over the wound. "Damn!" Cheated by pain and consciousness, he felt the blood ooze out between his fingers.

Somehow, in spite of the dull, deep hurt, he fell asleep again.

29

WHEN Phil began to wake, he couldn't fathom why there were people around him busily working and talking. The noises and smells were bright and harsh, as if he had fallen asleep in a warehouse or the middle of a shopping mall; it was unlike any of the other mornings he had found himself in unfamiliar surroundings. He tried to open his eyes. Before they slammed shut again he saw white ceiling tiles with gray metal runners.

I'll let them do what they want, he thought, I'm still asleep anyway. Someone rolled him onto his side and he felt a terrible groan coming out of him but didn't feel responsible for the sound. Without opening his eyes again, he knew his belly was against a rock that was pushing painfully against him, but he couldn't move. How did he come to be on a rock and why was there a pillow? The more he tried to sort out the fragments, the less he cared. He could only remember a sonata that Pam had once called wretched. A few measures of it were being played on a radio but it changed into a simple tune, the wrong key. How did it get into the wrong key? For a long moment, he tried to replay it in the right key but then realized that he was dreaming it anyway. I'll stay asleep, he decided, and move off the rock later.

It might have been a few seconds or an hour later when he saw a pair of woman's hands on a round metal rail just inches in front of his face. They were nice hands, pale, trimly manicured, hard-working but inexplicably feminine. He tried to move, but it hurt so much he groaned, not intending to make such an awful noise. The woman with the hands wanted him to do something but, whatever it was, part of him knew it was impossible. He could hardly breathe—something was ripping him in two or three parts.

Then he felt he had fallen asleep again but couldn't remember sleeping. Only that an empty spot had occurred in his wondering. He woke a little more this time, and the pain still existed but seemed to be at a great distance.

He looked for the hands. Who did they belong to? Then he saw them again, coming across the room. He trusted the hands and was comforted to see them. A face bent close to him, the profile of a young blonde who was as near to him as a lover might be but without even looking at him. In fact, she was upside down of sorts, turned toward his feet. He felt her touching his wrist, putting pressure here and there with curious fingertips.

He opened his mouth and moved his tongue, a dry alien thing between sticky gums.

The girl stood up straight and smiled at him. "Are you feeling awake yet?"

He was unsure of the answer.

"Can you tell me your name?"

He tried to smile. "Hello," he said.

"What's your name?"

"Phil."

"Phil what?"

"Benson," he whispered, exhausted from speaking.

"We can send you to your room now. You're all patched up." She patted his hand and walked away into the warehouse of wheels, poles, bottles, and boxes with lights.

He remembered. Like a kaleidoscope that at first only had two or three chips of colored pebbles—Pam, the match, the monk, the darkness in the pantry. As more pebbles fell onto the screen, touching each other and reforming, he recalled patterns.

OK. OK, he thought, taking a breath. I'm still here.

For the first few days, Phil couldn't really concentrate on what had happened. When the thought of self-destruction came to him, he could only pucker his face quizzically, embarrassed by and detached from the man who had done such a thing. Trying to imagine the state he must have been in made him angry with Pam. However, he gathered from the doctor's sprightly "Lucky your friend found you" that Pam had saved his life. Unable to reconcile it with what he knew about her scheme, he simply stopped thinking about it.

Though in pain some of the time, in a sedated haze more often, he found pleasure in the attention of the nurses—young and old, plain and pretty, friendly and brusque. He sensed that they viewed him as a sort of tragic figure. He couldn't help but respond with good nature to their tenderness and concern for his wound, his health and comfort; his cheerful mood seemed to perplex them.

Later, he realized that he had actually been *happy* in the

hospital. He wasn't thinking about money, Pam, Katie, pianos, or what to do with himself. He was alive and being fed, bathed and walked by nice ladies with white legs.

The social worker spent an hour with him, somehow opening him up to tell her everything he could think of about his life, from Mr. Tackett and Katie to his trouble believing in Pam. However, he told her the whole thing with the knife had been an accident, that he had been showing off and tripped.

"I thought you were alone when it happened," she said.

Phil grinned. "Some people show off even when they are alone. I'll bet you act in the mirror. Same thing."

She didn't reply but let his explanation pass.

He thought about Pam's finding him and wondered what she had felt. Pity? Disgust? Resentment? Detachment? The idea of returning to her became fixed in his mind. Over and over he fantasized going to her house, forgiving all things and being forgiven, and starting over. He remembered all the good—her sexiness, her fun, her wildly growing plants, her voice, and the tenderer moments.

I love her, he thought, knowing that it was a strange, compulsive and lonely love.

When the note came stating, "Your things are in your car—PR," he knew he couldn't go back. He thought about the words he had devised for this moment—I don't need you, I don't really love you, it would never have lasted anyway. You're a dangerous woman and I was just biding my time. But it all sounded hollow without her to say them to. He didn't need the words. He didn't need the protection. As soon as the note came, his hope was gone and he deliberately made her fade from his mind.

His roommates were a brain-damaged young man in for

an appendectomy who didn't do much but snort in a loud and incoherent voice whenever the nurses spoke to him, and an old man gently restrained in his chair with a knotted sheet. The old man masturbated constantly and futilely under the blanket they spread over him. Phil once heard him shout with surprise and then sleep through the rest of the afternoon, but he was back at it the next day.

The happiness that Phil had known in the first days began to wear away. His cockiness at having escaped lost its edge, and worry began to gnaw.

He learned all the views from the hospital corridor windows. In one direction, he could watch endless streams of traffic zooming along the expressway. Or he could stand and stare at the windows of another hospital. At night, he could see that a lot of things that occurred there were mirrored in the corridors behind him, as if each hospital had the same components of a basic organism and the only differences were the color of the brick and the trim around the windows. Another view gave him an awkward glimpse of a park. Even though it was April, through the glass it seemed to him that outside it was summer, warm and happy like childhood summers with bird songs, barking dogs and portable radios. Inside it was seasonless with a steady fluorescent sunshine, a constant low-key din of rolling wheels, and the high voices of women and young men accented with the chiming of glass bottles.

He got lonely standing at that particular window. Something about it reminded him of all the places he had lived and all the friends he had made. People had always liked him; he had always been grinned at, patted on the back, invited for drinks and dinner, sometimes kissed. He had found people to care about from the crazy film people in California to schoolteachers at the eastern edge of Pennsylvania to Greek restaurateurs in Miami.

And yet he knew no one deeply enough to be able to reach out to them and say, "Come and hold my hand." He was so remote from even his own son that Gordon had never found a way to address him—Philip? Hey, you? *Father?*

There was one person, an old and trusted friend, but he was afraid that he would have to waive his rights even to calling upon her.

The kid with the appendectomy was taken home by his long-suffering mother. Two beds in the room sat tall and empty with the green, ribbed covers tucked in tidily. Two beds sat low and rumpled—Phil sitting on the edge of his reading any books and magazines that he could find, while the old man sat tied in his chair opposite staring and staring at Phil as if trying to place which son, grandson or nephew he might be.

The social worker returned and told him that, because he had no insurance, no job and so very little money, they would have to make some monthly arrangements for the payment of his bill. Unfortunately, he was not quite a charity case. Phil told his doctor he had to be let out—he couldn't afford this expensive hotel any longer.

On his last night in the hospital, he restlessly scraped around for something to read. He wandered by the nurses' station and heard, "I think he went too far."

"But, Libya was just begging for it. We can't let them get away with that."

Libyans again, he thought. He still hadn't grasped exactly what it was that had made Libyans the new bogeymen— suddenly people had started talking about them constantly. At least it was a switch from the constant and exclusive battering of the Soviet Union. But why Libya? What about the Iranians and Syrians?

"Excuse me," he said, leaning his elbows on the counter. "May I have an orange juice, please?"

"Sure, Mr. Benson." One of the nurses got up and went to the refrigerator and handed him a sealed juice. "What do *you* think of the news?" she asked, as if she only wanted another vote for her side.

"About?"

"About what Reagan did."

"What's he done now?"

The nurse smiled knowingly. "You should watch television in the waiting room, Mr. Benson. We've bombed Libya. Isn't that terrific? I think we should have *nuked* Tripoli myself."

Phil shuffled back to his room. He put the orange juice on his bedside table and stared at it for a long, long while. Then he wept.

30

"YOU'RE becoming a much better driver now," Katie said to her daughter after watching her execute a left turn in a busy intersection.

"Thanks, Mom," Josie said drily. "I didn't know you thought I was that bad in the first place."

"Well, not *bad*, dear. You used to be a little too timid. That's why that man banged into the back of you."

"God, parents never forget *anything*, do they?"

"It was only last year." Katie laughed. "It may seem like a long time ago to you. When you get to be my age, everything seems to have happened yesterday."

Josie shrugged and pulled into the shopping mall parking lot. "Doesn't look like we'll get close to the doors today," she warned. Surrounding the confectionery-white mini-town of stores, the acres of asphalt were packed with cars, even in the middle of a weekday. "Want me to drop you?"

"No, that's all right. I expect your father is going to drag me all over Britain. I should start shaping up anyway."

Josie went quiet. Katie knew her daughter well enough to tell the difference between when she went quiet and when she just wasn't talking—it was a particular tightness in her face and chin.

"There's a place; is it all right?"

"Great."

Josie parked and unfastened her seat belt, which slithered back into its holder. She looked at Katie, questioningly. "Something wrong, Mom?"

"I was going to ask you that."

Josie made a quizzical face. "What do you mean?"

"What's the matter?" Katie gave her the "Mother can read minds but you still have to tell me, kiddo" look.

"Well, I was just wondering if you should go."

"Oh, my God, Josie, you don't think I'm going to stop this trip, do you? Your father has been talking of nothing else but going to Britain some day from the day I met him."

"But the Libyans might start blowing up airplanes. I mean . . . I don't mean to say scary things but . . ."

Katie folded her hands over the handbag in her lap. She wondered whether it would be wise to confide in her daughter the mood of impending disaster that she had felt since seeing the luggage ad on television. But isn't it so much milder than the feeling I had before the Cuban Missile Crisis? I cannot repeat myself. I cannot do it again. The first time I ruined Phil's education. Then I dragged Louis off to Japan, which was not what he wanted. Now, he's going to have his chance—he's been so good to us all, worked so hard all his life, and we've put off this trip too many times. One more time and he would really lose hope. Katie thought Josie might understand now that she was somewhat grown-up, but why make her nervous, too? Giving her daughter an appreciative smile, she thought about how much like herself Josie could be at times.

"They can only frighten you so many times, Josie, and you have to ignore it eventually. I'm not going to let crazy governments and terrorists ruin my life—or the lives of the people I love."

Patiently, Josie still seemed to be waiting for an answer. "Then you're definitely going?" She sounded a bit frightened.

"Yes."

"Will you call me when you get there?"

"Of course."

"All right." Josie sighed. "I'll let you go then."

They laughed together.

God, please let me come home to this lovely girl again, Katie prayed.

Wanderlust, he thought, his fingers hooked into the cold chainlink fence. Overhead, a jet roared up and away from Tulsa. Through the dirty exhaust hanging over the runway, he could see the griminess of its belly and landing gear and wondered what distant airfield had muddy runways. It wasn't this dusty one, nor was it Oklahoma red dirt anyway. No, it couldn't be wanderlust . . . this aching to be somewhere else. He had no interest in the next town other than a place to rest. He just knew he had to go on—had to find work to pay for gasoline, a loaf of bread, some sardines and a carton of orange juice. He only lusted to get away, not to wander.

The jet rumbled on, then banked north. He felt the power of its engines in his gut. A blast of air warmed and nauseated him. For another several seconds, he clung to the fence, watching the sleek white shape disappear into the clouds. Then he realized he wouldn't be able to stand up much longer. He stumbled back to his car and sat sideways in the driver's seat, feet on the ground, head between his knees. Eventually, the black blobs in his vision disappeared.

Leaning back, he found the pale blue shirt he was wearing irritating again. He had just pulled it out of the box that morning. Somewhere between Springfield and driving on to the Will Rogers Turnpike, he had realized that the shirt wasn't his. It was another one of Pam's jokes—to give him another man's shirt, as if she already had a lover whose laundry commingled with hers. And what did she tell the new one about him? "This asshole I used to go out with tried to butcher himself right there." Most likely, she had said nothing about him and wouldn't.

I am angry, he thought, staring up at the stained and torn lining of the car's roof. He rubbed his eyes vigorously until colors splashed across his mind. Angry, angry. He flung his arm against the dash.

The jet sounds narrowed off to the northeast. He sighed.

As he sat up, he had to pull himself with one hand, grasping the slippery edge of the vinyl seat cover. He flipped open the glove compartment and pulled out a map. He had been in this area years ago. One large town had been particularly profitable, having a great many churches with out-of-tune pianos. He refolded the map to expose the route, heading west.

Sore, he pulled his feet into the car and slammed the door. Here I go again, lusting to wander. He smiled to himself bitterly and turned on the radio to hear the news from

National Public Radio. He had begun to feel it was the only nonhysterical voice in the country.

They looked at each other the way people do who have lived together a long time, unconscious of the act of reading each other's faces. Phil knew that he appeared bedraggled and totally untrustworthy, but he didn't have the money for a motel room or a meal until he did some work. In this part of the land, he at least had the advantage of not being Indian, for they might not have opened their door to him otherwise.

"Well, it *has* been about five years, hasn't it?" the old man drawled.

The statement proved to be the answer. The screen door opened and they stood aside to let him in. Hot inside even to one with a feverish chill. Phil smelled a Sunday dinner at the grandfolks'—roast beef, carrots, coffee, homemade rolls. He followed the stout woman with thin, varicose legs and dull gray curls through the front room, which was expensively but conservatively furnished, into a more homely room. Rocking chairs, a modest television, fading ancestral photographs in gingerbread frames on a bookshelf, and a coffee table on a braided rug with a stack of *National Geographic*s made Phil feel nostalgic. It reminded him of the houses of his childhood. And in the corner, a friendly little blond spinet.

"Would you like some coffee?"

"Yes, ma'am, I would like that very much." Phil could feel his dormant Jackson voice returning with the sister sounds of the old couple's accent.

"Milk or half and half? Sugar?"

"Half and half, please, and two sugars." Half and half. He would have asked for three sugars to make it a meal, but politeness held him back. He sat down on the piano bench trying not to grunt audibly as he lowered his kit to the rug. The nurse who had wheeled him down to the front door of the hospital had told him not to drive or do lifting. She would be horrified to see what he had done in a day, including the miserable night in the back seat of the car just outside Springfield.

"Mind if I watch?" The husband, wearing a white shirt, a tie and the trousers of a charcoal business suit, settled into one of the rockers without waiting for the answer.

"Not at all." Phil glanced at him with a grin and fished through his gear. "Been doing this for so many years I had to stop being self-conscious."

The old man chuckled and lifted one freckled hand from the rocker arm then let it down in a restless gesture. Phil guessed that these two didn't have many visitors.

"Haven't had it tuned since our granddaughter got married. She used to come up from Atoka and stay with us every other weekend. We still think of it as her piano."

"She stop coming now?"

"Married a boy in the Navy. Nice fella. They're in San Diego. She plays the piano beautifully."

"Seems to be a well-loved piano." Phil tested a few keys and guessed that it may have been longer than five years since the last tuning, but it was definitely a friendly little piano. Intuitively, he knew the granddaughter and these grandparents through the sound of it and liked them all.

Holy hell, it's hot in here.

He wiped his forehead with his sleeve. Together he and the old man began to remove the photographs and ceramic ballerinas from atop the piano. The crocheted doilies puffed with dust.

"This is Wendy," the old man said, holding out a high-school graduation portrait of a brunette. She looked wholesome; no doubt she was the kind of granddaughter to have, if you could choose.

"Pretty girl." Phil shivered suddenly. Though his face felt flushed with heat, he had gone as cold as if someone had opened the door to the Arctic behind him.

The old man turned toward Phil, still holding Wendy's picture.

"Excuse me . . ." Phil tried to rise up from the bench. His healing muscles wrenched across his abdomen, and there was the deep dreaded pain and a cold misty sweat hovering over him.

Have to get out of here. Not going to make it anywhere. What am I going to do?

"Hey, son . . ." The old man put a burning hand on his shoulder, more weight than Phil could bear.

"I'll be all right." He fought the dark spots blotting out the wallpaper, the man's brow, wobbling and wavering. Sitting abruptly on the bench, he put his head between his knees.

Hurts like hell, like *hell*, dammit.

He saw the tuner slip out of his fingers and thud on the rug between his shoes.

Phil propped himself up on one elbow and took another swallow of coffee. "I'm feeling a lot better."

Mrs. Johnston, perched on the edge of her chair, smiled with solicitous satisfaction. "Why don't you stay for dinner? It'll be ready soon."

"I don't have the strength to refuse," Phil said. He tried to return her smile but suspected his might be a little watery from embarrassment.

"Had my appendix out, too," Mr. Johnston said, still lingering in the earlier conversation. "Long time ago. They were experimenting with a new drug then—sulfa. Saved my life. I was ruptured." Again, the nervous old hand raised up and dropped to his knee. "Had less trouble than when Mother here had her gallbladder out. All those new anti-bi-otics."

Mrs. Johnston frowned. "All right now. The nurses said that it was a worse operation than an appendix. He doesn't pay a bit of attention," she said to Phil.

"Was ruptured," Mr. Johnston repeated, nodding.

"So you were." She was plainly unimpressed. She kept a keen eye on Phil as he tried to sit upright. When he leaned back again, she said, "You're still awfully pale. I knew you weren't feeling right when you came to our door."

"That's the way with hospitals," Mr. Johnston said. "They always send you out too soon."

Mrs. Johnston rose to chase a timer buzzing in the kitchen. In a momentary loss for conversation, Mr. Johnston said, "Time for the news."

Phil followed him back to the study where his collapse had been tidied up—tools replaced in his box, pictures and figurines placed in a neat, temporary row on the edge of the piano. Restlessly, he watched the world going to hell on a color screen. Terrorists, terrorists, terrorists of all types. He felt the weight of it all coming down on him again. The death agonies of civilization gnawed at his abdominal wound.

I have to live through it. I've come through worse, perhaps, but I had hope then.

He heard Mrs. Johnston opening and closing the oven door, stirring in saucepans, getting dishes out of the cupboards. Ordinarily, he would have joined her. Helping out in strange kitchens made him feel as if he belonged.

"Dinner!" she sang out.

Mr. Johnston turned off the television and Phil followed him. They both shambled down the hall. The spread on the table in the breakfast room was a feast after the broth and Jell-O of the hospital diet, which had only graduated to shepherd's pie on his last day. Here he had honest-to-God meat and vegetables. He enjoyed the sight and smell of it almost as much as eating it.

"How long have you been tuning pianos?" Mr. Johnston asked.

"Oh, more than twenty years now. Sometimes I have jobs playing, too. Just finished a job in St. Louis with a theater."

"You travel a lot, then?"

"Mm." He nodded, his mouth full of buttered roll.

"Never been married?" Mrs. Johnston asked the inevitable question.

Phil shook his head.

Why did he *always* think of Katie, even after all these years, when someone mentioned marriage? Was this the rest of his life, thinking of Katie as the life he had barely missed somehow? He wouldn't marry her now if he had a chance, but the only wife he could ever imagine spanned the decades of Katie at sixteen with a violin tucked under her chin and funny glasses sliding down her nose; Katie at twenty-odd, hanging onto Gordon with one hand and Louis's little Josie with the other; Katie at thirty-odd shouting at her eldest not to run over the hose with the lawnmower and laughing at her balding husband, who had put a watercolor tattoo of a bunny on his pate.

I've wasted my life in a car, looking for something. At

least Chopin wasted his short life in interesting bedrooms
—I've had much less luck with that.

"What's the matter?" Mrs. Johnston leaned towards him.

He had been musing rather than eating. Fork poised mid-
air, he stared into the carrots and potatoes. "I . . . My appetite
isn't quite what I thought it would be. This is a terrific meal,
but . . ."

"Why don't you go upstairs and take a nap?"

"I could use a nap."

Mrs. Johnston showed him to a garret bedroom complete
with dormer windows and a padded window seat. She had
barely turned the light on before he groaned on to the bed
and curled up with a pillow held against his stomach. Must
be granddaughter Wendy's room, he thought vaguely,
watching a quilt float down over him.

31

THE doves strutted the rooftop outside the window, their voices rippling to one another. Phil rolled over slowly and watched one bobbing by, its gray feathers catching the sun dully. He saw buds on the tree branches that scraped against the tiles of the roof.

Spring. It didn't feel like spring. He remembered Wendy, the granddaughter, and her nice old grandma and grandpa downstairs. A smell of bacon and coffee hovered as if it had just found the top of the house an hour after breakfast. He yawned and struggled upright in the bed and found himself eye-to-eye with the mirror of a frilly vanity.

Is that me? It had been a long time since he had looked at himself. He was shocked. So gaunt and lined, so much gray in his hair and in the stubble on his face. Hollows deepened under his eyes; there was a flaccidness in his jaw. It couldn't have been fifteen years since I noticed my face other than to shave it.

He held his hands out in front of him. Long fingers, square palms, hairy and strong. He could have been a good carpenter or typesetter or weaver with these hands. Why was he a musician—a pianist without an instrument or anyone to listen to his music? What he really was, in the bare facts of the universe, was a drifter whom no one would miss even if he had pushed the knife in a little further and pulled it across toward his liver to cut some bigger vessels.

"I'm tired," he said aloud to the sunny room with the patchwork quilt and Winslow Homer prints. But he knew he could stop any time to rest. Perhaps even here, as a lodger.

He would suffocate, wouldn't he?

The Johnstons, the Wantabors, the Grebes . . . old people he had known who sat at home living their final days in a quiescence that Phil had always imagined he couldn't tolerate. It was always soothing for the time he was with them, trading stories and ditties and meals. Quite a few were decent pianists themselves, a few retired music teachers eager to talk and teach more. He learned from them, cared about them, was attracted to them, and considered some of the evenings he had spent in small towns with a piano in the parlor to be some of the finest moments of his life. And yet, he had always said, "I won't be like this. I must not be like them."

I can't stop. Not yet. I don't have it yet, whatever it is.

Wanderlust speaking? he thought, carefully lowering his legs over the edge of the bed.

Mr. Tackett had always said that the best warm-up after a long absence from practice was Bach, because Bach required precision. After this short hiatus he found his hands stiff. Playing "Brandenburg Number Three" loosened his fingers until he felt them becoming elastic again. Mrs. Johnston brought a tray of coffee and peaches; Mr. Johnston hadn't moved since Phil had started tuning that morning. He didn't say much, which Phil was grateful for, as his mind was laboring away at the next step.

The Johnstons sat appreciatively through the Brandenburg, Brahms's "Hungarian Dances," the entire "Emperor" piano solo adaptation and twenty minutes of various Rachmaninov.

When he wondered at last if he had made them weary, he lifted his face and saw a glow in Mrs. Johnston's eyes. She reached out and touched his elbow.

"We were wondering," she said. "Well, you seem to need a place to stay for a while. We were wondering if you wanted to stay here and then . . ."

Phil leaned toward her. "What would you like me to do? Name it."

The Association of Retired People met in the basement of a seventy-year-old church, an ancient building by Oklahoma's standards. He watched them file in and gather into groups, smiling uncertain toothy smiles. They fidgeted, holding handbags or hats in their trembling liver-spotted hands.

Phil sat in a corner, drinking weak tea and smoking a cigarette that he had lit after smelling someone else's cigar smoke. He listened as a jocular man with a polished manner, apparently a former local television personality, cited the dues situation. A few dragged out dollars and change from their pockets and plastic moneyholders. They talked about appointing representatives to visit members in the hospital.

"But, Charlie, when I went last week he didn't even recognize me. Or his daughter."

"Now, Mamie, you know that sometimes people understand more than they let on. I think we still should visit."

"Then someone else go." Mamie's three hundred pounds sat down again with the finality of her decision.

"All right. I'll go My cousin's in for her heart again anyway," a man said.

"Again! I didn't know that."

"Oh, you know . . ."

The show-biz man interrupted. "I have an announcement about the next meeting. We plan to meet on Tuesday instead of Monday because the youth group has a special meeting in this room. Is that all right with everyone?"

A thin assortment of moans followed. "I'll miss my program. It's the only TV I enjoy any more."

"I have a bridge club on Tuesdays."

"Have your son tape it. He has a video recorder, doesn't he?"

"I can't get a ride."

"*I* have one. But something always goes wrong when I try to use the fool thing."

"It's all right with us."

"I'll give you a ride, Tom."

"All right, all right. Now, after the meeting tonight we have tutti-frutti angel food cake and coffee and low-salt cheese crackers brought by the Taylors. Mrs. Hermann has promised cherry blintzes for May. Zeb has finally brought back his Space Invaders by popular demand." The cheering for Space Invaders was enthusiastic. "And tonight . . ." The speaker paused, showing his professional handling of introductions. "We have postponed our slide presentation to take advantage of an opportunity that might never come this way again. Our guest . . ."

"A what?"

"Guest," someone informed loudly.

". . . is a pianist who has been touring the country for more than twenty years. He's written film and stage music; he's played for ballet and so many other places, I can't even list them all." The man turned and held out his arm to Phil. "Ladies and gentlemen, Mr. Philip Benson."

"Oh, I've heard of him, haven't you?" a woman whispered.

Phil hoped that his face didn't look as red as it felt as he rose from his corner and walked to the old upright where they had placed it—just left of stage center on the concrete floor. Fortunately, he had come a few hours early and tuned it gratis. He hoped the choirmaster of the church would appreciate that during Thursday practice.

This is what I've come to, he thought, starting out with a little Schumann. They are nice old folks, but this is what I've fucking come to in my life.

A few coughs and shuffles echoed around the walls, but there was a rather surprising round of applause. Then he did Mozart. At least they like music, or are simply well-behaved. He had picked short, light works but something was feeding into him.

They were *listening*. He could feel it. It was odd to know that he was really performing for them and they liked hearing him. After the Mozart, he heard a murmured "Wonderful" in the applause.

He did his own transcription of a Vivaldi flute concerto. They warmed up with him. This was not playing background music for a two-bit drama or in an all-you-can-eat steak and lobster cafeteria or smoky lounge littered with booze and telephone numbers written on cocktail napkins. His audience was smiling and sometimes nodding. Each note of the Vivaldi went into ears turned toward him.

He worked hard. Like creating a sexual fantasy to improve a partner, he conjured Lincoln Center with himself in a tux and shiny black shoes, hot spotlights and a duchess in the box. Outside were the posters saying "Philip Benson Tonight" with a black grand in art deco graphics. He was the skinny kid from a small town who had worked hard, had tough breaks but had made it at last. All was polish and class and, afterward, red roses and champagne. He touched the keys with new feeling. The sentimental was missing; something strong welled into his hands and took over, fiercely sweating out the sweetness that Mr. Tackett had put into his hands. He let it have his fingers and wrists and feet, listening to the piano sing with a beauty that he had never before attained.

He held the last note just long enough, not too lingeringly . . .

Lincoln Center dissolved into the basement of an old church. Fragile people in folding chairs clapped, elbows jutting. One woman, tears in her eyes, stood. The man next to her rose also, leaning on his cane. Then another and another. Eagerness, life—years upon years of life—charged through them as they got to their feet, still applauding him. A man in a wheelchair rolled forward and held his hands as high as he could, slapping his meaty hands together.

"More!"

He saw the gnarled faces and wispy hair over freckled brows. He saw the shabby shoes and braces, walkers, hearing aids and pocket inhalers. He saw watery, faded eyes behind spectacles, and feeble, wavering legs. No audience, especially not in Lincoln Center, could have touched him more.

"Play some more, Mr. Benson!"

"More!"

"Beethoven!"

"Please, Mr. Benson."

Mr. Benson. Agatha, Harry and Ida, all seventy-plus, and he was *Mister* Benson. Breathless with gratitude, he trembled, fearing tears. He sat down at the piano once more.

He played the Katherine Sonata by Benson. Simple, elegant, a mysterious touch of morbid. And somewhere in the room was Mr. Tackett, covered in tobacco crumbs in his brown chair, nodding. "Well done, boy. You've shaken your training at last."

32

KATIE was cold; she hated to tell anyone that she was cold again because they always made a fuss, lighting gas fires and plugging in electric heaters to turn on her. Then she would get so hot that her legs and face itched. So she sat with Annie and Peter's cat on her lap, thinking, it's not really *cold*, it's just a chilly draft. There seemed to be something funny about the cat—she was so calm and affectionate. Katie had never liked cats much, never having had one anyway because of her sister's allergy, but this one was very nice. Perhaps English cats have different traits.

Louis came down the stairs and smiled at her. "Made a friend?" He sniffed the air. "I smell kippers."

"Kippers," Katie repeated. "Is that fish? Smells like fish."

"Yes. You'll love 'em," he said, tickling the cat's head.

Katie smiled. Louis was having a terrific time. He bounced as he hadn't bounced for years and was loving every minute of the trip. He was excited by everything he saw, tasted, heard, touched, and smelled from coal fumes to cathedrals, thatched cottages to bangers and chips. They had, in three days, made a zig-zag across England from London to York to Liverpool to Cambridge and back to London, then west to Peter and Annie's, seeing things that even his cousin hadn't seen. For years, Katie had felt guilty about the trip to Japan. They were actually having more fun on this "second honeymoon," although they were much too worn out to do as much as they had done on their first. It seemed a revival of what was best in both of them. Louis had never been funnier; Katie had never felt less neurotic.

She felt as if she were seeing spring for the first time, spring as it is *supposed* to be—miles of brilliantly green fields, soft rain, lambs on hillsides with their mothers, daffodils growing wild, close blue skies with wet but white clouds. All of England was beautiful, growing and alive but as kept up as a city park. They were especially lucky that Louis's cousin, Peter, lived in the countryside in a village near Swindon. They called their house a "terraced cottage," which charmed both Louis and Katie, though Peter pointed out that it was just the British way of saying row house. But row houses themselves were alien to both Katie and Louis, who had never seen any except years ago on a trip to Philadelphia.

Katie loved walking down to the center of the village with Annie. They stopped often to greet women weighted down with straw baskets or plastic shopping bags on their way back home. "Hello, Annie!" And Annie always introduced Katie as her "cousin from America," which cut out a lot of explaining about each of them being married to the real cousins. Katie found that the British always seemed pleasantly surprised to hear her say that she liked England very much.

Katie always came away from these encounters wishing that her own town in Colorado were still small enough to talk to people on the street. It had grown so much that she barely looked around the supermarket for a familiar face any more.

She also wished that she could bottle the friendly "bye-bye" she heard every time they left shops, take it to the local Seven-Eleven manager and have him replace the absentminded "Have a nice day" of the checkout clerks there.

Wishing that she had read more about England before she came, Katie tried to keep her mouth shut and ears open. She had assumed that Swindon was a small town because she had never heard of it except in the context of Peter's letters. She discovered that it was a rather important place in the west. Bristol was somewhere she had always associated with ships and sailors and had assumed it was on the sea. As they planned the trip, she studied the map and found it was on the River Severn and not on the sea at all. And she also discovered that Penzance was real—she had thought, if it existed at all, it might be in Italy. That was the price of being a snob about light opera.

And English cats were nice.

Annie came out of the kitchen. "Good morning, Louis," she said. "Katie, would you like tomatoes, too?"

"Uhm, OK, sure. Please." Every time Annie spoke, Katie automatically felt envious of her sweet, high voice. All the Englishwomen seemed to have beautiful young voices, while she felt she was growling out every word.

Tomatoes and fish for breakfast. Something else to tell the kids when we get home.

Louis sank into a chair and picked up the newspaper. In

a few seconds, he began to mutter, as he had every time he read the newspaper this week. "Old fool."

The cat stared up at her and blinked, purring with all her might. Katie picked her up and put her on the sofa pillow where she stayed, licking her back. "Guess I'll see if I can help Annie." She got her cane and limped to the kitchen. Her foot had been bothering her.

"I wish I could afford a subscription to this paper. Even to get it a week late . . ."

Peter came down in a rush. "Mind if I put the news on?" he asked and squatted in front of the stereo. He got it on just in time to hear the beeps that signaled the hour.

"Can I do anything?" Katie asked.

Annie had just pulled the grill pan out and was inspecting the splayed kippers crammed head-tail-head-tail on the grate. "You could take the toast through. I think it's ready. What are the men doing?"

"News." Katie took the toast rack and a plate of tomatoes and put them on the table. Louis and Peter were both staring at the radio, which was talking about Finland, Sweden, and the Soviet Union in a soothing voice. She returned to the kitchen. "I'll take the juice."

When she returned to the other room, Peter had suddenly turned the news off. Louis leaned far forward. They had a conspiratorial look.

"What's up with you two?" she asked.

"We're hungry," Louis said. "Is it time?"

"Yeah, come and get it." Katie poured the orange juice into tumblers as the two sat down quietly at the table. She glanced at Louis and knew that something had happened.

Louis gave her his look, knowing that she could see

through him. "There was a nuclear accident in Russia. A bad one. Radiation is blowing across Europe."

The cold, radiated wind seemed to blow right through her. Katie gripped the back of the chair with one hand and started as the ghost of a woman in a flowered, swirling dress screamed silently through her and disappeared again.

"Oh." Katie poured the rest of the juice and returned to the kitchen. "Help with anything else, Annie?"

Katie and Louis both watched a huge truck lumber by on the narrow road in front of the house. It paused, then drove up over the curb as a double-decker bus came from the opposite direction. Katie jumped back reflexively from the window. Louis glanced at Peter and Annie, who sat undisturbed, then smiled at Katie. She understood his look —they had already said enough about the narrow British roads and knew another comment would sound ungracious.

"We don't *have* to go to Stonehenge," Louis said.

"Of course we do. How can we go back and say we didn't see Stonehenge? It's so close!"

Gently, Peter said, "It's raining."

Katie was aching to do more than sit inside, watching ITV news then BBC news to keep tabs on the satellite photos of the Cloud. Radioactive British students who had been in Kiev were being decanted at the airport and handled with detectors and gloves. Peter and Louis read bits of the newspaper to each other. People in the local pub, the butcher's and the wool shop talked about Chernobyl, radiation clouds, contaminated milk, water and lambs. Yesterday, Annie had been nervous about hanging out the sheets on a pretty spring day.

Today, the radiation rained on Britain. Tomorrow, they would have to fly back to the U.S.

"I want to go to Stonehenge," Katie said slowly. "I am sick to death of fallout shelters. I am sick to death of living in fear. I don't believe in it any more. Let me out or I'll walk there myself. Wouldn't you like to go with me, Louis?"

As they put their coats on, Louis trapped Katie against the wall in the cage of his arms. "You," he said passionately.

Out of the door and in the back garden, where celandines, violets and periwinkles bloomed against an old brick wall, Katie saw tiny blue flowers on long curving stems. "Oh, what's this one?" she asked.

Annie bent over, hands on her wool-covered knees. "That's a forget-me-not." She always spoke of her flowers with a serious voice.

"Would it be all right if I took one of these to press? It would mean more than a photograph."

Annie nodded. "Yes, of course."

Katie plucked the flower with a few leaves. In her purse, she found a letter she had inadvertently carried all the way across the Atlantic with her. A letter she had written to Phil, just to keep in touch, which had come back the day before their flight. A feminine hand had written across the front, "Addressee unknown." She tore it open, shook the radio-active rain droplets off the forget-me-not and carefully tucked it away.